S0-APN-043

It was dusk, with Pelham's car lights pale gold against the lavender sky.

"Thank you, Dr. DeGraaf," he said. "We're not going far. It happened at the end of West Loop. Your block. Joe Cornish is waiting there and we have the place roped off."

"Is it that bad?"

"Yes. The boy's dead."

"Where do I fit in?"

"I want to ask you to act as coroner."

DeGraaf at last looked at the small body. It lay on its side, a little boy with brown hair, folded up in a fetal position, dead. DeGraaf looked past it, down the slope, through the night which was now deep indigo, and saw miles of darkening desert, flat and empty. It stretched away from the small body to the end of the world.

Also by Barbara D'Amato from Ace Charter
THE HANDS OF HEALING MURDER
A Dr. Gerritt DeGraaf Mystery

THE EYES ON UTOPIA MURDERS

A novel of suspicion by
BARBARA D'AMATO

ace books
A Division of Charter Communications Inc.
A GROSSET & DUNLAP COMPANY
51 Madison Avenue
New York, New York 10010

THE EYES ON UTOPIA MURDERS
Copyright © 1981 by D'Amato Productions, Inc.

All rights reserved. No part of this book may be reproduced in any form or by any means, except for the inclusion of brief quotations in a review, without permission in writing from the publisher.

All characters in this book are fictitious. Any resemblance to actual persons, living or dead, is purely coincidental.

An Ace Charter Original

First Ace Charter Printing: December 1981

Published simultaneously in Canada
2 4 6 8 0 9 7 5 3 1
Manufactured in the United States of America

THE EYES
ON
UTOPIA
MURDERS

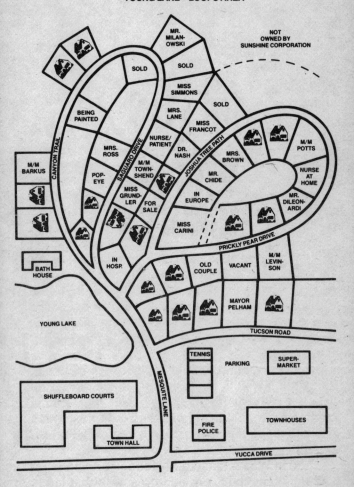

YOUNG LAKE—LOOPS AREA

NOT OWNED BY SUNSHINE CORPORATION

MR. MILANOWSKI

SOLD

SOLD

MISS SIMMONS

SOLD

BEING PAINTED

MRS. LANE

MISS FRANCOT

CANYON TRAIL

SAGUARO DRIVE

NURSE/ PATIENT

DR. NASH

JOSHUA TREE PATH

M/M POTTS

MRS. BROWN

MRS. ROSS

M/M BARKUS

POP-EYE

M/M TOWN-SHEND

NURSE AT HOME

MR. CHIDE

MISS GRUND-LER

FOR SALE

IN EUROPE

MR. DILEON-ARDI

MISS CARINI

PRICKLY PEAR DRIVE

BATH HOUSE

IN HOSP.

OLD COUPLE

VACANT

M/M LEVIN-SON

YOUNG LAKE

MAYOR PELHAM

TUCSON ROAD

TENNIS

PARKING

SUPER-MARKET

MESQUITE LANE

SHUFFLEBOARD COURTS

FIRE POLICE

TOWNHOUSES

TOWN HALL

YUCCA DRIVE

Chapter 1

Night in the desert is empty. The little girl in the ballerina costume felt more frightened by Halloween in the desert than she could ever remember being on Halloweens in the midwestern town they had left. Beyond the end of the short street the night was void and black. There was nothing for the street light to shine on, no dust, no moisture, no trees, nothing to show that the end of the street was not the end of the world. She was in charge of the other two children because she was the oldest, and already she had decided not to go quite to the end of the street. Two more houses would be enough. The other children would not complain. She could tell from the lack of shouting and laughing that they were frightened too.

They all pretended, though quietly, to be brave. The little boy with the funnel on his head and tin cans on his arms and legs marched right out in front, followed by a boy whose only disguise was a peaked green cap and circles of red rouge on his cheeks.

The Tin Woodman, closely followed by his sister and the other child, turned into a walk that led to a small stucco house. The porch light was on. That meant it was all right to ring the doorbell. The ballerina nodded and the little boy rang. Nothing happened. The porch light seemed weak and cold. It did not penetrate the night, but became lost in the blackness.

The little boy rang again. He looked toward the door, but the other two were looking back over their shoulders at the night which crowded up so close to them.

The door opened. In it was an old woman. The porch light raking across her face threw the shadow of her chin as a black slash across her neck; the wrinkles next to her mouth were deep black grooves. Her nose, caught by the light, became large and hooked. Without makeup or costume, she was the Wicked Witch.

The little boy made a small sound and pulled back, seizing the girl's hand. But the girl was determined to show her brother it was safe and held out her sack.

"Trick or treat?" she said.

The old woman brought a brown bag from behind her back. Holding it by the bottom, she put the neck of the bag into the girl's sack and shook it. Something dry and brittle fell into the sack.

"Trick!" the old woman shouted, and she slammed the door.

Something scrabbled in the sack. The girl stepped back on the sidewalk, looked in the sack, dropped it and ran. The other two ran after her.

Left on the sidewalk, the sack moved slightly, and shifted. There were dry, scratching sounds and then, one leg at a time, a scorpion felt its way out. It paused, testing the night air and the gritty concrete and then, satisfied, stalked methodically out into the night.

* * *

"Gerritt," said Mrs. DeGraaf, "I want you to go to Arizona and save your grandmother."

"If she needs saving, it'll be the first time in her life."

"Now don't be insensitive."

"I can't just walk out of here, Mother. I have obligations."

"Don't you give the poor things a spring vacation?"

"Yes. It starts Saturday. I teach my last class that morning. But I still have the interns to supervise, and besides that I have to cover the emergency room."

"My dear," she said, removing her gloves and putting them down on top of an autoclave, "don't be silly. I realize that the *hospital* never stops working. But that doesn't mean that nobody in it ever has a vacation."

"Your gloves are roasting. What makes you think she needs help?"

"Who?"

"Grandmother."

"Well, right after she moved into that absurd development in Arizona—"

"As I remember it, you told her last year that at her age she ought to get out of the Chicago climate and move to a retirement community where there would be people her own age."

"I couldn't possibly have said anything like that."

"Sorry."

"Well, she had hardly been there three weeks when the trouble started."

"What trouble?"

"Not that she told me about it right away, of course. In fact, she never did actually broach the subject. I had to learn about it from the *Tribune*."

"Now wait a minute. Gran Ross has been in the Tribune?"

"No, not personally. Thank heaven for something. But the problem has. The children and the old people fight, you see."

"What? Mother, really, I don't have time—"

"But it's serious. It's been in the *Tribune* twice. Of course I called her. And then she had to admit there had been a little bother. A little bother! People throwing garbage! And with mob scenes you never know when they'll get out of hand. So you see you really have to go."

Gerritt looked at his mother a few seconds. He was trying to decide whether it would be more trouble to ask her to explain or to go to the library and look up the *Tribune* articles. "You don't happen to have clippings of the articles, do you?" he asked.

"Well, of course. As a matter of fact I had to quote from them before she'd admit anything. They get so stubborn as they get older."

As she dug in her purse, Gerritt carefully refrained from saying that his grandmother had always been stubborn, and that she was stubborn because she was usually right.

"Here," said his mother. "I knew you'd ask for them."

There were two columns of newsprint. From the interesting scallops along their edges, DeGraaf decided that they had been clipped from the paper with fingernail scissors.

"Thank you, Mother," he said politely.

The first one was titled, with aggressive lightness, "Showdown at the Generation Gap." Gerritt read:

The three-color road sign that greets visitors to this small town in the desert says, "Young Lake—the most peaceful town in the world." But the billing is wrong. They are firing across the generation gap here, and the feud shows no signs of cooling down.

Young Lake is a middle income community some twenty miles west of Tucson. Built over the last fifteen years by a midwest developer, it now has a population of 9,451. Of these only fifteen are children.

"This was originally planned as an entirely adult community," said Peter Pelham, 72, who has been mayor of Young Lake for four years. "It is a retirement community, and very quiet."

Normally a quiet town, in recent weeks the threat of violence has hung over Young Lake, and violence has erupted again and again.

"I think it really started a few months ago, on Halloween," said Mrs. Timothy Barkus, one of the few people in Young Lake who has children. "The older folks started saying that the kids shouldn't expect Halloween candy, that they didn't want to be called to the door in the middle of the night. And of course the kids resented that."

"We worked out a system," said Mayor Pelham, "to handle that. People who wanted to give out candy would leave their porch lights on for Halloween. That's how we do things here—voluntarily."

But several parents disagree. They report threats to their children, even attacks on children by cane-swinging oldsters. On Christmas, a family's front-yard Christmas tree was destroyed. Garbage has been dumped by night on the lawns of homes where children live. The family of Mrs. Rena Claire moved out of the development two weeks ago. Contacted in Palo Alto, California, Mrs. Claire said, "I wasn't exactly afraid. It just isn't good for children to live in that kind of hostility."

Sara Carini, social director of Young Lake, said to the *Tribune:* "This is not a place for children. We have no schools, no parks, no children's activities. Our people have come here to find peace and quiet. For a family with children to move here, I would say is irresponsible. Children should be in a child-centered sort of community."

In most cases, those who have moved in to Young Lake with families have done so because they have inherited the property. Mrs. Amy Lane, a widow with two children, said, "My grandfather left us this house. And after my husband died, we had very little money. The children like the sun, and I work in the supermarket. It seems an ideal place for us. At least it did."

On Friday, seven of the families with children received tarantulas in their mailboxes. Henry Potts, father of an eight-year-old girl threatened retaliation . . .

DeGraaf skimmed the rest of the clipping. The father wanted to call in the FBI or, alternatively, to form a posse of parents. There were a few comments from older residents of Young Lake who swore they "loved children" or "deplored violence." Another loved children but was "too old to want them around all the time." Finally, the writer fell to considering housing values in Young Lake, up eighty per cent from the early days of the development, now ranging from $40,000 to $65,000.

The second clipping, dated a week later, took a less jolly tone.

Retirement Town Versus Its Children

The feuding citizens of Young Lake, a small retirement community in Arizona, some twenty miles west of Tucson, are viewing their problems as serious today in the wake of three unfortunate incidents.

'Fib' Levinson, aged 7, was treated and released at Scott Hospital late yesterday for a compound fracture of the right arm. He reported having been tripped on his way home from the school bus by "somebody with a stick or cane who was hiding behind the bushes."

Another Young Lake resident, Mrs. Cora Grundler, 78, was stung by a scorpion, which had been left in her mailbox by an unknown prankster. Treated at Scott Hospital, she was released, then elected to stay the night under observation because she anticipated possible heart problems. "It was such a shock," Mrs. Grundler said. "And very painful. I know the children did it."

The third incident occurred when an unidentified person hurled stones at the school bus which brings the Young Lake children home from their school just outside Tucson. Police Chief Joseph Cornish told the *Tribune:* "We don't know yet who it was. He was hiding behind a row of bushes at the edge of Yucca Drive. He or she ran away as soon as the stones struck the bus. We assume, therefore, that it was not meant to injure anyone. He had been gone five minutes before anyone called us. Fortunately, the only damage consisted of three small dents in the bus."

Dr. John Nash, interviewed just after the second incident, and himself a five-year resident of Young Lake said, "This is a retirement community. Most of these people are living on fixed, limited incomes. They fear the destructiveness of children. They fear the taxes they would have to pay for the support of schools if very many children lived here. They've worked hard all their lives, and now they've earned a little peace and quiet. Young Lake is not a place for children."

The children from Young Lake are bused to a school fifteen miles away near Tucson. There are no facilities for them in Young Lake. Since 1960, when they were first built, the value of Young Lake's modest retirement homes has nearly doubled. Some new and more elaborate housing has also gone up in recent years. A man-made lake near the center of town gives the little community its name. Young Lake and several other retirement towns were active over the last two years lobbying in the capital for legislation explicitly permitting restrictive covenants in communities such as this. On September 1 of this year Governor Raul Castro signed into law specific state legislation which gives local communities the right to bar children in their property deeds.

Children in Young Lake are permitted by its laws only to visit for certain specified periods of time.

The American Civil Liberties Union issued a statement to the effect that the organization was preparing a suit to challenge the constitutionality of the Arizona legislation.

Meanwhile, in Young Lake, children and adults walk in mutual suspicion.

When Mrs. DeGraaf noticed her son's eyes looking off into the middle distance, she said triumphantly, "So you see you have to go and save her."

"From a group of eight-year-olds?" he asked absently.

"No, of course not. Though they can be very nasty, I suppose." Her son burst out laughing. "Well, anyone can. What I mean, though, is that once things get to the mob stage you never know what will happen. People get hurt who aren't even involved, you know. And she might—" Mrs. De-Graaf stopped.

"You were going to say she might even get involved."

"You know how she is. She might make a *statement*."

"That she might. Old psychiatrists never give up. If she did *make a statement*, it's apt to be more sensible than some of these."

"I wish you wouldn't argue about it, dear. She needs you."

"Why don't *you* go?" he asked, but he asked it with his mind elsewhere. Four and a half months of winter were behind him and he could almost feel the Tucson sun. What was more, he liked Gran Ross. He found his grandmother more fun than, for instance, his mother, and had been rather lonely for the old girl since she moved to the southwest.

When his mother said, "But I'm no good at that sort of thing," he had forgotten what question she was answering. Oh, yes. He had suggested she go.

"You don't have patients to see," he said. "You're not on call."

"Of course not, dear. But I have no control over your grandmother. I couldn't make her leave."

"Neither could I," DeGraaf answered. But his mind was in Young Lake. The idea of children being illegal fascinated him. "I'll tell you one thing," he said. "I would never, never presume to tell Gran Ross anything, nor would I make her leave, even if I could."

"So you'll go," said his mother, who knew him rather well.

"Not until Monday. I suppose Gringo will cover for me. I did it for him when he wrenched his neck in November."

"However did he do that?"

"Halloween. Wanted to play the headless horseman. Had a lighted pumpkin under his arm for the head, and a graduation gown up over his real head. Walked around all night with his real head crooked over as far down and left as it would go. Took the getup off at midnight and couldn't get his head straightened up again. Three weeks bed rest. A trauma surgeon ought to know better."

He had told Gran Ross that he would meet her at her house in Young Lake, but he was not at all surprised to see her standing just inside the gate when he got off the plane in Tucson. His grandmother had been one of Chicago's leading psychiatrists in the nineteen thirties and forties and still wrote an occasional article on her favorite topic, cues to states of mind from posture and gesture. It had a new name now—nonverbal communication—but was otherwise the same study. Her articles were well-researched and clearly written. When dealing with the behavior of friends, however, she was instinctive; she jumped to conclusions from the least twitch of an eyebrow.

"You could use a drink," she said to DeGraaf before kissing him.

"As a matter of fact, yes," he said. "They had any amount of martinis on the plane, and no wine at all."

"I find airport bars fairly decent," said the old lady. "I suppose they make the drinks strong for the sake of nervous flyers."

They settled in a booth in a dark corner. "A bacardi," she said to the waiter, "and what wines do you have?" Finding that the choice lay between a bad Italian chianti and a good cabernet sauvignon from California, she ordered the second without asking Gerritt and then settled back.

"You know," she said, "for years I refused to order bacardis, even though I preferred them, because they were so pink. They looked like a ladies' drink. And of course that wasn't acceptable because I saw myself as fighting my way in a man's world. Now, since the women's movement has made that attitude a commonplace, it isn't interesting any more and I can order anything I want."

"I think I used to feel pushed into martinis for the same reason. That is, the reverse reason—"

"I understand."

"I never quite wanted to admit they tasted like bubble bath to me."

"Do you drink a lot of bubble bath?"

"I'm using my imagination."

The drinks arrived. Mrs. Ross took a long sip and said, "Beats bourbon any day. Now, how are you going to go about saving me?"

"Well, Gran, I thought I'd lie in the sun in your backyard. Then we'd have a steak dinner for two. Then we'd go to a couple of Mexican restaurants. Then I'd get some more sun. And by that time Mother would think I'd done what I could to save you, and I would have had a lovely time."

"Yes?" Two more sips. "You're not the vacation type, Gerritt. You aren't accustomed to wasting time any more than I am. Or was. What was it that interested you in the situation? I have to admit it has its nasty qualities."

"You tell me. What's been happening since the stories in the papers?"

"I don't know quite where the Chicago papers left off, but since you called me to say you were coming down, we've had some more garbage dumped onto children's lawns—that is, their parents' lawns. Another tarantula in a mailbox, an older person's mailbox, and a mysterious oil spill."

"What was that?"

"Well, it was just a lot of oil in a puddle on the

sidewalk. But I thought it was rather—I don't know—nasty, because so many of the old people ride those big three-wheeled things. Like large tricycles, you know."

"I've seen them."

"And this was right at a corner. If a tricycle went into a skid, it could skid right into the street. A lot of those old people don't see very well."

De Graaf smiled at her reference to 'old people', as if they were a breed different from herself. She smiled back.

"Lots of minor things, of course," she went on. "Curses, threats, community meetings and all that kind of thing, naturally. Grim looks. Oh, it's not the place it was, that's for sure."

"What sort of place was it?"

"Very sunny. Very safe. Quite dull."

"But I mean—surely this didn't start all at once? There have been at least a few children here for some years, haven't there?"

"Yes, and as far as I know there has always been some grumbling about them. That's why they wanted the law passed banning them, I suppose. After all, I've only been here six months. I think a few more children have moved in lately. Inherited the houses. A couple of larger families. Two children here is a larger family."

"Have you been calling yourself Mrs. Ross or Dr. Ross?"

"Mrs. At first they addressed me that way because they didn't have any other facts. You see, I'd signed the contract for the house as Adelaide Ross, so they put it that way in their Announcement of New People in the town paper, which is called the *Sunray,* by the way. I didn't bother to correct them.

Then I noticed that they bothered the couple of retired doctors who live here to death.''

"With symptoms?"

"Yes, that of course. But that always happens.
For drugs, really—prescriptions.''

"You have a drug problem in an old folks
town?''

"Really, Gerritt! They weren't *always* old. In
any case, why not? They've lived in society, haven't
they?''

"All right. Sure. Sorry.''

"It's for all the regular things. Valium,
barbiturates, dexidrine. Some painkillers. Nothing
exotic. We have an infirmary in Young Lake, but
it's staffed only by nurses—it's really intended for
emergencies, so they can't get drugs there. And it's
twenty miles to get to a doctor in Tucson. One of
our retired doctors practices in town part time, but
he's a very proper man.''

"Is that John Nash?''

"He gave the *Trib* a statement, didn't he? Yes,
he's the one. Were you interested in what he had to
say?''

"I guess so. Actually, he sounded a conservative
type.''

"He is.''

"So why make a statement at all then? Stick his
neck out?''

"Possibly somebody just happened to ask him.''

"I'm sure he's the sort who could look quite offended and say that he didn't think it was a fit topic
for comment.''

"You're right. In a way it's out of character. But
he's been one who's rather a militant on the subject
of children.''

"Oh?"

"Have you finished?" Adelaide Ross asked. "We could start, unless you'd like another. But you ought to see Young Lake before sunset."

"No, let's go. Do you have a car?"

"Naturally. I drove the Porsche down when I moved here."

"Naturally. Shall I hide the fact that I'm a doctor, then?"

"You won't be bothered for prescriptions. You're not licensed in Arizona. You're temporary."

"Oh. Just as you say."

"In your case, being a doctor shouldn't make any difference."

From Tucson to Young Lake they followed a road that was as straight as the edge of a razor. The last few miles were, to the eye, empty of life, except for an occasional Joshua tree; some dry bundles of spikes, and a few cacti.

"We'll have a rain soon," said Adelaide Ross, "and the whole business will bloom. And then in about three weeks it will go back to being brown again."

Far ahead was a bright green patch that slowly grew and differentiated itself until it turned into streets and houses.

"I'm in the new section," said Gran. "It's only partly developed, even now. Our section is called The Loops locally, because two streets bend around and double back on themselves. The two adjoining sections are teardrop-shaped. When the town was first laid out, the streets were all straight and at right angles to each other. But they found out people thought curving streets had more cachet, so now all the new ones bend. Ours bend with a vengeance. They also charge more for them."

"I imagine they should." Gerritt caught sight of the town sign: "Young Lake—the most peaceful town in the world." Somebody had splashed red paint on it. "Pop. 9,451" was just readable at the bottom.

Tucson Road ended at the edge of the lake, which was about a city block in size, still and blue.

"They found a spring here to feed the lake," Mrs. Ross said. "Otherwise I suppose the whole town wouldn't exist."

They passed the supermarket. On their left was a tennis court and behind it some buildings that looked official. Ahead, next to the lake, lay nearly a city block of shuffleboard courts, the largest shuffleboard display DeGraaf had ever seen, and next to them another public building. His grandmother turned right, up Mesquite Lane, heavily planted near the sidewalks with huge clumps of multiflora roses and boxwood and privet.

"Why all the bushes?"

"Psychological effect. Ninety per cent of the people here are midwesterners. They like the climate, but the Sunshine Company found that a lot of them became uneasy looking out over all that open desert."

"The bushes give them a feeling of intimacy?"

"Right. They come from places where the eye expects trees and woods and hills—and houses, of course. Trees mostly don't do very well here, though some people grow citrus. But the bushes are everywhere you look."

She took a right curve into Saguaro Drive and turned into the driveway of the fourth and last house on the left. Beyond was desert sand, marked off with white stakes and strips of white cloth dangling from strings.

It was a tidy little house, white stucco and cheerful, located on slightly sloping land. Beyond the loop, Adelaide said, the land ran down into a dry wash. The vacant lots were dusty and brown, but the lawns in front of finished homes were a painfully bright green, the flower beds jewel bright with zinnias and marigolds and portulacas. As Adelaide put the key in the door, a woman in a three-wheeler drove past on the sidewalk. Adelaide waved.

"Getting her day's exercise," she said. "Back home at this time of year she'd probably be shut in the house. The guest room is at the end of the hall. Not big, but it's what we have."

"I shall spend my time in the sun, anyhow."

"Also my paints are in there. But they don't smell much."

"I was wondering what you do here. I couldn't quite see you at shuffleboard. I had decided you did a lot of reading."

"I do. Thank goodness the old eyesight is still operational." The living room and entire hall were solidly covered with built-in bookcases. So was the bedroom into which DeGraaf stepped. It also held an easel and several clear, rather abstract paintings of cactus, stone, or bones.

"The light here makes you think of painting," said Mrs. Ross. "It's so uncompromising. Now, Gerritt, if you're really serious about seeing what's going on in this place, I suggest we have an early dinner. There's a Town Meeting tonight. Although I loathe meetings, I suggest we go."

"Democracy in action? Certainly. Let's go."

"I hope it's democracy. It may look more like mob rule. However. Dinner at five-thirty. Meeting at six-thirty. They start early," said the old lady, "so that people who wish to can be home in bed by nine."

The hall was nearly full when Adelaide Ross and Gerritt DeGraaf walked in—and they had tried to be early.

"You're very much encouraged to call people by their first names," Adelaide whispered. She waved to an acquaintance with one hand, held purse and glasses in the other, and looked around for a seat.

"Looks to me like two classes of people here," DeGraaf said. "About half of them look angry and the other half are so blandly unconcerned that they just have to be putting a good face on things."

"They'll both have something to say," said his grandmother, plopping her purse in one chair as she moved to sit in the seat next to it. Having secured both, she removed her bag and let DeGraaf sit down.

"The mayor usually presides. He's a gentle little man named Pelham. Tonight I'm sure he wishes he never took the job."

Gerritt singled out a short man with a smooth face. He was moving a chair on the platform in front. He looked as if he would find great delight in giving out a turkey at an annual raffle, but currently wished he could fly away.

"That's Peter Pelham, right?"

"Why, Gerritt, you've studied us."

"Not exactly. But when I read the article, I paid attention."

The hall was able to accommodate a thousand people. The seating was on folding chairs. DeGraaf assumed from the folding chairs that the room was used for many types of functions. The end where the mayor stood had a raised platform, stage curtains, a track on which the curtains might close, an American and an Arizona flag, and a large side door. The tall windows looked as if they belonged in a gym, and the hardwood floor would do equally well under square dancing or volleyball or card tables for duplicate bridge. Pieces of scotch tape on the walls evidenced past decorations.

"You're right," said Mrs. Ross into his silence. "They use it for everything."

"Do they, Sherlock?"

"Oh, come on, Gerritt! You looked at the stage, the windows, the floor, and the walls. Give me some credit for being able to see!"

By now it was standing room only, and DeGraaf marveled that in a community of nine thousand, at least twelve hundred must have turned out for this meeting. It suggested a lot of anxiety.

Peter Pelham was banging on a water glass with a spoon. The meeting was called to order.

"The secretary will read the minutes of last month's meeting," said Pelham. "Mrs. Dartmouth?"

A lady in the front, wearing a pink dress and holding a sheet of paper, stood up. "Now, Peter," a man on the left said loudly, "you know we've got more important things to talk about—"

"Abner, we've got to do this right. It isn't going to take that long to read the minutes."

"Minutes! She takes half an hour. Loretta uses the whole month writing up her minutes—"

"Now that isn't fair, Abner. Somebody has to do it. It isn't as if you volunteered to type them up."

"She doesn't need to make such a production out of it. Who needs chatty minutes?"

A voice from somewhere in the middle of the audience bellowed, "Why don't you both pipe down? The old lady'd have been through by now if you'd shut up."

"Nice people," said DeGraaf, under his breath.

"It isn't always like this. Really," said Adelaide.

In an uncomfortable silence the lady in pink, who had half sat down, then half risen again, stood up straight and began to read. She did it rather courageously, DeGraaf thought. She spoke in a clear voice, without hesitation; considering the interruptions, that alone required some nerve. Also, he began to think that she was editing as she went, for while some sections flowed easily with good connectives, others sounded like topic sentences without the paragraphs to go with them. Probably, he thought, the minutes usually included abstracts of any comment anyone present had made. People liked to hear their names repeated this way. The reading of the minutes was most likely a major amusement at these meetings. Usually. But this was not usual.

"Thank you, Mrs. Dartmouth," said Pelham. "We are now ready to consider problems from the floor. I ask you to hold any motions you may have until a bit of discussion has taken place. I think this may make things clearer." He produced this statement in one continuous breath, as if he expected to be interrupted at any moment. He was determined to do his duty. DeGraaf thought, watching him, that he had to lose, no matter what happened. No matter how even-handed he was, the aggressive faction would consider him too weak, and the pacifiers would think he was encouraging the radicals.

"Mr. Mayor. Mr. Chairman!" A woman of about sixty-five, wearing a brown dress carefully trimmed with ecru lace at the collar and cuffs, stood up. Several others were shouting "Mr. Chairman!" also, but her very distinct treble attracted Mr. Pelham's attention first. Gerritt had the impression that the mayor wished he had not heard her so clearly, but grimly intended to be fair.

"Mrs. Brown," he said.

"Despite all the shouting we've had," said Mrs. Brown, "and all the irregular behavior," here she looked at Pelham as if he might have prevented it, "I am going to follow our normal procedure and identify myself. I think it might be well if hereafter we adhered to this practice as we have in the past."

"I wish," said DeGraaf to his grandmother, "that I didn't have such an urge to kick her."

"She parodies herself," said Adelaide.

Mrs. Brown had scarcely paused. "Ellen Norris Brown, living on Joshua Tree Path," she said. "I would like to say that I came here two years ago—twenty-three months precisely—having been told I was buying a home in a retirement community. I might perfectly easily have bought property in another community elsewhere, but I relied on the claims of the development company here that they were dedicated to providing homes for retired and older people. We are now increasingly saddled with the noise and destructive behavior of a large number of children. I want to take this opportunity to ask the Sunshine Company formally what it intends to do to protect our rights. And if it is unable to give us the community it led us to expect, do they plan to buy back our homes, as they should, and provide us with moving expenses so that we can move to a proper community?" With a little breath that was not quite a snort, she sat down.

"My name's Levinson, Prickly Pear Drive," a man shouted. "And while we're asking questions here, I'd like to ask Chief Cornish exactly what the police plan to do to see that children aren't attacked. We had my boy over at the hospital this afternoon for a follow-up X-ray, and his arm isn't healing too well. What if he gets attacked now, while he can't defend himself?"

"Now, I don't think there's any real danger of that," Pelham said. "I wish that Chief Cornish and Mr. DiLeonardi would come up here with me, since some of these questions are clearly things they can answer better than I can. Joe Cornish? Oh, thank you, Mr. DiLeonardi. Chief Cornish. Here they are. Now let's see—"

"I'd just like to say—"

"Who is that, please?"

"Leila Townshend, Saguaro Drive. And I think I ought to say to Mr. Levinson that attacks on children can only be made by some *awful* person. That is, I don't want him to think that the *rest* of the retired people here would ever think of striking a child—"

"Oh, sure," somebody said.

"I'd rather just spank them," came a shout.

"I didn't *say* everybody," Mr. Levinson began.

"Now wait a minute," Pelham said. But the noise was increasing. "Just a minute, please," he called. But those who weren't calling out insults were explaining to their deafer neighbors just who was saying what. A couple of people stood up to make themselves more easily heard. Somebody pointed accusingly at somebody else. A man in front was waving his arms at a man two rows behind him. One wife was holding her husband back by his coattails, as if he intended to hit someone. Now half the hall was on its feet.

"Quiet!" It wasn't Pelham, and it came with such volume that it was heard above the roar. De-Graaf looked around for the voice of authority. It was Cornish, the chief of police.

"Quiet!" he shouted again. "If you want to fight, do it outdoors later on. We've had some questions asked. Let's try to answer them intelligently, if possible."

"Are you going to protect the children or the old people?" yelled a beefy, red-haired man. Red of hair, red of face, he was equal to Cornish in vocal volume.

"Mr. Potts," said Cornish, "we're going to try to protect everybody. It's not up to the police to pass laws. We're just going to see that no one gets hurt."

Pelham looked gratefully at Cornish. The hall was actually quiet enough for him to call on speakers by name. "Dr. Nash?" he said to a thin man with raised hand. About seventy, he was lean and carefully groomed.

"John Nash, Joshua Tree Path. I would like to ask Mr. Cornish something, since he so eloquently said that the police are not there to make law. Does he intend to enforce the law? If so, I refer him to the Arizona statute permitting zoning codes that restrict housing developments to adults only, and our local ordinance which does in fact restrict residence in Young Lake to those persons who are over eighteen years of age, excepting visits from direct relatives of residents and those for a period not to exceed thirty days. Do you intend to enforce these laws, Mr. Cornish?"

There was a mutter all across the hall, and De-Graaf thought he heard an elderly voice call, "Right on."

"Dr. Nash," said Joe Cornish, "from the police point of view, the situation is very confused. In order to eject a child from this community, we would have to take the child into custody and then take him out of town. That is, separate him from his parents. Now, the parents actually own the houses they are living in here, and have every right to be here. You might say that they are breaking the law by having their children with them here, but there is nothing which specifies what their liability is, if so. How can we arrest a minor whose only offense is living with his own parents? There's no basis in law for *that*. And we can't ship the *parents* out, since they are property holders. I don't mind telling you we don't know what we really ought to do. And quite frankly we don't know what kind of suit might be brought against us or the municipality if we acted hastily. I can imagine a considerable damage suit if we separated a child from its parents and the child suffered psychic harm—which could easily be claimed, since the child would certainly be frightened. I don't even know whether we policemen might be liable as individuals if we exceeded what could reasonably be considered our duty. We've talked about it among ourselves, and we've pretty well concluded that, unless either the town or the state—or maybe the Supreme Court— resolves what we're supposed to do, we're going to do the one thing we know to be our job. We're going to try to prevent violence. And we're going to see that whoever is guilty of violence, whether the person is seven or seventy, is caught and punished."

There were some cheers, some growls, and several waving hands. "Mr. Rogers," Pelham said.

"The trouble with what Joe said about justice," the old man said, "is that it only applies to adults like us. I can't do a thing without being sued or arrested, because I'm an adult. But the kids can run across my lawn, tear up my flower beds, leave popsicle wrappers and other garbage all over, and what can I do? They're minors. They're not even considered responsible. I just have to grin and bear it."

"Mr. Rogers, I believe if a child has caused actual damage, in law the parent has a liability and has to pay for the damage."

"And what if he won't admit his kid did it? That's happened to me. Or what if he says all kids do that? Boys will be boys, you know. What if he won't pay for it? Am I supposed to hire a lawyer for three hundred dollars to collect twenty dollars to repair my lawn? What if it's all the kids in the neighborhood who do it? Who's going to divide up the cost? Who decides? And the worst thing is that if I don't like it, I'm just an old grump that hates kids. What kind of fool do I have to be to sit around and watch my flowers get trampled and just smile?"

There was a swelling, roaring cheer, across the entire hall.

"He's absolutely right!" a man shouted over the cheer. "I came here from Chicago, where I had a nice house and a yard I loved. But the kids in the area cut it to ribbons. They tore across the lawn and made it into a bed of mud. Trampled through the hedge. Broke branches off the crabapple trees and used them to hit each other. They picked branches when they were blooming and took them home. How was I going to get rid of a hundred kids? I couldn't, short of fencing in the whole place and turning it into a fortress. But I was getting to retirement age, so I picked a place where I thought I could do a little gardening without being vandalized. I *thought*. Now what am I supposed to do?"

"Listen, we've worked hard all our lives," said a woman with a metallic voice. "We've come here for some peace and quiet at the ends of our lives. And we've paid our savings for these places. What are you going to do about it?"

"My question, I believe, was never answered," said Ellen Norris Brown. "If the properties were misrepresented, Mr. DiLeonardi, do you intend to give us our money back?"

"Mrs. Brown," DiLeonardi started cautiously, "you must realize that you could sell, right now, for more than you paid for the house. Certainly *I* would buy it back. It would be a fine investment for me. As it is for you."

"But not," said Dr. Nash, with a cutting edge to his voice, "*not* if everybody started selling at once."

DiLeonardi looked ill and started to speak.

"It's not a question of selling," someone else shouted. "We've settled here. It's a question of being promised something we haven't got."

"The children are *not wanted,*" said Mrs. Brown. "And they're not legal. If I kept an illegal herd of cattle on my lawn, they'd be ejected immediately. Why aren't the children out?"

DiLeonardi turned to her but was cut off again.

"People here are on limited incomes," yelled a man. "We can't be paying for schools. And besides we already did all that years ago."

"The parents should be fined!"

"My children," said a young woman, "don't walk on other people's lawns. When children deface property, somebody ought to talk with the parents. Children are not savages—"

"What about finding out who threw garbage on my front lawn?"

"Well, I think we're making a lot of fuss—" began an old lady, who was quickly shouted down and did not fight back. Her lung power was not equal to it.

"I think we ought to get a legal opinion."

"We've had legal opinions—" DiLeonardi began.

"Lawyers just want to sue," somebody yelled. Another screamed "Dead right!" Two more retorted that it wasn't so, but you never knew which way a judge was going to go, and somebody added that reasonable men differed but the fact was that if you asked five lawyers you got five different opinions. While this dialogue was going on, several other conversations started up all over the hall. DeGraaf heard Cornish say to DiLeonardi and Pelham, "Oh, what the hell. Let 'em talk."

"People are the same at any age," said his grandmother.

"Yes. This seems to go pretty deep, though."

"I suppose so. They thought they had Utopia and it turned out to have earthly problems after all. Poor things."

"You're a snob, Gran."

"I hope not. But I don't believe in Utopias."

"Should we stay?" The hall was resolving itself into knots of arguing people.

"Oh, I think so. They promised coffee and doughnuts afterward."

"You'd stay through this screeching for a doughnut?"

"Well, *you* want to."

"Will you stop reading my mind? All right, you old fake. Let's stay."

To DeGraaf's surprise, after some fifteen minutes of verbal brawling, a few people started to leave, but others drifted to a side room where there was a smell of coffee and doughnuts. DeGraaf took a swallow of the coffee and gulped. "Is it instant, or what?"

"Oh, I'm sorry," Adelaide said. "Did you get it from the big pot?"

"Yes."

"That's the caffeine free stuff. If you look around they'll have a small pot somewhere of the real thing. They just assume everybody will have trouble sleeping if they drink real coffee. Old people, you see."

"I'll get used to this place some day."

"Popeye!" said his grandmother. "I didn't see you. Meet my grandson, Dr. DeGraaf. Gerritt we call him. Gerritt, this is my best friend in Young Lake."

"Well, now we're getting somewhere," DeGraaf

said. He was looking at an elderly, rather scrawny man, and the reason they called him Popeye was evident. The thin neck, the toothless look, the squinty grin, even the pipe, all were there. Not the sailor clothes. He wore trendy white jeans and a red plaid shirt. "I'm glad to find somebody here Gran really likes. I was beginning to wonder." They shook hands with gusto.

"Good gal she is, too," Popeye said. "Of course, I keep an eye on her. Ladies shouldn't be living alone. Need a man to look after things."

"Oh, absolutely," said his grandmother with complete and bland deceit.

"Though it might be I don't have enough to do, too," he added frankly. "I water her garden sometimes. She's great at planning and planting. But when it comes to daily watering, well, her interest sort of lags."

"Always been my failing. Routine. I must discipline myself. If I just keep at it, I'll learn some day."

"Well, I'm glad *somebody* is happy around here," said a voice behind them.

"Peter!" said Adelaide. "Peter, this is my grandson, Dr. Gerritt DeGraaf. He knows who you are, of course, already."

"Mayor Pelham," said Gerritt. "I don't envy you."

"Damn right. You shouldn't. What am I supposed to do? Outlaw children? They'd be making up children's stories with me as the ogre for years to come."

"Well, it's one form of immortality."

"Sure. But not one I'm looking for. Actually, I'm not so much worried about posterity as I am about the next few weeks. I keep thinking that if we can just hold on long enough we'll come to some sort of resolution. If we can only get there without something worse happening."

"They're not shooting at each other yet."

"No, not yet. But the children are outnumbered. A war wouldn't have to happen. It's just that so many accidents could occur when tempers are like this."

"And you have the discomfort of sympathising with both sides?"

"Yes. It's nice of you to say that, Dr. DeGraaf. Yes, it would be a lot easier if I believed one side was clearly right and all I had to do was bring the other side around. Or even sneak past them. Whatever."

Gran Ross was glancing at the size of the crowd.

"Have you enough doughnuts to go around, Peter?" she asked.

"Pretty much. We had a lot more people than usual. But some of that was expected. And then, more people than usual got mad and went home without eating. That's the bright side."

"It's nice you can find one," DeGraaf said.

"Oh, I'm just whistling to keep up my spirits. After all, I came here to retire in peace and quiet, too. I'm no different from the rest of them in that respect. I really thought I had found it. The cottage at the end of the road. No problems worse than whether we were going to put marigolds or zinnias in the beds around the flagpole at the Hall. Always a faction for each. But now—I guess I'd be better off if I really retired. Well, see you again, folks. I've got to circulate. Give everybody a crack at me."

"Don't worry so much," said Popeye suddenly.

"People argue a lot. But they never do anything serious."

"I hope to God you're right, Popeye. Goodnight."

"He frets," Popeye said. "He shouldn't. People here are bored, you know. Retired. No job. This whole squabble keeps them busy."

"That's your theory of it, then?" DeGraaf asked as they strolled to the door, he with his hand on his grandmother's arm.

"Sure. They enjoy it. Look at the stuff that's happened. Pranks or accidents, mostly. Halloween stuff. I don't worry."

The night was warm, but cooling rapidly, as desert nights do. From the hall they walked up Mesquite Lane, the main street. The shuffleboard courts were on their side of the street, a smaller layout of tennis courts on the other side. There was a moon and some discreet street lighting, and the courts looked silver. Beyond the courts was Young Lake, large and perfectly still.

"They claim to have called it Young Lake because it was man-made and new, you know," said Popeye. "But it's really to make all those old people feel younger. Damn fool nonsense, if you ask me," he chuckled.

They went slowly up Mesquite Lane, savoring the air and the clear view of the stars. Prickly Pear Drive bent away from them to the right. They followed the curving course of Saguaro Drive. At the house just before Adelaide Ross's, Popeye waved goodnight and let himself in. Gran Ross and her grandson let themselves into the next house, talked a little about family affairs and went to bed.

Chapter Two

The next day was still, warm, and peaceful. Gerritt got up, aware immediately from the brightness of the sun that it was late. He felt rather guilty. When he found his grandmother scrambling eggs for him, he felt even guiltier.

"Gran, you don't have to do that."

"I do very few things that I don't want to do, Gerritt, including this. It's a failing of mine. Please sit down and spare me the abashed look."

"All right, but it's a damn poor way to go about saving you."

"You haven't a white horse, I suppose?"

"Nope."

"Or a motorcycle? That's very popular these days."

"No motorcycle."

"I suppose it's hopeless then. I am not going to be saved."

"I'm a failure."

"So let's do something we enjoy."

"Although," he said, "I think some people are going to get themselves into a nasty mess over this thing. Still, I don't see why you should be involved."

"So what shall we play?"

"Tennis?" he said tentatively. He would not quite have asked it straight out, but he was uncertain what activities his alarmingly agile old grandmother was equal to and what activities she was too old for.

"I'm not the tennis player I once was," she said.

"Shuffleboard."

"Heaven forfend. I shall never set my hand to a shuffleboard pusher-thing. I don't even know what they're called. To me they always looked like the poles they used to raised and lower the windows at my grade school. No, I said I was not the tennis player I once was, not that I was extinct. If you can stand a bad game, I'll play. If you want a better game, there are a few youngsters, sixty, seventy years old, who play pretty well."

"I am filled with charity this morning. I'll take you on."

"In most cases," said Adelaide, producing her tennis racquet, "I have found charity to be another name for guilt feelings."

The courts were hot. It was Tuesday, though it did not seem like it to DeGraaf. Tuesday meant students, and later a seminar with residents interested in forensic medicine. But instead he was out under the sun. After a while his grandmother sighted a young man leaving the police station across the street. Waving furiously, she attracted his attention, and introduced him to DeGraaf as George, a policeman and friend fortuitously off duty from the three to eleven A.M. shift. She induced the two younger men to play tennis, while she sat in the shade of the bench house. About two, she and DeGraaf adjourned to the tea shop for lunch and George went on home.

"The menu here is heavy on such delicacies as stewed prunes, custard, and rice pudding, but they have a thing they call chicken pancake that isn't far from a decent crepe stuffed with chicken."

There were three brands of caffeine-free coffee on the menu, but they served the real stuff also, and all was well.

"We'll walk home," said Mrs. Ross, "and then you can sun bathe."

It was not until 5:45 that the horrors began.

They started rather unremarkably when the young policeman, George, poked his head over the back hedge of Gran Ross's property. DeGraaf, who was trying to get a suntan, looked up at the sound of rustling bushes.

"What's up?" he asked. "I thought you were off duty."

"I got called back. We're missing a child."

DeGraaf walked over to the hedge, telling himself the sinking feeling at his heart was nonsense. "Missing how long?"

"He came home on the school bus at three. Had a couple of cookies or something at home, and went out to play. Hasn't come back."

"At that rate he can't have been missing more than an hour or two."

"A little more than that. Call it two and a quarter. He ate his cookies fast. His mother wanted to go to the store, but he said he had something he absolutely had to do first. He'd promised somebody. So she told him to take fifteen minutes. He said he'd try and if he couldn't do it that fast he'd come back and do it later. That meant by three-thirty he should have been home."

"Kids get involved. They don't know how much time has passed."

"I know. The Chief's pulling out all stops anyway."

"How old is he?"

"Seven. Brown hair. Red and white striped shirt. His name's Timothy Barkus."

"Is his mother usually excitable?"

"I don't think so. But she had his promise to come home. So she started to worry. And what with all this other business—"

"Sure."

"That's the trouble, of course. After what happened to Fib Levinson, his mother naturally has visions of him lying behind some bush with a broken leg."

"I guess I shouldn't keep you. I haven't seen any small boys at all. A little girl peeked over the hedge a while ago, about where you're standing. Wouldn't say a word, either, which struck me as very like a child. Pigtails out to here."

"That's the Potts girl, probably. Let us know if you do see him. OK?"

"Of course."

"Maybe you could check whether your grandmother saw him. Just call."

"Sure. Good luck."

It was seven when he got the phone call. Mayor Pelham said cautiously:

"Dr. DeGraaf? Could you come over to—no,

could we pick you up? We've got a problem and we'd like you to help us. I'm sorry to call you out of the blue like this, but I think you'll understand."

DeGraaf agreed to be ready in five minutes and excused himself to his grandmother, who was making chicken cacciatore.

"Pelham," she said, "is not given to flights of fancy, so I guess you'd better go. Let me know. I'll stick some of this in a casserole. It'll keep."

"Thanks, dear. There he is. I'll run."

It was dusk, with Pelham's car lights pale gold against the lavender sky.

"Thank you, Dr. DeGraaf," Pelham said. "We're not going far. It happened at the end of West Loop. Your block. Joe Cornish is waiting there and we have the place roped off."

"Is it that bad?"

"Yes. The boy's dead."

"Where do I fit in?"

"I want to ask you to act as coroner."

"How do you know I have the experience?"

"Oh, your visit and who you were was in the *Sunray,* the town paper. I also heard through the grapevine. Listen, we're here already, and the parents are here. I'll explain later." People were starting to surround the car.

"But don't you have a coroner?" DeGraaf asked.

"Sure. But—look, we don't want to move the body until somebody who knows his business has seen it. I've *got* to explain this later."

"I don't have a bag. I don't even have a thermometer."

"Joe has a whole kit. Come on."

Half a dozen older people crowded around the car, asking over and over in brittle voices, "What's the matter?" "Peter, what's wrong?"

A man of about seventy, in overalls, shouted, "I live here, Pelham, and nobody'll tell me what's happening. I *live* here." From the waving of his arms, DeGraaf guessed he meant the house that stood a couple of hundred feet east of where they were parked.

In the distance, out of sight, someone was screaming. DeGraaf noticed three spotlights strung up to a generator; two policemen, including his friend George, stood near the upper part of a giant trapezoid made of ropes tied to bamboo stakes. One side of the trapezoid ran along next to the sidewalk and the rest of it down the slope where the light was fainter.

The elderly crowd, now four men and nine women, was like no mob DeGraaf had ever seen. They twittered, cackled, chattered and squeaked. They picked at the mayor's sleeve and tapped DeGraaf on the shoulder. They knew something was wrong and they wanted to be told whether it threatened them directly. One couldn't push them or shout at them, for while they chattered they were polite. And yet while they were polite, they picked and picked. And they would not let the men through.

"Please," DeGraaf said. "We've got a very sad thing here. If you want to wait, we will tell you about it as soon as we know anything. But I imagine it will be about half an hour to an hour. That's a long time to stand here. If you could come by the police station later, it would be better."

There was a twittering in the crowd.

"Have coffee at somebody's house," DeGraaf suggested. "Near the police station. Then come over." He took Pelham's arm and turned away. About to step over the rope, he asked George, "Where do you want us to walk?"

"Go ahead. We've been over this part. So have the dog and Mrs. Lane, unfortunately."

"The ground looks like rock."

"Sun-baked mud. Next nearest thing to brick. We didn't find as much as a scratch on it."

DeGraaf and Peter Pelham walked and slipped down the incline to the dry wash.

"What in hell are the parents doing here?" DeGraaf whispered in Pelham's ear.

"Apparently the mother was waiting at the police station for word when—well, when word came."

"Their name is what? Barkus?"

"That's right."

DeGraaf, for a moment ignoring the screams of the woman, watched Mr. Barkus. He was standing with his arms folded, looking as if he wished he were somewhere else. Mrs. Barkus caught sight of Pelham.

"You said you'd protect everybody," she screamed hysterically. "You didn't really care! All you old people care about is yourselves! You *never* cared about the children!"

"Mrs. Barkus—"

"Why couldn't you protect them? Why didn't you protect Tim?"

Pelham took a step toward her, but he didn't know what to do.

"Look at him! Here! Look at him!" she shrieked.

Mr. Barkus said, "Judy, please," and she turned, clawed at him and pushed him. He lost his balance, staggered down the incline, then caught himself.

"Don't be nice to him," she shouted at her husband. "He doesn't care!"

Barkus plodded back up the slope, his eyes bright in the floodlights. DeGraaf walked over to him.

"Do you have a car?" DeGraaf asked.

The man stared at him blankly for a moment, then answered, "Uh—yes. We followed the police car over."

"Can we get your wife to wait at home?"

Barkus looked at his stricken wife. "I don't know," he replied. "How can this be happening?"

"We have to get her home," DeGraaf said. "This is no place for her."

Barkus drew a long breath, and began slowly to walk to his wife's side. Coming up behind him, Gerritt touched the woman's elbow. "Mrs. Barkus?"

"What do you want?" she sobbed, clutching at her husband's arm.

"Mrs. Barkus, I'm not from Young Lake. I don't know what's going on here. But I'm acting as coroner in this case." He started to turn up the slope, still talking. "If you will wait at home, I'll find out as much as I can as fast as I can. And I'll come over and see you when I'm done."

She was forced to turn up the slope to hear what he was saying. "I can't," she said. "I have to stay here." But she took a step or two along with him.

"We'd get through much faster if you could wait at home. I understand your feelings, but there's nothing you can do here. If you want to find out what happened as quickly as possible, try it this way. I'll call on you *tonight*. I promise."

"I *know* how this happened," she said grimly. But she was no longer shrill.

"In that case we'll want to hear what you know, too. Will you and your husband wait at home? Please." They were now fifteen feet from where she had first been standing. DeGraaf had accomplished his main goal: to get her away from the body.

A kind of numbness seemed to be setting in. "All right," she said woodenly. "But come whenever you can. No matter how late it is."

"I will. You have my word."

Arm in arm the two Barkuses stumbled up the slope. DeGraaf turned to find Pelham and Joe Cornish watching him.

"Okay," DeGraaf said to Mayor Pelham. "You've got me into this and now we're alone. Tell me why. And while we talk, I need a body thermometer and an air thermometer."

"I've done the air," Cornish said. "Here's the medical kit."

DeGraaf at last looked at the small body. It lay on its side, a little boy with brown hair, folded up in a fetal position, dead. DeGraaf looked past it, down the slope, through the night which was now deep indigo, and saw miles of darkening desert, flat and empty. It stretched away from the small body to the end of the world.

The police, he thought, knew their procedure. The hands were already covered with plastic bags, to protect anything that might be under the nails. This on the possibility that the child might have fought with and scratched whoever killed him.

Killed him? DeGraaf realized he had jumped to the same conclusion the mother had. It was the atmosphere in town. But the child might have stumbled down the slope and struck his head. He might have been bitten by a poisonous snake or insect. Or he might have been bitten by a commonplace insect, a bee or a hornet, and gone into anaphylactic shock. There was no point in guessing.

He squatted down next to the body and inserted the thermometer. From the boy's face, it looked like strangulation. Still, some snake poisons also made the face puffy and blue. There were abrasions on the face and hands, he noticed. Dust on the clothes. That didn't tell him much, yet. If the child had fallen, he would have rolled down the slope of the dry wash, over rocks and dust. If he had been bitten, he could have rolled on the ground in pain. He didn't want to move the body before everything necessary had been done.

"You have all your pictures, Cornish?"

"Everything."

"Searched the area?"

"Oh, sure. Not a clue. But the light is bad. Two of the boys will stay here all night and we'll get it again in the morning when we can see better."

"Just wanted to know whether I could move him a little." He took out the thermometer, noted the temperature. He turned the body over on its back. There were bruises on the neck, but the light was so distorting that he merely noted it for later. "Well, let's go, then. I want to watch them pick him up. And let's get a shot of the ground under the body, just in case."

"Good by me."

In a few minutes they moved back up the hill.

"You never answered my question, Pelham," DeGraaf said as he and the mayor took the stairs to Cornish's office. "Why do you need me if you have a coroner?"

"Let me have Cornish explain. I'm not trying to get out of it, but I don't know the slander laws, and this whole business has me upset."

"Sure. But I want to know before I start the autopsy."

Cornish, who had come back by police car, was ahead of them.

Pelham said, "You two didn't really meet. Joe Cornish, of course, Gerritt DeGraaf."

"Call me Joe," Cornish said, sticking out his hand. "Sulfur fuel allergy."

"What?"

"You'll find out, if you haven't already, that half the people around here, except for the very old, have come here for some medical reason. In fact, if you're young and you don't have a medical reason, people wonder what you were running away from. Anyway, mine was an allergy to sulfur fuel, especially the high-sulfur kind they burn in Illinois."

"Public buildings in Illinois are required to burn the stuff because it's mined in Illinois. You're not unusual in reacting to it."

"I left a police position in a city south of Chicago and came here."

"You know your police business. I can see that."

"Well, thank you. We try. But of course in a town this size we don't get homicides. I haven't had anything that looked like murder since I've been here."

"And you think this is it?"

"It sure smells like it, but I'm waiting for your report."

"All right. But before I do the autopsy and before there's any report, you two are going to tell me what all the mumbo-jumbo is about."

"Mumbo-jumbo?" Cornish asked.

"I want to know why Pelham came hurrying over to get me. Look, you say you never have homicides. I'll buy that. But in a place where most of the population is over sixty-five, you must have a fair number of sudden deaths. Therefore, you must have a coroner or medical examiner. You didn't call him this time. Why?"

Cornish looked at Pelham. Pelham looked at Cornish. For a moment the night seemed darker and colder. Pelham said, "You tell him. You're the police."

"Our regular coroner, Gerritt, is one of our residents. He's a doctor, semi-retired. Has an office and sees patients about three days a week. His name is John Nash."

"Oh."

"From your tone of voice, I guess you've seen him."

"At the meeting."

"Of course. Well, he's been one of the Young Lake people most upset by the children. He isn't one of the loudest, because he isn't a loud sort of person. But his remarks are more vitriolic than most."

"Yes?"

"A week ago Tim Barkus's mother came to me with a complaint. Tim was afraid of something Dr. Nash had said to him.

"What?"

"He said that if he caught Tim running over his lawn again, he'd break his legs."

"Wow! That's an extreme remark. Still—people speak to children differently from the way they speak to adults. I certainly see your problem. You can't have a person acting as coroner who might use the position to cover up a homicide. His own homicide."

"Hardly," Cornish said dryly.

"All the same, you don't seriously think he'd go that far, do you? To murder a child to protect his lawn? It's incredible. Aside from whatever scruples he may have, he strikes me as a fairly cautious person, too."

"Sure. But what if he struck the kid, not meaning to kill him, and the kid's head hit a rock and he died? Or say he laid a trap for Tim, intending to frighten him, but it worked too well and killed him?"

"He's a doctor. He ought to know where the danger lines are."

"Things go wrong. And then, Tim may have had some special sensitivity. You hear of people with exceptionally thin skulls—"

"Yes."

"And besides, while he might know the danger line in the normal course of events, this wasn't normal. Tempers have been high. He might have lost his sense of caution. We don't know what Dr. Nash is like when he's in a rage."

"No. Well, there's no sense speculating without facts. Am I supposed to use the infirmary as an autopsy room?"

"Can you? It's not perfect, but it's well equipped."

"I guess. I'll have to send specimens to a major lab, though."

"No problem. Label 'em and George or Sergeant Fish can drive 'em to Tucson when you're done."

"Two other things."

"Yes?"

"Why don't you want to call in outside help?"

"Peter? You want to answer that?"

"Okay. We don't want to call the state police into it, because the case would be totally outside our control from the moment they got involved. I hope we don't have a murder, but if we have, I want Joe here and me to be giving out the interviews to the papers. If anybody else does it, they'll blow up this generation gap thing and make us look like fools here. You've seen what their articles are like. And what it would do to property values I don't like to think."

"I see," Gerritt said rather stiffly.

"Maybe you don't approve. But our people mostly have their life savings tied up in their houses. I wouldn't suggest we stay in charge—at least I hope I wouldn't—if we didn't have a capable man on the spot. But Joe has a big-city homicide background, and he knows his onions."

"I agree with that."

"Besides which, he knows the people here better than any outside man could, even with a month of work."

"I'm sure that's true, too."

"I believe we are more likely to get to the bottom

of this with Joe on the job than if we go outside."

"Speech, speech," Joe applauded.

"All right," DeGraaf laughed. "The second thing is this. I wish you would tell Dr. Nash the reason you've called me in. Professional courtesy. I don't want to take over his job without him knowing why."

"He'll know why," Joe said grimly. "I saw him last week about the kid's complaint."

"What did he say?"

"Said it wasn't true."

"Hmmmp."

"But, sure, I'll tell him it forces me to turn to you."

"Good enough. I'd better get to work. I think that deputation of old people is outside. My fault. I kind of thought they'd go home to bed. But at least it cleared the scene long enough to get something done."

"I'll tell them about the accident," said Pelham. "It's nearly eight now. When will you have results?"

"Two hours at the very soonest."

"Wait a minute, Peter," said Cornish. "We're going to have to get together on how much we give out, before we talk with anybody. Even the parents."

"The parents?" Pelham stared.

"It wouldn't be the first time a parent has beaten a child to death and tried to cover up," Cornish said, and DeGraaf nodded in agreement.

Pelham looked stunned for a second. "Nice places you fellas come from," he said.

"It happens everywhere."

"Well, I'll just tell the old folks who it is and the

fact that he's dead. I'll tell 'em we'll have more details in the morning."

Young Lake had a full-time infirmary, staffed by three full-time nurses. The three took eight-hour shifts and were on call to visit homes, also. There were four beds and a small laboratory in the facility. However, this was not intended as a hospital, but rather an emergency room, a place for treatment of minor problems, and a sort of holding station if someone were very ill and waiting for an ambulance from Tucson. Actually, the most important function of the infirmary was non-medical: it reassured nervous old people that, even out here in the desert, medical equipment and medical opinion were always available. Oxygen was stored rather prominently. There were a number of breathing problems in town, as this was a climate where asthmatics and chronic bronchitis cases were often sent. In addition, there were heart problems and a prevalent fear of heart attacks. Without the facility, the town could not have grown as successfully as it had.

The equipment was excellent and new. The lighting was good. There was no autopsy table, of course. A standard autopsy table has a system of water sprinklers at the slightly raised upper end and a system of drains at the lower end, to carry away liquids.

On the table, under a sheet, was the small body.

DeGraaf had asked that the body be transported and placed in the same position that it had been found. He wanted the postmortem lividity unconfused.

He looked more closely at the body. In a way, he

experienced the same feeling as with an emergency patient. In emergency cases there was the added urgency, of course: discover what had gone wrong and correct it before it was too late. But here still was the puzzle. What had gone wrong? If it was murder, how had it been done? Who had done it? The body called out to him to work back from the facts he could see and find out. Ultimately, it was a request for vengeance.

He photographed the abrasions on the elbows, legs, and even the clothes. In detail, he noted everything external that marked the body—dust, scratches, stains. He photographed the bruises on the neck.

As always, he had a moment when he knew he was taking extra time over the externals. It was the moment when he should make the first cut, and after all these years still dreaded it. It was worse with children, too.

He put down the feeling, focusing on the puzzle. What had happened to the little boy with brown hair? What was the body trying to tell him? He made the first cut.

Chapter Three

"Strangulation," DeGraaf said in Cornish's office at ten that night.

"No accident, then," said Pelham.

"Not even a joke gone wrong," said Cornish.

DeGraaf said, "I thought you'd be home in bed, Mayor."

"I couldn't have slept anyway. So it's definitely murder?"

"Definitely."

"Okay," said Cornish. "Tell us what we need to know."

"Right. I exposed about three rolls of film, by the way. Abrasions, lividity, the condition of the face. You'll want them developed for your own use and a set held for evidence, I should think."

"Yes."

"I also left a row of specimens on the counter that should be sent to a lab. They might eliminate a few far-out possibilities, but I'd be surprised if they told us anything new or unusual. More to be thorough than anything else."

"Good."

"The test for the potassium concentration of the

vitreous humor of the eye may confirm the time of death, but only approximately."

"I thought you got the time of death from the temperature," said Pelham.

"Only roughly. It can take a full day for the body of a fully clothed adult to reach room temperature, for instance. But the variations are enormous. Larger or fatter people cool more slowly. Some causes of death actually *raise* the body temperature after death, which very few people realize. Cholera, typhoid, stroke, strychnine poisoning and strangulation all do. And we're dealing with strangulation here. Now we have a thin, small body, lightly clothed. Generally, you assume that a body loses two to two and a half degrees for each hour after death up to three hours. After that, one or one and a half degrees. But if the body is in a very cold room or outdoors in the cold, the heat loss is faster. If there is a wind, it may be *much* faster. And yet it isn't evenly faster. By that I mean you can't really predict that in a much colder spot the heat loss will be proportionately that much greater. If the air temperature is at all near body temperature, of course, heat loss is pretty meaningless."

"And yet you took his temperature."

"Sure, it's one factor. It confirms other facts—or not. These things can be expressed best as probabilities. If you have two separate facts tending toward one conclusion, that conclusion is much more probably right than if you have only one. You triangulate your data, you see. It is still only a probability. It's never a hundred per cent, but with enough data you can get close. Take the time of death, for instance. His body temperature was 82.1 degrees. That's a loss of six and a half degrees. The air temperature when we got there was 62 degrees. But at four o'clock this afternoon it was 85 degrees. You know how fast it cools in the desert in the evening. As soon as the sun started to get low the temperature began dropping. Maybe it was 75 degrees at five o'clock and 68 degrees at six. You see how complicated that makes the influence of the air temperature on the cooling of the body? What else? There was no wind. One other complicating factor out of the way. There was no moisture, which might also cool the body by evaporating. Taken all together, from the *temperature,* I would say he was killed close on four p.m., but that's only a general idea. It may be that the sun on that dirt bakes it so hot that a body falling on it is actually *warmed* at first. I can test that tomorrow by going out and seeing how warm the earth really is and how long it stays warm if you cover it with something. What is really valuable, though, is to take this temperature indication together with other facts."

"Like what?"

"His mother said, didn't she, that he had a snack at a little after three? Cookies? They had started to digest, but were still in the stomach. So we have two facts tending to tell us he died about four. A third test is the clouding of the eye. There was a filming of the eyeball, which you often see as soon as fifteen minutes after death, but no clouding of the cornea. The clouding of the cornea, lack of it, that is, is not much help, since it doesn't begin usually until about twelve hours after death. But his eyes were open, and both drying and filming suggest two to three hours passed before he was found. In other words, there is no reason, from the evidence of the eye, to think he was killed much later than we thought. It checks. Three facts."

"Okay."

"When we get the report on the potassium concentration from the eye, it will probably tend to the same conclusion. It operates on the idea that the retina releases potassium after death. The problem with it is that individuals vary a lot in how much potassium they put out. Same problem as temperature, you see. But within certain limits it should help. If so, it will be a fourth fact."

"They all sound extremely variable."

"Oh, they are. There is a fifth—rigor. There was some stiffness about the face and neck. That was all. Rigor mortis proceeds faster in hot weather, but it's extremely variable also. It can come on fifteen minutes after death, but that's unusual. Or sometimes not for twelve to fifteen hours, but that's unusual too. This amount of stiffening in a normal child under conditions that aren't too extreme suggests about two to four hours. You see how much guess work is involved?"

"I certainly do," said Pelham, looking a little sick.

"But there are no strange effects in this case. Nothing is way out of line. None of the figures are unusual. We can say that the weight of probability is *very* strong that death occurred between quarter of four and five."

"All right," said Cornish. "What about the cause? How was he strangled?"

"By hands. There are no cuts on the neck. No cloth burns. No deep marks. No abrasions. My impression is that he was choked by bare hands, or hands and an arm crooked around his neck. The bruises are somewhat confused and there is a possibility that it was both. I would think the killer wrapped his arm around Tim's neck from behind and squeezed, and the pressure on the carotid sinuses made the boy unconscious. Then, with thumb and fingers pressing in and the heel of the hand pushing, the killer shut off the windpipe. The hyoid is broken."

"How much strength would that take?"

"Not a good question, because when the choking was done, the boy was probably unconscious. The easiest way, then, would be with the child on his back and the killer leaning down on him. Anybody with a little weight, a very little weight, would do. It would have to be someone who could bend, I suppose. Not a *very* feeble person, or the boy would have got out of the arm hold around his neck. Nobody with severe arthritis, for instance. But the limits are not very helpful."

"What size fingers?"

"From the bruises, average, though there was quite a lot of shifting, and the impressions are blurred. Overlapped may be the word. Probably not a child. Certainly not any seven-foot, three-hundred-pound, ham-handed football tackle. There'd be more deep damage. Anybody with markedly long or very short fingers won't do."

"Scratches from fingernails?"

"No, but they aren't all that likely. Try it yourself. Put your hand to the front of your neck and push in with the heel of your hand and the flats of your fingers. The nails don't contact. And this would be even more true with the child lying flat on his back. Of course if you run into some woman with long, pointed, mandarin fingernails, she didn't do it."

"Mrs. Corbin is out," said Pelham, breaking his silence.

"Oh, god, yes," said Cornish. "And a pity, too."

"Who's she?"

"Oh, a grand woman. Lavender-blue hair. Has it done three times a week. Silver shoes with three-inch platforms. Fingernails at least two inches long and bright rose. She's seventy-two if she's a day. You can't miss her."

"I have the picture."

"What else do you know?" Cornish asked.

"I can guess at quite a bit. There was a rough spot on the back of the head, with a little bleeding. Considerable roughing up of the hair on the back. Lots of roughing of the hair on the left side of the head, and abrasions of the scalp in the same place, *without* bleeding. Abrasions of the left elbow and side of the left arm without bleeding. He was wearing a short-sleeved shirt, you remember. Abrasions of the *point* of the right elbow with no bleeding. Roughing of the left side of the left sock over the anklebone. Some abrasion of the left cheekbone. No bleeding. Considerable roughing up of the outside, that is, left side, of the left leg of his Levis. Dust on the shirt and pants. Now—postmortem lividity. We found him lying on his right side. The top of the body, or left side as he lay, had paled, which it will do as gravity drains the blood to the lowest places. The reddish hue of the right side, that is, lower side as we found him, confirms that he had been lying on his right side for some time. In the internal organs, however, there is some clotting on the left side of some spaces. Now, postmortem lividity takes a little while to develop. You almost never notice it before half an hour after death, and a couple of hours is more likely. If a body is moved after that, after lividity develops, and the position is changed, you get a conflicting pattern of staining and you can make a good guess about the position before it was moved. When it's moved during the first half hour or so, you can't guess accurately. But that's what I think happened."

"How? What do you mean?"

"I think he was killed somewhere else. In an area with a rough surface—something like a street, sidewalk, or baked mud ground. That's why there was an abrasion on the back of his head, with bleeding. Whoever leaned on him to close off his air, rubbed the back of his head on a moderately rough surface. Of course, if it had happened after death there wouldn't have been any bleeding. As it is, there isn't much. I took samples from the abrasion. Maybe there are particles that can tell a lab what sort of surface he was lying on when he was killed."

"What you mean is, maybe and maybe not."

"I'm afraid so. Anyway, I think he was then bundled into a fairly small, partly or entirely closed container and transported. On his *left* side. From that he received the abrasions on his left elbow, left side of the left pants leg, left anklebone and sock, shoe, cheekbone, and roughing of the hair and the abrasions on the left side of his head. Without bleeding. He was dead. I think it was a fairly deep container, and closed, or at least narrow, because the point of the right elbow was abraded also. You see, both elbows were rubbing against the sides of whatever he was trundled along in. It must have been quite a small space, or he would not have been folded up enough to be forced against the sides sufficiently firmly to rub both elbows and both knees. And of course he was left side down. This is consistent with the slight internal clotting.

"When he got to the bank where we found him, he was either lifted out or dumped out, and either lay where he fell or rolled down the bank a way. I would like to try rolling a rag doll on that slope, just to see whether it picks up the same amount of dust. But it isn't too important. Whichever way he got there, he came to rest on his right side, and from the lividity patterns it is quite clear he was not moved again."

"Well, that's—uh, very interesting." Pelham spoke with admiration tempered with some reluctance. He was uncertain how to express approval of the deductions without also expressing cheer in the presence of death.

"Any chance he scratched the person who killed him?" Cornish wanted to know.

"I've scraped the fingernails. The lab might use neutron activation analysis and see what's there, but it'll be a bitch."

"Why?"

"Well, he was a little boy. I've done each fingernail separately, and labelled the samples separately, but I was amazed. There was what looked like poster paint in four different colors, orange predominating. Some sandy dirt. Glue—probably white glue. Something I'll swear was dirt mixed with peanut butter. Something sticky and purple. We might ask whether he had peanut butter and grape jelly for lunch. Two of the nails were broken. Didn't look like they'd broken today, though. The edges were somewhat smoothed. Ballpoint pen on the palms, which I didn't scrape. I made a note on the report. Most of the other nails badly needed cutting. There was nothing that looked like fiber, skin, blood, or hairs. Some milk was on the left elbow. A small stab wound, partly healed, maybe about four days old, on the right wrist."

"I'll get the stuff off to the lab right away. Most of the guys are out in the cars looking for tramps. I'll call one in."

"You figure it's some tramp?" Pelham asked eagerly.

"Nope. But I have to check."

DeGraaf said, "I promised the parents I'd see them. I can't really back out."

"Right. We have to decide what facts we're going to use," said Cornish.

"Use for what?" Pelham asked.

"Well, you can't give everything you've got out to everybody. You have to keep some of the facts to yourself. To be able to eliminate false confessions, for example—"

"Who would want to confess to killing a child?" Pelham gasped.

"Probably nobody here. But you just never know with people. Also, it's nice if you know a few things the killer doesn't know you know."

"Personally," DeGraaf said, "I feel we owe it to the parents to give them the information on how he died. That he was strangled, I mean. That he was unconscious first, because that may be some comfort to them. And the approximate time. That may help the mother feel that it would have done no good to start the hunt earlier. I don't believe in sitting on information that could make relatives feel a little better."

"No. Okay," Cornish said. "But we don't give out any deductions or other details."

"Even to the papers?" Pelham asked.

"Even to the papers, Peter," said Cornish.

"You're coming to the Barkus house with me, aren't you?" DeGraaf asked Cornish.

"Sure. You can't be very eager to go."

"No. But it's possible something important may come out. And if they had anything to do with it, we'll really want to have seen them early."

"You ever run into a parent who killed a child but hadn't beaten it plenty before?"

"No, but there's always a first time."

"How right you are. I'll get Fish to watch the store."

"And I," said Pelham, "will go home and try to sleep. Damn that John Nash. I'm out of sleeping pills and that stingy Scot will never prescribe more than a thimbleful at one time."

"He's right. They won't do you any real good. Read if you can't sleep," DeGraaf suggested.

"Hmmp. All I have left is *Desert Plants of the Southwest.*"

"Dry reading. It'll put you right to sleep."

* * *

They drove out to the Barkus house in Cornish's car. The house was on Canyon Trail, which formed the west half of West Loop, DeGraaf's grandmother's loop. Apparently the builder had thought it would be confusing to have the same street name extend all the way around the loop and back to the beginning. So while Adelaide Ross lived on the inside of the loop but the east side, she lived on Saguaro Drive; the Barkus house was on the outside of the west side and was on Canyon Trail. Facing it, across the street, but still on Canyon, were three undeveloped lots. Just behind those were Popeye's house, and next to it, DeGraaf's grandmother's.

"Dr. Nash's problem," said Cornish, "was that the Barkus kid used to cut through his yard to get to the east side of the East Loop to play with the Potts girl. Sometimes Tim played with the Lane kids. They live across the street from your grandmother."

"Kids all over the world take short cuts."

"I know, but the people here expected to have a Garden of Eden, I guess. There's the house."

The Barkus house looked barren in the dark. Every light inside appeared to be on, and the drapes were open. Instead of making the place look cheerful, it looked hollow.

Cornish sat in the car a couple of seconds.

"I don't enjoy this," he said.

"Neither do I."

"Whatever it's worth, Gerritt, I appreciate your being willing to step in like this. You're here on vacation, and it isn't your job."

"Well, I'm curious, though. I can't resist trying

to find out what happened in a case like this."

"Be my guest."

"What do you mean?"

"Nose around yourself. Solve my case for me, if you can."

"Aren't you a little bit deficient in ego problems?"

"Yup. I used to be somewhat jealous. About people messing around in my territory. I got over it when my asthma attacks started. You can't know how frightening those things can be if you've never had one. You just can't draw a breath."

"I can imagine."

"I doubt it. It sounds like such a trivial illness. There were so many times I thought I wasn't going to get another breath—my attitude toward my job changed. Don't know why. Anybody who had a suggestion that could get the job done, God bless 'em. Maybe I started to think that if I weren't there the job would still have to get done, so why not? Then I chucked it all and came down here. And, sure enough, they *are* getting along without me."

"What about the asthma?"

"Haven't had it since. But my feeling about help is the same. That is, if the person is qualified and doesn't get in the way."

"Good enough."

At the door of the Barkus house, DeGraaf had the odd sensation that the place was unlived-in. The husband opened the door at their knock, looking apologetic, though there was no reason why he should. Mrs. Barkus was seated on the sofa, holding a glass with fluid in it the color of bourbon. But there was no suggestion of drunkenness, only an unnaturally vacant quality as she echoed her husband's words.

"Yes, come in."

Barkus waved his hand vaguely at the room. Taking that to mean they should find a seat wherever they wanted, DeGraaf and Joe Cornish moved quickly to the nearest they saw.

"Well," said Mrs. Barkus, "I don't know why you're here, Joe. You failed. I told you they were dangerous. I told you over *and* over, and you didn't do a thing to protect Tim."

"Are you sure 'they' hurt him, Mrs. Barkus?" DeGraaf asked.

"The old people killed him. It was no accident."

"How do you *know?*"

"From the way he looked."

"But didn't you say it was murder before you even saw the body?"

"Sure, I did. There's murder in this town. There has been for months. It just got—it got Tim first."

DeGraaf thought for a moment that she was going to cry, but he misread her emotion. She was angry. After a time she said, "We could have got out of here, too, if Bill had any guts." She looked at her husband with contempt.

Her husband cleared his throat and looked at the lamp.

"He had a chance of a job in Phoenix, and he didn't take it," she said.

"It would have meant taking a cut in salary. And the houses in Phoenix cost a fortune," Barkus said, staring at the place where the carpet met the wall.

"And how much was Tim worth, I wonder," said Mrs. Barkus impassively, looking directly at DeGraaf.

"A lot, I should think," DeGraaf said.

"How was he killed?"

"He was strangled, Mrs. Barkus."

She said nothing for a moment, then realized she had said nothing and said, "Oh," quite carefully.

"He was unconscious before he was strangled. Made unconscious by pressure on the carotid. He wouldn't have suffered. We think it happened around four o'clock."

"Oh."

"Could you answer some questions about Tim, Mrs. Barkus? I wish you would believe that we very much want to find out who did this. Would you like Chief Cornish to ask the questions, or shall I?"

"Joe blew it. I'll talk with you. Not him."

"Okay. You have to realize I don't want to hurt your feelings when I ask something. If something is just too hard for you to talk about right now, please tell me. Otherwise, I'll go ahead. Talking helps some people and hurts others. So you'll have to let me know."

"All right."

"And you, too, Mr. Barkus. I wish you'd tell me anything you can think of that might be important." He wondered why he hadn't noticed Barkus enough to include him in the conversation before this.

Barkus moved his eyes to DeGraaf for a second, nodded, then transferred his gaze to an electric plug. Mrs. Barkus turned the wedding ring on her finger over and over.

"Can you tell me about today? Was Tim acting at all unusual when he left for school this morning?"

"Yes. But he's usually pretty hyper," she said.

"Reacts to things. If he doesn't feel like going to school, then he hates school. If he's got something special for show-and-tell, then he can't wait to get there. This morning he was enthusiastic, but he didn't say what about."

"So he walked to the bus stop?"

"Yes."

"And you didn't see him again until when?"

"Well, the bus gets here almost exactly at three. It takes Tim a couple of minutes to walk home from the stop. The stop is on Mesquite Lane, so it's not more than a city block, really. What time he actually gets here depends on how much time·he spends talking with his friends first. Most of them have the habit of running home to eat something before they play."

"So he actually got here—"

"I was trying to think. Maybe five after. I wasn't watching the clock, but I was waiting for him, and it was about usual. Not late or early."

"And then what?"

"He was hungry, naturally. He had cookies and apple juice. He didn't like milk and I didn't like to give him soft drinks. Oh, hell—" For a moment tears filled her eyes. Then she said, "Damn!" and went on. "He gulped his food. He always did. I had to go to the store. I was out of everything, bread, milk, you name it. Tim wanted to go out and do something, and I said I had to leave for the store by three-thirty."

"Couldn't you have gone without him? Left him out playing?"

"Sure. But he liked to go. So I said he could take fifteen minutes."

"Fifteen minutes for what?"

"I don't know."

"Did he give you any idea what *sort* of thing he wanted to do?"

"No, not a word."

"Well, how did he say it?"

"He said something like, 'I promised somebody I'd take care of something.' "

"That's vague enough."

"Well, it seemed he had a secret. Nothing bad, but the kind of thing where you promise a friend you won't tell."

"And then what did you say?"

"I said that if he could get it done in fifteen minutes I'd wait and he could go with me."

"And he said?"

"I'll do the best I can to remember. He said, 'Okay. If I can't do it in fifteen minutes, I'll come back and do it later.' And I said, 'All right. Hurry up, now.' And he said, 'It isn't something you can do in a hurry, but I'll be right back.' "

"It isn't something you can do in a hurry?"

"That or words pretty close to it."

"And then?"

"He ran out and I waited. Had a cup of coffee, but he didn't come back."

"Children often lose track of time. Why did it worry you?"

"I can answer that one for sure. The atmosphere around this place. It's rotten."

"But nothing really serious had happened."

"You don't think so? With that kid having his arm broken? And the scorpions in the mailboxes? And somebody left Mrs. Lane a note that they'd put a tarantula in her *house* some night!"

"Tarantulas and scorpions aren't usually deadly."

"I've heard that one before. Not usually. But our hiking guide always said they could be, to children and old people."

"Sometimes, yes."

"Well, that's what we're talking about here, isn't it? Children and old people?"

"Yes. Yes, you're right."

"We could have had something serious happen before this. It just happened now. And it just happened to my Tim. And it *enrages* me."

"What was Tim's attitude toward the atmosphere in town?"

"It's hard to say. The children, all of them, seemed to think of it as a sort of challenge. Exciting, like a feud, you know."

"What did they do about it?"

She hesitated. "I don't know whether they *did* anything about it. They talked a lot. And that isn't the same thing."

"What did they talk about?"

"Oh, getting even. Taking care of themselves. I once heard them saying they should go around in pairs. Buddy system. They got that from summer camp swimming rules. I sure wish they had done it."

"Yes." He waited to see whether his silence would cause her to come up with anything else.

"They talked about identifying their enemies. I don't know exactly what they meant by that. It was pretty obvious who their 'enemies' were. That venomous little dried-up Dr. Nash, for one. Sweet people, like Abby Francot and Becky Simmons—

and I told Tim this—were old folks, too, but they never made fusses about the children. They said they liked to hear them around. It was cheerful, they said. Oh, you knew who your enemies were."

"Did the children plan to retaliate? Against Nash, for instance?"

"Oh, no, no. Nothing like that."

"But children *do* talk big."

"No. Nothing like that."

For some reason that question had dried up her conversation. He had come to the end of what he wanted to ask, anyway, with two exceptions.

"Which direction did Tim go when he went out after the cookies?"

"I don't know. He went out the front, and I was in the kitchen."

"What did he usually do after school?"

"He played with the Lane kids, or Fib Levinson, or Libby Potts. There isn't much choice around here."

DeGraaf rose. Cornish got up, too.

"Well, thank you, Mrs. Barkus. If you think of anything, will you let me or Chief Cornish know?"

"Sure. But I know what to think already. Nash killed him."

"Well," said Cornish uncomfortably, "we'll check out every lead we have."

"You do that," said Mrs. Barkus. "Lock the barn door."

The two men headed for the door. Barkus followed them.

"Say. *Where* did they play?" DeGraaf asked.

"What?"

"After school. Where did the kids play?"

Barkus turned to his wife, who was now standing in the middle of the room, holding on to her elbows with both hands. "Everywhere," she said. "Sometimes in the park. They *call* it a park. It's really empty land in the middle of the East Loop."

"Okay, Mrs. Barkus. Thanks again," DeGraaf said. They went out the door, and Barkus closed it after them, without a word. They walked to the car and didn't speak until they were in it.

"I thought he was going to come after us and tell us something," Cornish said.

"So did I."

"Odd. I know they're under stress—"

"But they don't react the way they should. Or he doesn't. I know."

"I'll drop you home."

"No, I'll just cut across the vacant lots. It can't be a hundred yards."

"If you want."

"Are you serious about me poking around in this thing? I'm fairly irrepressible when I get started."

"Of course I'm serious. Life isn't long enough for stupid jokes. Just tell me what you find out."

"Naturally."

"Good night."

Cornish's car pulled away. DeGraaf was left standing on the sidewalk in front of the Barkus house. He looked back at it. Barkus crossed in front of one window, probably the dining room, then crossed another, heading for the back of the house. As DeGraaf stood there, he came back again, apparently carrying nothing, through the

dining room, past the living room window, and
around to the back on the other side. Doing nothing. Aimless pacing. There was no sign of Mrs.
Barkus. DeGraaf turned away and crossed the
street.

Away from the porch light and street light, the
stars jumped into view. Barren land appeared, in
high relief now from the lights that struck it
diagonally and at a distance. The terrain sloped
away unevenly down to the north, toward the end
of the Loop, and the slope to the dry wash where
the body had been found. Between DeGraaf and
that spot were lots equivalent to seven houses. The
boy had been killed near home.

On the west side of the street three of the seven
lots had been built upon, the Barkus house and two
others nearer the wash. On the inside of the Loop,
there was just one house, about halfway to the
wash. The rest was dust and scrub and stakes with
white rags marking lot lines.

DeGraaf had been thinking that the child had
been killed almost within sight of home, but in fact
that was not quite the case. The unevenness of the
ground and the scrubby growth combined to limit
visibility. In addition, wherever there were houses
there were the inevitable bunches of landscaping
bushes between the sidewalk and the street.

The lots had at first seemed small to him, laid
against the backdrop of the entire desert as they
were. But in fact, compared to the fifty or a hundred front feet that a Chicago house might have,
even in its expensive suburbs, these appeared to be
a hundred and fifty. He supposed land here was
once so cheap that large gardens were possible.

And the privacy this afforded would be an attraction of the place, too. One would not easily see what one's neighbor was doing. It also reduced the likelihood of someone having witnessed the murder.

Slowly, watching for ditches, cacti and strings that might be tied between stakes, DeGraaf made his way toward his grandmother's house. Come to think of it, he only hoped that it was his grandmother's house. He was a newcomer here, after all, and had seen these places from this angle only in daylight. Possibly he should go around in front and check the house numbers, rather than barging in the wrong back door and scaring some little old lady to death.

Then he saw a shadow move, ahead of him.

Instinctively, he stopped dead and froze, watching for the movement to come again. The shadow resolved itself into a figure, bent over, and DeGraaf heard a scraping in the dirt. DeGraaf moved forward cautiously, keeping behind a dead saguaro cactus. In the yard of the house next to his grandmother's, someone was digging.

The street light near his grandmother's house threw wide shadows of the houses over the back yards. DeGraaf could not see what was going on in the next yard without going closer. And in order to get closer, he had to cross the strip of light between the houses.

Quickly, he decided the best resolution of the problem would be to walk directly over, openly, like a neighbor on a late stroll, and see what would happen next.

Noisily, he scuffed the underbrush as he went towards the yard. He didn't rush it, but he kept going, so that once the figure heard him it would be too late to cover up whatever was going on, and, by the same token, little reason to think DeGraaf was sneaking up.

The figure didn't move.

"Hi!" called DeGraaf, now some fifteen feet away.

"Oh. 'Lo there." There was no start, no rush on the part of the figure to cover up anything. De-Graaf realized that his carefully reasoned approach had been a waste, for the person was rather deaf and had not heard the scuffling. It was Popeye, pipe clenched in his teeth, holding a garden trowel. He was dressed in bib-front overalls that even in this light looked very blue, and a red-and-white checked shirt, with checks two inches square.

"What 'cha doing?" DeGraaf asked bluntly.

"Plantin'. What're you doing?"

"Walking."

"Hmm."

"Got your gardening outfit on?" DeGraaf asked, and thought of a cartoon he had seen years before of a gentleman farmer in similar attire, holding a small trowel, working the pots in his penthouse window sill garden.

"Sure thing."

"How can you see, this time of night?"

"You're seeing me, aintcha?"

"You've got a point there." DeGraaf let the conversation die, though it had never been lively. He hoped silence would force some revelation. Apparently this was not the sort of person that such a technique worked with, for they stood together, gazing into the middle distance, Popeye to the north and DeGraaf to the south-by-southeast. Finally DeGraaf thought he had backed himself into a corner, and said, "I know a couple of farmers up home who think it's better to plant on nights with full moons. They say they get better germination that way."

"Not me. The problem is I don't sleep. At night, that is. I can take a dandy nap in the daytime. Two or three some days. But I can't sleep at night. So I work. Why not?"

"Why not, indeed?"

"I was night supervisor at a factory. A pottery factory. Thirty-five years. You know, the kilns stay hot. You can't just go home and leave the stuff, like—oh, sewing machines. I ran the whole place at night. Nearly as many workers as we had by day. But I guess I never learned good sleep habits that way. I'd nap in the daytime, but I never got the hang of sleeping straight through, day or night. Days were too noisy."

"Not here."

"Nope, not here. I figured when I came here it'd all be different. But you don't change your spots that easy." He picked up a hoe from the ground and leaned on it.

"Planting flowers?"

"Nope. Stupid things, flowers. No use. Vegetables are just as nice looking—if you aren't prejudiced. Kale is pretty. There's flowering kale that's pink in the middle with a white border. The leaves *themselves* are pink, I mean. It's a little hot here for kale, but you can put it in the shade of something. Then there's tomatoes. Grow like weeds here. I

picked up a couple of rotten tomatoes the supermarket was throwing out. I put 'em out here and
just stepped on 'em. Squashed 'em into the ground,
you follow me?"

"Mmm-mm."

"And I've been eating tomatoes ever since. Not
one penny spent. Not *one penny*." He chuckled.

"That's pretty good."

"Eggplant. You ever see eggplant flowers?"

"Lavender?"

"Yup. Like little lavender stars. Not so little,
either. These have two-inch blossoms. Pretty as
any border flower and you can eat the results. People mostly haven't got any sense. I could *live* off
what I grow."

"I suppose. Hey, Popeye, you see any kids
around today?"

"That little Potts girl came nosing around.
Why?"

"The one with braids? What about Tim
Barkus?"

"I didn't see him today. I guess I'm not on his
regular patrol. They say I'm lucky." He laughed.
"Kids! Reminds me of my grandson. Used to pick
the neighbor's flowers and then give 'em to her because he liked her so much. 'Course, he's outgrown
that. He's twenty-seven now."

"Well, I was wondering—"

"What's the matter?"

Popeye, DeGraaf reflected, was not slow.

"To tell the truth, he seems to have been killed."

"Omigawd. How?"

"Strangled."

"Jeez, I thought you meant by a car or something. When and where?"

"This afternoon. Down there." DeGraaf pointed toward the end of the Loop and the dry wash, not too specifically.

"I must've slept through the whole thing."

"Did a policeman ring your bell this afternoon?"

"I didn't hear it, if he did. I might have been taking a nap. My hearing is pretty good, but it used to be better. My daughter says I hear what I want to hear. People around here all say their kids say that. Heh!"

"Well, listen. If you think of anything odd you saw around here today, will you let me know?"

"Sure thing. But listen, son. Ain't I supposed to tell the police?"

"Tell them, too. Them and me is buddies. Tell either of us, but don't tell anybody else."

"Okay. Goodnight."

DeGraaf waved and was inside his grandmother's front door before he realized that Popeye had never actually told him what he was planting.

His grandmother was still up. He watched her come to the door, not looking young, and he felt it had been a very long day for both of them.

"I was just going to make you a hot toddy," she said. "They were very popular about 1910, I think."

"Should you be up late like this? It's the witching hour."

"The witching hour is midnight. It's not quite that late yet."

"You'd rather be accurate than relevant. Lead me to my toddy."

"Toddies are very nice for after skating. You really should have seen the skating rinks in Chicago fifty years ago."

"All right. All right. You are very pointedly asking me nothing about what happened. I'll tell you."

Which, briefly, but with full technical detail, he proceeded to do. She listened all the way through, asking no questions until he had finished. He took her up to his conversation with Popeye.

"Did you ask the parents whether they knew what Tim had for lunch?"

"No. I never thought of it."

"No harm. You can do it later. Why didn't you push on the question of what games he played with the other children here?"

"She was very unforthcoming on that."

"I'll bet."

"What do you mean?"

"Tim was one of the reasons we've been having trouble. It isn't *only* the crochetiness of old people, although there's enough of that. Tim was the sort of child you feel was not valued at home. Unloved we used to call it, but I'm not sure that's quite the right word. I think it has something to do with whether the parents listen to the child when he talks. Or else there's some major problem in his home."

"What did he do specifically?"

"He was the sort who *would* run through flower beds. Because they were flower beds, I mean. Not because he forgot or was in a terrible hurry and needed a short cut. He'd especially run through the gardens of people who cared most for their gardens. I have the feeling the other children were not too fond of him, really, but you could check that."

"Hmmp."

"His mother had *plenty* of complaints."

"Who did he bother the most?"

"Oh, the grouches, of course. They'd react, you see. Dr. Nash. Cora Grundler. Cora lives diagonally south across the street. Ellen Norris Brown, who wasn't on his direct route to anywhere. She's in the upper part of East Loop. Oh—and Sara Carini. He teased her just unmercifully. She lives at the point of the East Loop and her lawn makes a kind of point in front for that reason. Well, he'd habitually cut across it on his bike. Unnecessarily, I mean. She had a perfect *track* worn there. One time somebody left a few old cholla cactus branches in the track and his bike went over them and he fell in the rest. She always claimed they had just blown in. And you know, it didn't stop him."

"But Gran, you don't seriously think somebody killed a child just because he ran over a flower bed or some grass?"

"How do I know? According to your autopsy, *some*body killed him."

DeGraaf swallowed the last of his toddy and stood up. His grandmother rose too, and took his cup. He put his arm around her shoulders, kissed her pink, smooth cheek, and said good night.

Chapter Four

DeGraaf woke up early the next morning with a feeling he knew well. He thought of it as not being able to wait to get to work. Sometimes, in the past, he had taken time off from his regular job to work on a case. People would substitute for him. Or he would do both jobs, hardly sleeping, feeling fuzzy day after day. His supervisors reprimanded him occasionally for exchanging shifts with another man when he wanted to take off time for a murder case. He would point out that he invariably subbed for other doctors when they were sick, and generally the supervisors had the sense to stop complaining. Behind the complaints, though, was the fact that taking outside cases, not as a doctor but as a medical investigator, was not respectable. A physician was supposed to do only doctoring, ever. He was almost as bad as a renegade colleague who had, for years, written a series of gothic romances under a pen name. When the dirty fact came out, the poor man brought a bag lunch to work and ate in his office for seven weeks because the atmosphere in the doctor's cafeteria was intolerable.

So it was exhilarating to be away from Chicago, and free. At least for a few days while spring vacation lasted. The game, he thought, was afoot. Go!

But there was his grandmother.

"Gran," he asked, "if I go out and poke around in this thing and leave you here tatting, I would be a very inconsiderate guest, wouldn't I?"

"Oh—fish and house guests spoil in three days, they say. This is your third day, if you count Monday. Perhaps I'd just as soon you'd get out of the house."

"I was going to take you places."

"Actually, I thought you were going to rescue me."

"If so, things have got worse since I arrived."

"I have the perfect solution. I shall be your Watson if you need one."

"Oh great. We'll expose you to more danger. Mother would be so pleased."

"She won't know. I'll invite suspects to tea, or whatever. Martinis might be more up-to-date."

"Well, we'll see. This coffee is very properly made."

"Drip."

"Who, me? Oh, I see. The coffee. You are one of the few people these days who tries to do things properly."

"It is now the style to do them adequately."

"Gran, does Popeye—now, I know he's a friend of yours—does he usually go around digging up his garden in the middle of the night?"

"He doesn't sleep regularly, I know that. Naps on and off in the day. If I call him there's always a chance of waking him up. Not that he seems to mind."

"But have you ever seen him gardening in the dark?"

"No. But I haven't looked, either."

"You mean you've got 9,450 people in an area that small?" DeGraaf asked, looking at Cornish's wall map of Young Lake.

"Sure."

"But it's not more than two miles in any direction. In half an hour you can walk from the middle of it out into the desert."

"Look, if a house has a quarter of an acre to a lot, that's four lots in an acre."

"Right."

"Six hundred and forty acres in a square mile gives you 2,560 houses in a square mile. In four square miles—two miles by two miles—you'd have over 10,000 houses. That's plenty. Considering you have more than one person per house. Even leaving some room out for streets."

"So the murderer could have walked, driven, pushed a wheelbarrow, ridden a bicycle, or run a golf cart to that dry wash from anywhere in town without spending much more than half an hour on it."

"Barring arthritis. And definitely not walking. They'd sort of notice if you walked through Young Lake carrying a body. But with any vehicle, less than half an hour."

"All the same, he wouldn't want to go far afield, would he? He'd be noticed outside of his own neighborhood, don't you think?"

"Yes and no. People do a lot of walking and tricycle riding around here. Taking their constitutionals. But generally they either go around their own couple of blocks or down to the stores and back."

"What about the kids?"

"What do you mean, 'What about the kids?' "

"Do they play beyond their own area?"

"Not too much. They go farther than in most places, because there are so few kids to choose from. After all, if there are fifteen kids in the whole town, they all have to sort of know each other. They usually seem to be within a couple of blocks of home, though."

"How many are there in the Loops?"

"Five. Uh—sorry—now four. They played together mostly, from what I've seen."

"Guess your search for tramps didn't turn up anything?"

"Oh, lots. We found a kid, an eighteen-year-old kid, in the desert west of town about half a mile. He was on a walking tour, left the highway and went out into the open, slipped on some loose rock and got his foot wedged between two boulders. Been there for thirty-six hours. If we hadn't been out looking for suspicious characters, he probably would have died."

"You're absolutely certain he was trapped that long?"

"Gangrene in two toes. They amputed both at Scott hospital last night. No doubt at all."

"Peter Pelham better get used to the idea that this is local."

"I think he has. You can't expect him to leap at

the idea with delight. "

"And more than local. It's likely to belong to the Loops."

"I agree with that, too. Have you been out walking?"

"A little bit. Why?"

"You'd be even more convinced that it was a Loops problem. Look at the map."

DeGraaf looked.

"What's that?" DeGraaf asked, as Cornish pointed to markings that ran from the lake due northward, between the west side of town and the Loops.

"It's a gully of sorts. Young Lake—the lake itself, that is—and the spring that feeds it are both lower than rest of the town. Part of that low formation runs north out of Young Lake, between the Loops area and the west side of town, and then fans out into the dry wash where the body was found. That's why the land slopes down beyond your grandmother's place. The point I'm making is that it would be hard to cross the gully from the west of town with a dead body, to dump it in a wash near the Loops."

"Right. You'd have to come by road. The area beyond the Loops is entirely undeveloped. Why is that?"

"Somebody else owns it. Not Sunshine Company. It's owned by a Chicago firm or syndicate. They must have bought it for next to nothing."

"Can't it be built on?"

"Oh, sure it could. There's no road now, but building one would be easy. Even where Mesquite Lane runs across the gully there's only a little arch bridge. Doesn't even deserve to be called a bridge. It's more like a culvert. To make a road over the gully they could either take a curve or use landfill and go straight down."

"Okay. But as it stands now the only road entrance to the Loops is where they merge with Mesquite Lane."

"Yup. And I really don't see why anybody would take a dead body from one of the other streets in town all the way to Mesquite and then up into the Loops to dispose of it."

"No. Especially since they wouldn't know the Loop people well. It might turn out that they were all home, watching the street, sitting on their porches or something. They'd notice an unfamiliar face."

"And besides that, the streets in the north part of the rest of the town end in the same gully system. You could dump a body there just as well. As a matter of fact, all the streets in town either end in a gully or run out into the desert in a maximum of —let's see—eight blocks. Except Tucson Road, of course, but Yucca is right next to it and ends in the dump. I mean, the sanitary landfill."

"Yes. And the boy came from the Loops, too, of course. But I don't imagine we can just rest on the assumption that it's somebody there."

"Who's resting? I've got people going over the whole town. I want to find out whether anybody, anywhere, saw Tim Barkus yesterday after school. And whether they noticed anybody acting odd."

"You mean you're asking everybody in the whole place?"

"Not immediately. I don't have the manpower.

We could do a total canvass in two weeks or so, but I want some facts now. An appeal in the paper I've got already. Notices in the stores. And we'll start questioning nearest to where the body was found and work outward. Before I moved here, I always wished I was in a small enough place to do this—to make sure *everybody* knew what we were after. So often somebody knows something but doesn't quite like to *bother* the police—"

"I know. They don't want to make a fuss."

"Yes. I always thought, if we could just *ask!*"

"I agree."

"And we may turn up something soon. It isn't such a big place, the Loops."

"Get the samples to the lab?"

"Sure. We can't afford a neutron activation analysis on all the stuff, but we'll do it on a few. A couple of the fingernail scrapings especially. Everything else gets the regular lab work."

"Can you find out from the school what Tim had for lunch?"

"Sure."

"Listen, about the body. Who actually found it? You said something about a dog."

"Yes. The Lanes live on Saguaro, the east side of West Loop, across the street from your grandmother and a little north. Mrs. Lane's grandfather left her the house when he died here. I guess she moved in because it was inexpensive. She has two children. And a sheep dog. The dog usually stays indoors out of the heat of the sun. Last evening it was let out at six, when the day was getting cooler, and it didn't come back. Apparently that was unusual, so the kids got worried and went looking for it. That was about 6:45. They got to the bank near the dry wash and saw the dog sitting near something down the slope."

"Did they see the body?"

"Not exactly. Mrs. Lane said they saw something that disturbed them. So they called the dog."

"Who still wouldn't come, I'll bet."

"Right. That made them even more uneasy, so they went and got their mother. She came and climbed down there. And found the body."

"What did she do? Leave it?"

"No, she sent the children home, telling the older one to call me and have me come over. She didn't tell the children what had happened, I guess. Then she pulled the dog away and went up the bank a little way. Sat there and kept watch, with the dog, until we arrived."

"Sensible woman."

"Yes."

"Have you talked with the other neighbors?"

"Jeez, it's barely nine a.m. I figure there are at least thirty houses that face directly on one of the Loops. I'm starting out in about ten minutes. George takes shorthand and he's going along."

"Three of us together would be a little intimidating to people, don't you think? Shall we leave George behind and I'll take the shorthand?"

"Multi-talented, aren't you? Sure. George has plenty he can do right here."

"You'll find the old people here rather emphatic," said Cornish as they walked up Mesquite. "I mean their characters are very definite."

"Even their vaguenesses are definite?"

"Well, yes. The older people get, the more like themselves they become, if you see what I mean."

"I know. I've seen it."

"Even your grandmother?"

"No, she was always definite," Gerritt chuckled.

DeGraaf and Cornish strolled up Mesquite, past Young Lake and past the proposed site of the bath house, which was being levelled by bulldozer. A young man with hair like straw sat in the bucking seat of the bulldozer and grinned while plumes of dust rose from his work. A grey haired lady in a motorized wheelchair passed them on the other side of the street. Her wheel chair had a basket attachment on the back, with two wheels of its own. The basket was aluminum, DeGraaf thought, and appeared to be about twenty-four inches wide and thirty or so deep.

"Hi, there, Joe!" she called in a reedy voice.

"Hi, Abby. Going to market?"

"Naturally. Every day. Bye-bye."

DeGraaf watched Cornish's eyes touch the basket. They walked on.

"Now, Abby Francot is from the East Loop," Cornish said. "But here she is running down the West Loop. Out for air, probably."

"Or visiting."

They turned into Canyon Trail, the west side of West Loop, and were approached by a younger woman, about fifty-five, with pepper-and-salt hair.

She asked, "Who's there?"

"Joe Cornish, Miss Simmons."

DeGraaf took in the three-wheeler she rode, a guide dog on a leash attached to one handlebar. She steered with one hand and took signals from the dog with the other.

"I'd talk, but I'm going to market," she said. "Who's with you?"

"Grandson of Mrs. Ross. Dr. DeGraaf."

"Nice. See you both later."

She rode off, cautiously but steadily.

"Hmmm," Cornish said. "*See* you later. They get along so much better here, you know. In a normal city with a lot of hurrying people and fast traffic, and nobody to care—sometimes I think this place isn't so bad."

"I'd wondered why they built a ramp into every street corner. But it's necessary, isn't it? Those things don't go over curbs well."

"There's that, and other reasons too. People with canes who walk very poorly, but want their exercise. Crutches, walkers, the whole lot. And some don't hear and some don't see."

They looked after her as the tricycle ran down the next incline and into the street, the dog striding ahead. And they watched the carryall basket on the back of the tricycle, a big, square affair, built on between the two rear wheels.

"Mmmp," said Cornish as if he didn't enjoy his own thoughts. "There are hundreds of those baskets in town."

The sidewalks were unusually broad, the streets clean and entirely without the rubbish DeGraaf was used to. On their left they passed a vacant but graded lot, then the Barkus house, its blinds now all drawn. Then some undeveloped space, two lots wide, dry as the desert beyond and prickly with hostile looking plants. Across the street was the unbuilt land DeGraaf had cut through the night before, and north of that, a house.

"I don't think they're home," Cornish said.

They went up the walk to a tan stucco house. There was a truck in the drive with a ladder on top and a legend that read "Sun City Painting and Decorating." The door was open. They knocked, were not answered, and went in.

"What's up?" said a skinny little man wearing a paint-stiff pair of overalls.

"I'm the chief of police. Are the Larsons home?"

"Nope." He ducked his head like a desert bird.

"Will they be home later today?"

"Nope."

"Were they here yesterday?"

"Nope."

"Where are they?"

The man was silent.

"He only answers yes-or-no questions," De-Graaf suggested in a whisper.

"Do you know where they are?"

"Yup." The little man ducked his head, extruded his tongue, and replaced it, as if he'd caught a fly.

"Maybe they're in Tucson getting away from the paint smell until you're finished."

"Yup."

"Have you seen them at all in the last two days?"

"Nope." He ducked his head sideways, then put his brush down ostentatiously and folded his arms.

"You have drop cloths over the furniture in the bedroom, too?"

"Yup."

"So they wouldn't be likely to come here for the night, would they?"

"Nope."

"See anything that makes you think they were here last night? Water drops in the sink? Bed uncovered?"

"Nope."

"Know where they're staying in Tucson?"

"Nope."

"Well, that's fine. Thanks for the information," Cornish said, walking back out, trailed by De-Graaf. They left the door open, as they had found it, for ventilation. "Thinks he's Gary Cooper," Cornish muttered.

"No, he figures he only does what he gets paid for. You don't pay him for answers."

"The hell of it is, you can't swear at a guy if he's telling you *some*thing."

From inside, the slap-slapping of a brush could be heard.

Towards the end of West Loop was another undeveloped stretch on the east side of the street. There were two houses on the west. Nobody was home in either house.

"I think they work. And if they were at work yesterday, too, that's going to let them out."

"If," DeGraaf said.

"Sure, sure. I'll check it."

At the north end of the Loop on the inside was a triangular lot that was evidently sold, for it had been levelled and some low-grade lumber lay about, of the sort used for framing poured concrete. Directly across the street was the spot where the body had been found. Without consulting each other, both men started to the slope.

The ground was baked hard. DeGraaf knew in one look that there was no need to ask whether there had been rain recently. There was no evidence of water anywhere, or even tracks from old runoff. Far down in the dry wash, the bottom looked flat enough to suggest that many months ago a hard rain had made a temporary river, and that the river, as it dried and sank back into the earth, had puddled there. That was all. All the ground now had that, soft, suede-like, nappy look of baked clay over which birds, mice, and spiders had scratched and run for months.

"Wouldn't you think there'd be some sign of a track in the damned dust?" DeGraaf said.

"There might be, but there isn't any dust. Not on the slope. The breeze takes it all into the lee of things, or into the gully."

There were claw marks on the rise, as of a large dog digging in his toes in a big hurry to get up the slope. Bird droppings. Some dry grasses, a dead grey-green color, a few of them broken off and pointing due north.

"Not enough of these grasses to tell how wide a thing might have gone over them," DeGraaf said.

"Nope."

"Now don't *you* start that."

"Well, we can keep it roped off. Nobody uses it anyhow. It hasn't been sold—"

"What the hell are you doing there!" somebody shouted. And almost immediately, "Oh, it's you." The last words were not especially less angry than the first, but they were uttered in a lower volume.

"Abner!" said Cornish. "I'm glad you're home. We were working our way over to see you."

"Not very fast you weren't."

"I want you to meet somebody, Abner."

"I don't have time to meet anybody. I'm leaving for work."

"Well, what are you doing out here, then?"

"I thought you were the murderers returning to the scene."

"No kidding." Cornish looked skeptical. "Now, come on. You can work ten minutes extra tonight. Everybody knows your time is your own."

"My time is at my disposal. That doesn't mean I fling it about carelessly. I give a full day's work—though it's for about half a day's pay. At least that's more than you can say for most people."

"The work or the pay? Let's head up the slope."

"You already are."

"This is Dr. DeGraaf, Abner. I imagine you might call him Gerritt."

"Oh, well, if I must, I must."

DeGraaf found himself grasping a hand that was more like a tree root. The face above it was grooved like the bark of a pine, had very much the same color, and was about as yielding.

"Abner Milanowski," Cornish announced.

"You might as well come in," Milanowski declared, and led them up the slope to a house that was about a hundred yards away over the rise.

The house was as prickly as its owner, as inaccessible as its owner, and its landscaping was utterly unlike the others DeGraaf had seen in Young Lake. Desert plants do not grow thickly together. Nature has shaped them to be standoffish, each to its plot of hard-won soil and its chance for a few square feet of raindrops. But as far as such plants permitted crowding, they crowded around Abner Milanowski's house. Dry sage made a thicket in the front. There were saguaro cacti, prickly pear, and barrel cactus. The tangles of ocotillo around the walls recalled nothing so much as Sleeping Beauty's castle. Along the lot line were the forbidding elbows of Joshua trees, and red cholla lowered its horns around the gate. A dry flagstone path, overhung with thorns, made its way to the door.

"How do you get these to do so well, Mr. Milanowski?" DeGraaf asked.

"They're supposed to do well," said Milanowski, opening the door and marching in. "They live here. The damn fools—" for a minute DeGraaf thought he was referring to the plants— "the damn fools'll spend a fortune on water to bring plants here that are totally unadapted. Does that make sense?"

"Well, it reminds them of home."

"If they wanted to be reminded of home they should have damn well stayed home. This is a different place. The stupidity of transporting grass and petunias from the midwest to a place like this just makes me mad! Spend the rest of the time watering and feeding and weeding and for what? For something that looks unnatural when you get it done. The damn fools!"

"It's a hobby for them."

"The native species of cactus are an excellent hobby. And beautiful, interesting plants."

"I agree with you."

"You don't have to. It's true whether you agree or not. I do a little article on one or another of them in the paper from time to time. Some people even pay attention to it, too. But where do most of them keep their cacti if they do get interested in them?"

"Let me guess," said DeGraaf. "Don't tell me. In pots?"

"Right! The idiocy of it. Say, he's a bright boy, Cornish."

"We wanted to ask you a few questions," Cornish said stolidly.

"I suppose I have to ask you to sit down. I don't entertain, you know."

"Well, we're not here for tea," said Cornish.

"Don't have any. Tea. Utopia."

"What?" DeGraaf asked.

"Utopia. That's what they want. All the things they liked about their old homes but with dry clear air and warm weather thrown in. Sunny skies forever. Well, it won't work. It's not a hybrid, it's a mongrel. Little patches of bright green in the desert. Deface it. That's what they do."

"I notice you're way out here alone at the end of the Loop," DeGraaf said, smiling.

"Sure. Wish it would stay that way. But they'll sell. All those lots'll sell. Then I'll have neighbors." From the tone of voice he might have been saying, "Then I'll have smallpox."

"Yes?"

"And naturally they'll have grass right up to my lot line. And then what? They'll be asking me, ever so subtly, whether I'd like to have a lawn put in. No, I would not like it, thank you. Say! The murder might keep them off for a while, don't you think?"

"Mr. Milanowski—"

"The lot next door is sold, they say. It won't be long. I suppose you don't like me looking on the bright side of a murder."

"Actually, we wanted to talk with you about it."

"That dreadful child. Bothered me when he was alive and now he bothers me dead."

"How did he bother you, Mr. Milanowski?"

"Oh, now your ears prick up, huh? He bothered me because he liked to tip over cacti, that's why. And why should anyone try to kill a plant that's a hundred years old? Some of 'em are, you know. All the same, I hear he was even harder on lawns, so I guess he wasn't all bad. This looked like nothing valuable to him, I suppose."

"I suppose."

"And I was cannier than the others. I never said anything to him about it. If he'd thought I valued the plants he'd really have been at pains to knock them over."

"Really?"

"Sure. Ask anybody. Did you notice the cactus on the corner of the lot near the sidewalk? He'd knock it over every now and then. It was an old man cactus, you see, white and fuzzy and not very spiny, so he just pushed it with his hand. After this had happened once too often, I went out and found a variety that was about the same size but full of little spines. So when he gave that one a push he got himself covered. They're hard to get out, too. He never tried it again. And you know what? He probably never even knew why it happened. Never knew it was a different cactus. Because he never really looked at the plants, you see. Not really to *look*. He just hit things. If he'd cared about them at all, he'd never have hurt himself."

"Yes. I can imagine that."

"I suppose you think that's pretty rotten, too?"

"No, as a matter of fact, while you were telling the story I found myself rooting for the cactus. What did you do with the other one?"

"The cephalocereus senilis? Planted it out in back."

"You mentioned working on the paper, Mr. Milanowski. Do you just do the cactus column, or other things too?"

"I do everything that comes up. The *Young Lake Sunray* has four paid employees and God knows how many volunteers. I'm a retired newspaperman, myself."

"What do you call your position?"

"Business manager. But I do about twenty per cent of the articles, too, I would guess."

"May I ask something that's probably rude?"

"I do. Why shouldn't you?"

"How's a misanthropic fellow like you find himself doing community-minded work on a small town paper?"

"Like 'em."

"That's all?"

"If I were *forced* to answer," said Milanowski, and he turned redder than normal around the neck, "I would say that the general criminal stupidity of mankind can be slightly lessened by getting out a sensible, informative newspaper."

"I'll buy that."

"Not," he added hastily, "that you don't have to print a lot of tripe to get 'em to read it. Social stuff. You know."

"Yes, thank you. I do." DeGraaf paused. Cornish coughed. "I think Joe would like to know what you were doing yesterday afternoon."

"I wouldn't kill a child for pushing over a cephalocereus, you know. But of course, you don't know."

"Can't know for sure."

"Naturally not. What times? After lunch I worked in the office for about an hour and a half.

Say until a quarter of three. Went out to get a story
on the guy who says he caught a fish in Young
Lake. Took a drive over to two houses on the west
side. Social note. Guests. Sometime in there I
stopped to look at the crack people say is developing in the bridge. Can't say it looks like much to
me. I think I did that on the way to the second
house. There were a couple of interesting cacti under the bridge. You get different species where
there's water now and then, like that. Do you know
most of 'em probably aren't even named yet? I
hung around the bridge for a while. Maybe twenty
minutes. Went to that house, and back to the office
to type the tripe. For the social column. It was after
five by then. Came home about six. That enough?"

"It covers the time period. Though not exactly
like a blanket."

"The people I called on could probably give you
some help."

"Yes. Did you see anything strange around here
when you got home? Notice anybody hanging
around?"

"One of the Lane kids went past not long after I
got here. They don't tip cacti, by the way."

"I'm delighted to know that."

"Then about seven all hell broke loose. I was
trying to make dinner. Tacos. I believe in eating
something interesting. Just because one is a
bachelor, one does not have to live on boiled eggs
and TV dinners."

"I agree."

"Well, everybody was milling around out there,
and talking. All the neighbors. So I stayed in.
Could hear every word, though. Finally joined 'em.
Humph."

DeGraaf got up and strolled to the windows. There were three facing in the direction of the dry wash, two in the living room and one in the kitchen. With his eyebrows he asked permission to go into the kitchen, and Milanowski shrugged a "Why not?" From none of the windows was there anything like a good view of the slope or the dry wash. Instead, there was a thicket of ocotillo receding into Joshua tree spikes, like bales of barbed wire.

"Well, it's my kind of view," Milanowski chuckled. "If I want vistas I can take a walk."

"Abner," Cornish said, "you want to get to work. Can you send me over addresses of the people you visited yesterday? When you get to the office and can look them up? If Gerritt doesn't want anything else, we'll be getting along."

"I've got just one more question," DeGraaf said.

"What's that?"

"How has your paper been handling the feud between the retirees and the kids?"

Milanowski's eyebrows shot up. "I don't see why you—however. We don't exactly have a policy. We report actual news. Like the kid who broke his arm. I suppose basically we sort of try to play it down."

"Why?"

"Well, we have a circulation that goes to every house here. We're supported by association dues. So we don't sell additional papers by being sensational. And we don't knock the place. The letters give us our biggest problems."

"Letters?"

"Letters to the editors column. Everybody who writes one thinks it has to be printed. Nasty, some of 'em. Make things worse, if anything. Some we print; some we don't."

"Do you save them?"

"You mean the ones we don't print?"

"Yes."

"Yes, we file them in the basement. Behind the Coke machine."

"May I go through them?"

"If you can stand it."

"That bad, huh?"

Milanowski nodded. "It's a lesson in just how stupid people really are," he said.

They had only just broken through the cholla thicket on to the sidewalk when Cornish shouted, "Damn!"

DeGraaf looked around and saw half a dozen cars cruising slowly around the Loop. On the sidewalk stood four people, looking down the slope into the dry wash. Even as he watched, two more cars turned into Saguaro Drive from Mesquite.

"Damn! The Tucson papers are out. I should have thought of it."

"Some local people, too, aren't there?"

"Yes, and it'll get worse. DeGraaf—would you stand over there near the rope and look official?"

"Oh, I've even got an official voice. 'Keep moving, please. Keep moving,' " he intoned. "How does that sound?"

"Just great!" Cornish pulled out his walkie-talkie. DeGraaf sauntered over to the ropes. "Fish! Are you there?" There was a sputter. "Oh—what? —fine. Listen. I want both Loops closed off. No, wait a minute. We'll do it politely. Put up some sawhorses at Mesquite by the lake, where both

Loops turn off. Just north of the Tucson Road junction." There was a short squawk. "Right now. And send me George and somebody else to guard this place until I clear these people out. Now what I want you to do at the roadblock is this: stop every car, and only let people who live in the Loops through. Stop pedestrians too. Tell 'em you're sorry, but the area is closed for two days for investigation. Otherwise we'll have a herd of reporters stampeding through the scene. Don't get them upset. We don't need any angry stories in the papers. Tell 'em we'll hold a press conference this afternoon at—oh, hell, when? Tell 'em five. Say that nothing will be given out until then. If they tromp through the area with their fat feet we'll arrest them for destroying evidence. Think of a polite way to say that. And get those two men out here on the double!"

Cornish found DeGraaf standing at the top of the slope, just inside the rope. His hands were joined behind his back and he rocked placidly up and down on the balls of his feet. The feet were planted about eighteen inches apart. Every now and then he would say mechanically, "Move along now, please. Now, now, there's nothing to see. Move along, please," in the best constabulary tradition.

The situation otherwise was growing worse. Cars extended all the way down Saguaro and Canyon Trail. The street was congested with slow-moving, stop-and-start traffic, and what the jam must be like where both Loop roads ran into Mesquite, DeGraaf didn't like to think.

Then, suddenly, he was aware of reporters. Distinguished by their business suits and their look of righteous, eager alertness, they began forming a blue and grey broadcloth knot around DeGraaf. They bombarded him with questions.

"Have you arrested anybody?"

"Do you have any suspects yet?"

"Is it one of your old codgers?"

"Is this part of the feud?"

"How much more serious are you going to let this thing get?"

"Have you made any move to stop it?"

"Will the parents retaliate?"

"Why haven't you declared a curfew?"

DeGraaf stared placidly into space and declared, "I'm sure I couldn't say," with now and then, "That's a matter for the Chief," thrown in. Since he could no longer see the automobiles because of the crush of press men, he gave up telling them to move along.

Cornish repressed a great desire to go back to the station and leave DeGraaf to his role playing. He straightened, marched over, and said, "I'm Joe Cornish, Chief of Police."

Some flash bulbs went off.

"Have you taken in any suspects?"

"What are you doing about the feud?"

"Listen," said Cornish. "The investigation is just beginning. You realize that. And I don't want anybody walking on the evidence around here. I know *you* people know better," he went on, hoping he wasn't sounding too insincere, "but the civilians don't. We can't have souvenir hunters foraging around down that slope. So—if you want a picture of the area, though God knows it'll be dull enough, take it now from here. I'm closing the area for forty-eight hours. We're holding a conference this afternoon at five at the station. Until then I will have no comments at all. That isn't because I want to be unfriendly, but because I have work to do. And unless I get it done, I probably won't have anything to give you then, either."

"Do we take it you have no comment now because you don't know anything at all?"

"What are you doing about the feud?"

"Are the old people trying to drive all the kids out of Young Lake?"

George and an older policeman appeared behind the reporters.

"I don't have answers yet. See me at five. George! Hey! You two! Now, gentlemen, if you're finished with those pictures—I'm sorry, sir, but you can't step over the rope. George, you can stand guard at this end. I'm sorry, sir, but nobody is allowed down the slope but the police. Now the entrance to this road is going to be closed off, so I'd like to ask that you all get back to your cars. We'll be issuing citations to any cars of non-residents found on this street after ten o'clock this morning. And really, you know there isn't anything to see here. Now let's all go. I'll walk you back to the station," he added, deciding he had better pull them off. "Don't let anybody down the slope, George." He went over to DeGraaf and spoke into his ear. "Can you work your way around the Loop houses? See about alibis. I'll try to catch up with you when I get rid of these parasites."

"Good enough," DeGraaf said quietly. Then he said more loudly, "Very good, sir."

"Hmmp." Cornish walked away, taking the reporters with him.

DeGraaf, for his part, was visited with a great enthusiasm. He had been turned loose to rummage among the suspects—or witnesses—call them what you might and never mind the fact that most of them were probably neither. He was free to poke around in his own way. Cornish's forces were tied down, not because they were insufficient for an investigation, but because they were insufficient for both investigation and major crowd control.

When he had finished mentally rubbing his hands, DeGraaf realized that he also had a problem. Who was he to any of the people he was about to visit? He had no standing and no identification. He didn't even know the names of the people in the next house.

There was a solution to that, though; the truth. And when he realized that he had thought of subterfuges before considering it, he was faintly ashamed of himself. He would announce that he was acting coroner, and that Joe Cornish himself was temporarily tied up with protection problems. He would have them call the police station and confirm. Simple.

The lot next to Abner Milanowski was vacant, but, as Abner had said, sold. A sewer line was being dug into it. Beyond the lot stood a pinkish stucco with white trim. There was a green lawn in front, and a rectangular bed of zinnias in aggressive bloom. He went up a walk of crazypaving pattern on concrete to the edge of the front terrace. There was green indoor-outdoor carpeting over the terrace and part way down the front walk. A matching green mat was in the recessed doorway. It looked for all the world as if the lawn were trying to elbow its way into the house. But it was cheerful. He knocked, and when the door opened, noticed that the green carpet went on inside.

A woman he had seen somewhere stood in the doorway, a German shepherd dog by her side.

"Hello. I'm Gerritt DeGraaf," he said. And then he remembered. She was the woman they had seen on the three-wheeler earlier. She and the well-behaved dog stared at him, but neither caught his eyes. He recalled in the same instant that she was blind.

"I was with Chief Cornish this morning," he said, and explained his errand. "I wish you'd call Cornish at the station if you have doubts," he finished, "since you really haven't any way of knowing who I am."

"You know, I think I will. Just wait here, please."

She disappeared past the corner of the door. With one ear DeGraaf listened as she dialed the number. He studied the thick green rug through the screen door. Beyond it was the calm, solid dog, looking every bit as competent as a good receptionist. Beyond the dog was a large mirror in the entry hall, and his own reflection looked back at him. Possibly the mirror was the door of the coat closet. Leaning against the edge of the mirror was a white-tipped cane.

"I'm sorry I had to do that," said the woman, returning briskly. "It's just that in my position it's difficult—"

"Not at all. It makes it easier for me if you get official confirmation, I think."

"Come in. Tara won't bother you. She's very intelligent."

"Terror?" He looked at the quiet dog.

"Tara. As in *Gone with the Wind.*"

"Oh, right."

"Are you allowed to tell me anything about what has happened?"

She was a neat woman, with a few grey hairs mixed in with the dark, a pepper-and-salt coloring. Tidy and competent, like the dog. She looked directly at his face, though sometimes she missed his eyes and stared fixedly at his ear instead. Now she walked directly to a chair, touched the arm lightly, reaching behind herself, and sat down. When De-Graaf himself sat, his chair gave a little creak, and the woman smiled and nodded, approving the fact that he had made himself at home.

DeGraaf said, "I don't see why you shouldn't know. The child was strangled. There's no doubt that it was murder. I don't want to alarm you by saying so, but I imagine it's better to know."

"I asked. Yes, it's always better to know where you stand. As far as unpleasant facts—I was a legal secretary all my life. Until my accident, of course. And I guess I've heard just about every unpleasantness there is. Who killed him?"

"We haven't the least idea. May I ask about your blindness? I'm filling in the background of everybody in the area, you see."

"Yes, of course. I'm glad to have you ask. You can't imagine how tedious it is to have people constantly avoiding the subject. As if *I* could avoid it!

They even try not to use the word 'see' in my presence. It's so frustrating. And so stupid!"

"I can see that it would be pretty irritating."

"Well, yes, and it creates such an unnecessary barrier. You just want to scream. Suppose a friend gets a new dress and starts to tell you about it. Then she realizes you can't see it and awkwardly changes the subject. So you have to say, 'Well, dear, I know I can't see it, but it would be interesting if you would tell me what color it is. May I feel the fabric?' "

"That's going the long way around, certainly."

"And, it's hard to believe, but there actually are people who speak louder because a person is blind. I'm not *deaf,* after all."

"I've heard of that. I've seen people speak louder to someone who's been paralysed. They think 'disability' and can't think beyond it."

"Isn't it ridiculous?"

"Tell me—I ought to know this—what is your name?"

"Becky Simmons."

"You're much younger than most Young Lake people, aren't you?"

"Somewhat younger, at least. I'm fifty-six. I had to retire because of my accident. So I looked for a place to retire to that would be—easy to negotiate. I don't have to worry about getting over snow and ice here. And there are practically no fast cars on the streets. It's just ideal, and I'm lucky I could afford it. I could never have saved enough, but the insurance claim from the accident and the settlement of the negligence case made it possible. Where else could I find a place where I could cross the street without worrying? Or—being honest about this—go to the store without a chance of being mugged? I had my purse snatched twice while I was still back home in Hammond, just after the accident. And that's frightening. This place is heaven for a person in my position!"

"So you have no sight at all?"

"Well, I can get an idea of bright light in the left eye. No dim things, or even shadows. I can get an idea of whether it's day or night, if it's sunny."

"An injury to the cornea?"

"You have to be a doctor to act as coroner, don't you? I hadn't thought of that. Yes, it was actually a combination of things. A steam pipe burst in the building where I worked. I was hit with the steam and then a room divider blew out and I was knocked through a glass door and down a short flight of stairs. I had a head injury as well as some burning of the eyes. The janitor was killed and the woman who worked next to my desk was burned so badly that she can't use one leg at all any more."

"How ghastly!"

"Oh, it was horrible! The accident itself happened so fast I hardly had time to be frightened. But the recovery was long. Or seemed to be. I had some burns on the left side of my face. They thought they did very well on that, though. You can hardly tell, can you? People say it's a very good job, and I can't feel any scar tissue any more. I did at first, and I thought I must look like a monster, but it was just swelling and it went down after a while."

"No, it looks like an excellent job. There's a little redness near the left ear still. That's all. And your hair covers most of that."

"It's a relief to talk with somebody who's frank."

"I know. There's nothing worse than the friend who says, 'Now, don't think about it, dear.' "

"Have you had an accident? It sounds like it."

"No, but I see quite a few cases."

"Oh, I suppose you would."

"You have an advantage over people who are born blind. They have no natural instinct to look toward the people they're talking with, and it sets them apart a great deal."

"Oh, yes. I know. At the institute they sent me to for Braille, they were trying to teach some of the children to watch people. To look at people when they talk. It's so sad with children, isn't it?"

"Yes."

"We had a little girl in the office. A case, I mean, before my accident, who had been blinded when she was hit with some sort of chemical at a product demonstration in a shopping center. There was carelessness, and she got an incredible amount of money. Half a million I think it was, which seems incredible, but I thought at the time that however much it was it wouldn't repay her. It isn't enough."

"Was there negligence in your case?"

"Oh, yes. Or I'd never have won. It turned out, though we never heard about it in the office until the accident happened, that the building inspector had been in six months before and a week before, and both times he'd ordered them to replace the steam pipes. Wouldn't you think they'd have had the sense to do it? But I guess their insurance company paid."

"That's everybody's way out."

"Isn't it!"

"Miss Simmons, if I may say so, you strike me as an extraordinarily brave woman. Would you mind if I asked you some questions about the Barkus boy's death now?"

"Oh no, of course not. I've been inconsiderate, talking on like this. You have a lot of people to see."

"I'll get to them. No hurry. First, could you tell me if anything out of the ordinary happened around here yesterday afternoon?"

"Out of the ordinary? Well, I can't say anything did. Of course, when you're going only by sound and perhaps smell—"

"But that's what I think might be so useful. People who can see are likely to disregard sounds and smells unless they're very obtrusive. But you might notice something fairly subtle."

"Oh, dear. Now I feel stupid. Do you mean I should have heard a scream? I don't think I did."

"Not necessarily. A scuffle, maybe. A dragging sound. I don't want to put ideas in your mind, though. If there wasn't anything, don't think of anything."

"Oh, dear."

"Well, let's try it this way. Where were you from, say, two-thirty on?"

"My alibi?"

"Call it that, maybe. But I'd like to see whether you might have heard anything."

"Let's see. I went for a ride. No, the ride was in the morning. I think it's important to get out of the house. Keep alert. I went to the grocery store about two-thirty, on my tricycle. I go nearly every day.

It's not so much that I need things that often, but I like the exercise, and I see people there to talk with. I didn't check the clock. I have a clock with exposed hands, but I can't help thinking that handling it all the time isn't good for it, and I'd checked it about twelve-thirty."

"Fine."

"I didn't notice anything special along the way. I don't think the children were home yet, while I was on my way to the store. Usually you hear them when they are. Even if they're a block or two away. I think they were back when I started home. I wasn't paying much attention to them, though. They weren't anything unusual, after all."

"Anybody else?"

"Mr. Quirk was at the Mesquite corner."

"Who's he?"

"He does yard work for quite a few of the houses. You're bound to see him. He didn't speak. He's a bit of a grouch, so that's not unusual. But he may have been working behind somebody's house, because I didn't hear him, either."

"Then how did you know he was there?"

"The smell. He has a big tool cart with supplies in it. And it always smells of manure."

Chapter Five

The house directly south of Miss Simmons showed a small bicycle with training wheels on the walk and a set of play dishes on the porch. So unusual were such objects in Young Lake that De-Graaf stared at them on his way up the walk and missed the fact that a woman was backing out the door, punching the lock. She turned and started down the top of the three steps just as he was reaching the bottom one.

"Oh!" she said.

DeGraaf sidestepped, noticing a healthy tan, healthy looking brown hair, and youth. "Sorry," he said.

"If you're a reporter, I haven't got anything to say. At *all*. And besides I'm on my way to work and I can't stop."

"I'm not a reporter, though." He explained. His suggestion that she call Cornish to confirm who he was didn't check her sideways movement down the sidewalk, all the time he was talking. And he also was moving sideways, mirroring her.

"Well, I believe you," she finally said. "And I would talk with you, really I would. Only I have to be at work, at the supermarket. It's only two and a half blocks away, but I'm almost late now."

"When do you get home?"

"Two-thirty. That way I can be here before the kids get home. It's a beautiful arrangement, and I'm not going to stand here and be fired for being late." She started to walk away, then stopped. "Anyway," she added, "if you come around three you can talk with the children, too. That should be much more useful." And she left.

Finding himself in front of the next house, De-Graaf shrugged, walked up and rang the bell. As he waited, he looked at the pink stucco facade, and the carefully manicured lawn. Still no one answered. Inside he could faintly hear a television program. He rang again. Finally a woman in nurse's uniform answered the door.

"Yes?" she asked. Inside, turned lower, the television was still on.

"My name is Gerritt DeGraaf," he said, and he explained his errand.

"Oh, dear," said the nurse, with a prim little rustle of something starched. "I don't want her disturbed." The word "her" was accompanied by a twitch of one shoulder toward the back of the house, and another rustle. Clearly it meant not only her patient, but her rather fractious patient.

"Would she be so disturbed if I asked her just a question or two?"

"Well, it's her heart, you see. She only got home from the hospital last week. Betty and I have been doing twelve-hour shifts because it's so difficult to find anyone to come out here."

"But she must wonder about the disturbance. Or

didn't she hear anything?"

"Actually, no. She had heard about the—the trouble, of course."

"Which trouble?"

"The children and the old people. Fighting, you know. But she hasn't heard about the murder. And I don't want her to. Not yet. She gets excited so easily. The storm in Duluth, for instance. That's where she's from and her children still live there. It wasn't even much of a storm, but the power was out a whole day. You know how the papers love to report those things here. You know, to show what wonderful weather Arizona has?"

"Yes, I understand."

There was applause on the television set and the nurse sneaked a furtive look in its direction. "She got so upset about the storm. You'd think she'd know from living there what a couple of feet of snow was. Nothing would do but we had to call both children. And with some phone lines out, it was just impossible. The longer it took, the worse she got, naturally. You'd think she was going to have another attack. Crying and asking for cups of cocoa. You know how they get."

"Yes."

"Well, when we finally got them, one of the girls had been out shovelling, and she was pretty annoyed to be called running to the 'phone. The other one was upset because her freezer was defrosting. Because the power was off, you know. And she wouldn't talk more than two minutes. It was all so silly. Then we had another little tantrum because the children wouldn't talk long. Honestly!"

"Well, it was sort of inconsiderate of them not to chat, after she had called long distance. Wasn't it?"

"I'm not so sure. She calls every other day at seven a.m. I imagine they feel as if somebody's always looking over their shoulder."

"I guess. What are your hours here?"

"Seven to seven. Which is too long. We're trying to get somebody else so we can have proper eight-hour shifts."

"Then you were here yesterday afternoon?"

"Oh, of course."

"And were you out at all? Or your patient?" She had an ear turned to the television, and he waited for his question to sink in.

"Oh," she said. "Out of the *house?* She doesn't even get out of bed! And I'm supposed to walk her around the living room twice a day. I have to literally drag her out of bed. She'd like it if I carried her. I *told* Dr. Gilpatrick she wouldn't do it. He thinks that if you just say to them they won't get well without exercise they'll jump right to it. That's the trouble with doctors. They give orders, but they don't have to implement them."

"That's true."

"And she fights getting up. I don't know whether it's fear or she just enjoys being an invalid."

"A great many people like being sick."

"That's so true."

"But she *can* walk?"

"Oh, dear, yes. But she doesn't *think* so."

"Were you right near her all yesterday afternoon? Could she have left the house without your knowing?"

"I never leave her. I sit in the living room, but her bedroom door opens on to the living room. She's still on her blood thinners and I have to watch her constantly. *Constantly.*"

"You don't stay in her room, though?"

"No, she naps a great deal. She calls me when she wants something. I know what you're getting at, of course. But she really is somewhat weak, and on top of that, if anybody ever had an alibi, she has."

"I'm very glad to get things clear, Miss—"

"Pettijohn."

"Miss Pettijohn. Did you hear anything unusual yourself yesterday afternoon?"

"I don't think so." She looked very much as if she wished she had.

"I thought since you're in the front room here, you just might."

"I just can't think of anything at all."

DeGraaf was fairly certain that she would hear nothing all day but television.

"Well, thank you," he said. "Try telling the patient that it would be very brave of her to take her exercise. Sometimes that works where nothing else will."

In the drive, he studied Miss Pettijohn's car, a tan Volkswagen, very clean, with a red rubberized interior. The windows shone. It even looked as if the sides of the wheels were washed. Probably she maintained a very tidy sickroom.

The mailbox at the next house south was black. On it was lettered in white, "George and Leila Townshend" in flowing script with curly tails. The walk curved and on the lawn was a plaster donkey pulling a plaster basket filled with vinyl geraniums. In the driveway was a grey Bentley with chocolate-colored leather seats. A guest? DeGraaf rang the bell. On the other side of the door a set of chimes played the first thirteen notes of "Home Sweet Home."

The door was opened by a portly man, his face the color of good sherry. He wore a camel hair jacket in a light weave.

"I'm Dr. Gerritt DeGraaf. You don't know me, but I—"

"I don't know you but I've seen you," the man said. "Night before last at the meeting. Come in and state your business. Whiskey?"

DeGraaf's first thought was that it was far too early for a drink. A second thought led him to see what he might be accepting.

"Splendid," Townshend crowed. He led the way to a fiberboard cabinet of walnut-grained vinyl in a Spanish colonial design. The whiskey he poured was Chivas Royal Salute.

"Excellent," said DeGraaf, and he meant it.

"Now what can I do for you? Oh, Leila. Come in, dear. My wife, Leila. Dr. DeGraaf."

"I'm so happy to see somebody under eighty, Doctor. May I join you, or is it terribly personal? Or private? Or even—horrors—business?"

"None of those. I'd be happy if you would stay, Mrs. Townshend."

"I will absolutely rush from the room unless you call me Leila."

"Delighted," said DeGraaf, wondering whether he was very much obligated to offer to let her call him by his first name. He decided to take cover under an air of preoccupation.

"Now, fire away!" said George Townshend.

"Well, I have been commandeered, you might say. Made acting medical examiner."

"Ha! Couldn't very well let old Nash loose on

the corpse when he'd threatened to break every bone in the kid's body, huh?"

"It did seem more prudent this way. Anyhow, I'm surveying everybody in this area because Cornish is tied up right now with an army of aggressive reporters, and we want to find out whether anybody saw anything suspicious. Before they have time to forget."

"And check out alibis, too, huh?"

"Yes, that too."

"I like a straightforward type."

DeGraaf sipped his drink, then realized that Mrs. Townshend did not have anything to drink. He hesitated a split second, looking at her. Townshend caught the look.

"Leila isn't drinking," said her husband.

His wife, saying nothing, stared brightly at DeGraaf. For his part, uncomfortable, he let his eyes move away. They passed over a sofa of pink plush covered with a vinyl protective cover, a slat table holding a piece of driftwood on which were glued a ceramic mushroom and an elf. On the walls were prints of two children with big eyes and, over the sofa a seascape, the kind that appears to be three-dimensional. There was a beige carpet, beige curtains on traverse rods, and a ceramic bowl on the table that said "Please pass the nuts" and had handles shaped like hands.

He realized the Townshends were waiting for him to speak.

"I hate to ask this kind of thing, though I'm sure you understand. I wish you would tell me where you were yesterday afternoon."

"We were here, most of the time. We drove in to Tucson in the late afternoon."

"What time was that?"

"We must have left here around three. What do you think, dear?"

"Around three. I didn't look at the clock."

"You went to Tucson? When did you get back?"

"Let's see. We went to the liquor store. That was really the reason for the trip. Then we went out to dinner. Spanish restaurant. La Hacienda. If you get time while you're here, go eat there. No place to eat in Young Lake at all."

"You were going to estimate when you got back."

"So I was. It couldn't have been much later than nine. I don't recall exactly."

"You see, Gerritt," Mrs. Townshend said, "since there's nothing to do in Young Lake anyway, there's really no point in keeping track of time. Is there?"

"I imagine not. In my position, though, you have to hope that people do, sometimes. Let me take you back to the hour before you left. Say after two-thirty or so. Did you see anybody on the street or sidewalk?"

"You know, a couple of those old biddies spend their whole damned day taking constitutionals up and down the street," Townshend said. "I didn't notice anybody special. And I was taking a sun-bath in the back most of that time anyway. So I didn't see what went on in front."

"Did you see anybody out in the back?"

"Yes, that abominable little girl with the braids stuck her head in the yard. How she thinks she can just walk into somebody's house, I don't know."

"She didn't quite walk into the *house*, dear," said his wife.

"Practically. The yard is enclosed, after all. It's the same thing. She's as bad as the Barkus kid was. Though I shouldn't say that. Awful brat."

"Did she say anything?"

"Not a word. Pop! In and out. Looking for somebody, I suppose."

"I don't imagine you could give me an idea of the time she was there?"

"Towards three. It was about then, or maybe because of it, that I got up and went on inside. Leila said she'd had enough sun and we cleaned up to go to Tucson."

"Too much sun wrinkles the skin, I think. Don't you, Gerritt?"

"I believe so, yes."

"We're both sixty, though you'd never think so," George said. "We don't believe in pushing our luck, see," George laughed. His wife looked out the window.

"Can you think of anything else that might help the police? Both of you, as general observers of the scene here?"

"They're all crazy," said Mrs. Townshend. "Otherwise they're unremarkable."

"Crazy in what way?"

"Making such a fuss about children being around, for one thing. What's it to them? Nobody's asking them to babysit, are they? I think they're just bored."

"That may be very true."

"And the kid got bored to death?" asked her husband.

"George, that's not in good taste."

"Neither is murder," said Townshend, with considerable sanity. "Have you ever thought about the kids? There's nothing for them to do around this place. Maybe they get to playing games they shouldn't. Maybe they play Indian games and tie each other up. Maybe it went too far and some other kids killed the Barkus kid. Who knows? This is a funny town, DeGraaf. You don't know it yet."

"I'm learning. Well, I appreciate your help." He rose.

"Always glad to help the police," Townshend said. To DeGraaf, there was something familiar about the way he said that.

"How long have you people lived here?" DeGraaf asked, passing by a gold Cupid holding up a circle of glass that formed a small table.

"A few months. Five, I guess. We travel some, don't we, Leila?"

"Oh, yes, dear. We just can't bear to settle down, Gerritt."

"Though we love Young Lake, too," said her husband.

"We both do," she said.

DeGraaf said, "Goodbye, and thanks for the scotch."

The house south of Townshend's could have been called Our Spanish Model. It made great use of tan stucco and irregular brick. Out in front, wielding a hollow cane of weed poison, was an elderly lady. She was bent over like a bittern about to skewer a frog, and when she spied an offending weed, she stabbed at it venomously. Then she stepped back, nodded victoriously, and stalked a little farther. DeGraaf coughed. No result.

"Good morning," he called out.

She swung around and pointed the poison cane at his navel.

"What do *you* want?" she asked. She had bright blue eyes and pale blue hair. She so clearly doubted that he could want anything worthwhile, that he had to fight down a desire to walk away. Instead, he forced a nice, jolly bedside manner—precisely the sort of thing that had made him decide not to go into private practice. He explained his mission, and parts of it twice. She was slightly hard of hearing.

"Very well, I'll call Joe," she said crisply. Stabbing her weed killer at him—it took him a second to realize that she meant him to hold it for her—she stumped off into the house to phone Cornish. He inspected the mechanism, tried it out cautiously on something that looked weedy, and then she was back, waving him to the door curtly, with an imperious claw.

"I haven't got time for this sort of nonsense, you understand," she said. "But let's get it over with."

Bedside manner, he thought, might be wasted here. Try a straight attack.

"Would you give me your name, please?"

"Didn't Joe even tell you that? What kind of police service are we paying for here?"

"They're getting my services free, which is something of a bargain."

"More fool you then. We'll see if it's such a bargain. My name is Cora Grundler."

"And you moved here when?"

"Two years ago."

"What did you do before you came here?"

"I ran a diner in Niles, Illinois. Lunch and sup-

per sort of thing. I was not a waitress, you understand. I ran the damn place. And schlepped
through the snow five months of the year, all hours
of the day and night."

"So you came here because of the snow?"

"I came here because of the *lack* of snow."

"Yes, yes, of course. Arthritis?"

"In spades. I'm sixty-seven, and I just won't
struggle with the weather any longer. I have very
little money, Dr. DeGraaf, but it's properly in-
vested. If I'm careful I can stretch it for as long as
I'm likely to live. It is possible to live inexpensively
here, as long as one's tastes are modest. One has to
resist impulse buying, of course. By impulse I mean
such things as Saturday night steak. I live on whole
wheat bread, cheese, and California oranges."

"Some other things surely."

"Not really. Sometimes margarine. For the
bread. Sometimes tuna fish. I drink water. I am not
exaggerating. Would you care to see my refrigerator?"

"No, I'll take your word for it. Why are you
making such a point of it?"

"Because in just a minute you are going to ask
me what my attitude toward those children is. My
attitude is negative. I don't want children here;
they cause damage. The damage, though trivial, is
too much for me to afford. Three dollars buys a
tiny package of grass seed. It would buy two packages of cheese."

"I see."

"If the number of children increases, we'll be
asked to build playgrounds, and eventually even a
school. I can't afford it. Taxes and association dues
for those fool shuffleboard courts and Sara Ca-

rini's social programs are plenty as it is. People who *use* those programs should contribute to them. Not the rest of us. I'm willing to pay for police and fire protection. I use those things. But that's as far as I go. This town was established by retired people on limited incomes. There's nothing here for children. People with children can go someplace else. And for the sake of the children, they ought to."

"I think that's very clearly stated."

"But you don't agree."

"You won't believe this, but I really haven't decided what I think about that question. However, a child was killed yesterday. I am against *that*, unequivocally. I have to know where everybody was between two-thirty and five."

"Well, I was here."

"Doing what? Were you out front?"

"Didn't happen to be. If I'd done the weeds yesterday, they wouldn't need it today, would they? I'd gone to the store. Drugstore, not the market. Going to one or the other is the main form of excitement here. You pass everybody on the way, or meet them there."

"What time was that?"

"Three or three-fifteen. I saw Abby Francot on my way over and Becky Simmons on my way back. Or was it vice-versa? Doesn't matter. It's amazing how those two get around."

"Did you see anything else?"

"Later on this Potts girl came running past me. Asked me where I'd been. The idea!"

"Where was she headed?"

"Oh, north on Saguaro. Right out in front. Towards where the Barkus boy was found."

"And what time did you say this was?"

"I didn't say."

"Would you care to hazard a guess now?"

"Yes, young man, I will. I saw her on my way back from the stores, so it must have been after four. I may have talked with the pharmacist rather a long time."

"By the way, Miss Grundler, how do you get to the stores?"

"Walk or use my tricycle."

"You have one of those big three-wheelers?"

"I certainly have. No gas and next to no repairs. And according to my doctor, the exercise is very good for the joints."

"It certainly is. Motion but not much strain."

"And much less expensive than cortisone."

"But if you use cortisone, isn't it covered by Medicare?"

She seemed loath to admit it. "They don't pay the cost of going all the way into Tucson to get to the doctor. They can't pay everything."

DeGraaf stood at the point where East Loop and West Loop came together into Mesquite Lane. A hundred yards south of where he stood the red-and-white-striped sawhorses blocked the road. Two patrolmen were methodically turning back sightseers and letting residents through. There were comparatively few residents and a great many sightseers. It was about eleven. DeGraaf wondered whether rumor that the murder scene was closed would filter back to Tucson and dry up the stream of the curious or whether lunch hour would bring many more cars. Cornish had intelligently put the barricade just north of the spot where the Tucson Road entered Mesquite. The cars could be turned back south along Mesquite, then east on Yucca to get back to the Tucson Road and go home. Just the same, there was a lot of shouting and blowing of horns. That was an unusual sound in Young Lake.

Popeye passed on the other side of the street and waved. A fluffy little lady in a motorized wheelchair passed him, heading north into East Loop. Miss Simmons and her dog and tricycle passed Popeye, also heading south. The dog gave her a cue by moving to one side just as they passed Popeye. She called out and they exchanged a few brief greetings. Then she gave the dog a command and they started away again. Like most people, De-Graaf thought for a second that the dog was a marvel. Miss Simmons, though, shouldn't be out on a day when there were so many cars. He hoped the men at the barricade would keep an eye on her when she crossed.

An older man crossed the street and started up the west side of East Loop. Apparently everybody went to the stores every day.

DeGraaf turned up West Loop. He rang the bell of the house on the point. He rang again. No one answered.

"She's not there," called a man's voice, some distance away. It was the older gentleman DeGraaf had seen. And now he thought he remembered who it was.

"Do you know whether she's expected back?"

"In a few days. She's in the hospital. Insulin reaction."

"Oh. Has she been there long?"

"Three days. She overeats and then tries to take extra insulin. One of those."

"Are you by any chance Dr. Nash?"

"That's right. Who are you?"

"Dr. DeGraaf. I'm afraid I've taken over your job, somewhat unwillingly."

"Oh, I know about you. Come over to the house. Let's not talk out here."

They crossed a few yards to the point of East Loop and turned up Joshua Tree Path.

"Which is yours?" DeGraaf asked. Nash pointed to an impeccably groomed mini-neo-colonial four houses up. Because of the bushes the development used for landscaping, it was only partly visible. DeGraaf cast a glance at the intervening houses.

"Surveying, are you?" said Nash. "Well, there are three old teachers—Latin teachers, mind you—in that one. They go about together like the Three Fates or Furies, or what have you. Unless the three of them did it together they're out of it, because they didn't do it separately."

"I'm not a great believer in clubby murderers."

"Nor am I." They strolled on towards Nash's house.

"What about this one?" DeGraaf asked. He pointed to a low shuttered stucco painted in a shade of blue he considered unfortunate.

"For sale. Coronary occlusion. Called me, but there wasn't anything left to do."

"And how about this place?" It was the last one before Nash's.

"They're in Minnesota, visiting their children and grandchildren. Better than having the children come here. An overweight daughter with a cadaverous husband and three children who always look sticky."

"This house is identical to Abner Milanowski's.

I'm getting used to the models available here. For a housing development, they certainly have a large number."

"They try. I believe the actual number of models is eight. Most developments have three or four. As a matter of fact, they started with four, but when they upgraded—and raised prices, of course—they went for the larger number. This way you don't see identical houses next to each other, or facing each other, at all. Though you choose your own model, so presumably you could pick one exactly like your neighbor."

"Do they discourage that?"

"They may. But I find that people have a sense of what is expected of them. Usually they have, at any rate. Come on in. We don't lock doors much around here. Though I expect that will change."

"Why?"

"The kids. They're putting insects in people's houses. I don't mean flies, I mean scorpions."

"Don't the adults do that also?"

"Possibly. Well, sit down. You were saying that they roped you into this business?"

In a house full of uncompromising chairs, De-Graaf picked a grandly uncomfortable Queen Anne side chair with a straight back. Briefly he studied Dr. Nash. The man looked as if he spent his nights laid out in a pan of formalin.

"I suppose you understand why," DeGraaf said.

"Oh, sure. I called the little monster a little monster. They were absolutely correct to get you."

"I understood you also offered to break his bones."

"Yes, actually I did." Nash looked at his hands .

distastefully. "But I understand that in the end no bones were broken."

"The effect was worse, I imagine, than whatever you threatened him with."

"I do not kill children. As a matter of fact, I don't kill adults, either. But I think you should know that a good many people would have liked to break that particular child's arm, if not worse. He was a spectacularly uncivilized, uncivil, destructive child. He not only appeared to be poorly raised, but appeared to have no natural aptitude toward being properly raised."

"Can you explain that?"

"Oh, certainly. He was the sort who had to make a mess. If there were marigolds in a row, he must rush through them. You might find in some people that such an impulse sprang from a feeling that a row was unnatural or rigid. Not so this child. Milanowski's yard, which was, if anything aggressively natural, felt the damage too. And it wasn't just yards he savaged. I've seen him kicking over cacti in the open areas. He shot at birds with his slingshot, and while I'm certain that he was exceedingly inaccurate, I have seen him a couple of times with dead birds. He was the sort of person who does not do anything, but undoes many things."

"He might have outgrown it."

"Possibly, if something had happened to change him enormously. But I doubt it. I am not fond of children, but, *have* met some who were civilized. The Lane children, for example, are not neighbors I want to have, but they are not basically destructive, either. They may walk across a lawn when they're in a hurry. They certainly make noise. But not on purpose. They are tending a small vegetable garden. The girl, I have noticed, is learning knitting. And the boy builds airplanes. The Barkus child did not engage in such pursuits. As a matter of fact, he smashed one of the airplanes a couple of days ago."

"In playing with it?"

"So he said. They were all screaming about it out in the yard. He said it ran into the wall. But I was in back at the time and I saw him step on it. The Lane girl told her brother to forget about it, but I think she knew."

"Nice fellow."

"There are some like that. Nevertheless, I agree that the strangling is an abomination. What do you know about it?"

"Not enough. I'm going around checking alibis. Cornish may be along later, if he can get free of the ravening newspaper reporters."

"He isn't up to this sort of thing. Poor Cornish. He's experienced, and he's bright enough. But he came here with the idea of becoming all-but-retired. And now look what he finds himself coping with."

"And not just the murder, but the town feud. Which isn't likely to go away."

"Maybe somebody hopes that after this nobody will dare criticize the presence of children."

"You can't possibly think that somebody would kill one child to win acceptance for the others?" Gerritt asked incredulously.

"How do I know? It's a possible result. People are crazy. Look at the reasons some people kill. Look at the motives you read in the papers. How do I know what a fiercely protective mother might do?"

"I don't think it's likely."

"*I* don't think it's likely, either. I wouldn't give it one chance in a thousand of being true, but it's possible."

"Where were you yesterday afternoon?"

"I came home from the office about two. I am semi-retired."

"And you were here the rest of the time?"

"Why do you sound so doubtful? This is where I live."

"It seems everybody else makes shopping trips every day."

"I can see you've been around a bit," Nash laughed. "I picked up a paper on my way home. I didn't need anything else. The others don't have anything else to do, you see, so they go to the store. Besides that, they feel they must go there to get the gossip. If I need something I just pick it up before I start home. I don't feel I have to keep going back for the day's news."

"You don't hear gossip?"

"I don't pass it around. For instance, I've sat on your grandmother's secret ever since she moved in."

"Her secret?"

"She calls herself Mrs. Ross. She's Dr. Ross and a very well-known lady. I imagine she's hiding it so that she won't be buttonholed at every affair to pass judgment on people's psyches."

"I guess that's it. How did you know?"

"Adelaide Ross isn't a very common name. And she's from Chicago. And the right age. And even though she doesn't flaunt it, she's obviously an unusually intelligent woman. As to how I knew there *was* such a person—I read. She has an article in this fall's *SDP Journal,* by the way. I probably should have done what she did, and hidden out. Practice here isn't very lucrative, and people spend most of their time trying to get drugs out of you that they shouldn't have."

"Like what?" Visions of elderly acid parties passed through his mind.

"Oh, the whole pharmacopoeia. Pain-killers. Somebody who needs a limited dose for arthritis wants unlimited access. Pep pills. Tranquilizers. They're very, very offended if you give them a limited prescription. They're like everybody else in this society. They want to just gobble up whatever they please. Tired? Don't eat right? Take a pep pill. Stiff knee? Don't exercise, take a painkiller. Nervous? Don't go out and try to be some use to society. Take a tranquilizer and watch television. Phooey. Winston Churchill said he was not elected to preside over the dissolution of the British Empire. I did not go into medicine to help people go to rot!"

"What do they do then? Go to Tucson for the stuff?"

"I don't know. Some do. I like to fool myself into thinking that some of them try to get themselves in hand."

"What did you do yesterday afternoon? After you got home?"

"I made lunch. My wife died two years ago, and I do my own cooking."

DeGraaf thought of expressing sympathy, but the man's manner did not invite it at all. "Then what?"

"I read. The *JAMA* and a couple of other things. Must've spent about three hours getting through six articles."

"Up to five o'clock, do you mean?"

"Yes. Pretty close."

"Well, that covers the period nicely. Did anyone visit you? Did you notice any noises? Anything like that?"

"Not a damn thing. I am trying to overlook the constant yammering of those children, in any case. I certainly didn't hear or see anything unusual. And I don't encourage visitors."

DeGraaf looked about, wondering. There was absolutely nothing discordant here, and no way to check up on Nash. It would be useless to ask him about the articles. He might have read them any time and his memory for detail, DeGraaf guessed, was likely to be very good. "Do you really feel that no children at all should be allowed in Young Lake?" he asked.

"Certainly. We have paid for our homes. The area was established with this very thing in mind. We aren't asking for assistance. We aren't asking for subsidies from the government. We're quietly taking care of ourselves and we ought to be allowed to do it in our own way. Do you think Miss Francot, who's unable to use her legs, could go shopping and do her daily rounds in a normal city? Or Miss Simmons, who's blind? They'd either be run over or mugged. Probably they'd need public assistance. We keep our streets clean here. Where else is that true? We keep the streets safe. We're not asking for help in any of those areas. We pay for it ourselves. We just went to be let alone. We don't want the problems other cities bring on themselves.

We don't need the crime or the littering. Why should we?"

"You think children bring crime and litter?"

"Litter for certain. And it will certainly lead to the rest. We'll have schools first, then teenagers and fast cars and additional stores. Increased traffic. Then some manufacturing. Houses springing up. Hamburger stands. Teenagers having battles in the streets. Teenage drug problems, which are much less quiet than the kind of thing I complain about. We *know* children litter. The only kind of junk I find in my yard or on the sidewalk is their stuff: ice cream bar wrappers, the sticks too, candy papers, and broken toys. They leave things anyplace they finish with them."

"Can their parents be asked to supervise that?"

"Don't be naive. They could be asked. They have been asked. But they can't be forced. Their usual response is, 'It can't be my child.' They're not going to run all over town picking up their kid's gum wrappers. The owners of the yards have to do that."

"But the parents legitimately own these houses. What do you suggest they do?"

"Sell 'em. Have you ever thought of what they're doing to the children? This is *not* a child-oriented town. No playground. No schools. No parks. Why bring children here in the first place? They're not doing the kids a favor, whatever they think. And if they think they *are* helping their kids because it's clean here and there's no crime, they're using what *we've* built and paid for, and they're decreasing its value to those who have done the work."

"If you allow all-senior towns, what's to stop all-white towns or all-rich towns?"

"In the first place, both of those exist. But why ask the question that way? You're using the bugaboos. Try it this way. If the Sioux Indians would like a village of their own, to live in and preserve their arts and customs, why not? If they maintain and support it and aren't asking for anything, like us, why not? If somebody establishes a Mackinac Island where automobiles aren't allowed, everyone thinks it's a great idea. They applaud Greenfield Village, a place that's frozen in time a hundred years back. Why not have ethnic enclaves and cultural enclaves and age-group enclaves and the whole business? I can imagine a village inhabited entirely by people with very young children. Think of the advantages to them. They could have streets with extremely low speed limits, or no cars at all in certain areas, and huge common areas for playgrounds. They could pool their babysitting skills, so that no parent would be tied down all the time, the way it is now. As it is, if a parent needs to go out for a couple of hours, it's either hire a private babysitter or take the child to some nursery. I've seen mothers in town with squirming kids travelling to nursery schools miles away. What's the sense of it? Most of the huge transportation systems our cities have are required because facilities are so scattered. Different age groups need different facilities. Old people don't need the same things as young children. And teenagers need quite different things. And young adults. It's inefficient to jumble them all. Look at Young Lake. Everybody walks or bicycles everywhere. Because the things *we* need are here."

"Well, personally, I think that growing children need to see different age groups, to find out about roles at various ages. And different ethnic groups, too. I remember how important my grandfather was to me when I was growing up. And I learned things, like how people got around before there were automobiles. It gives children a sense of continuity to know their grandparents."

"So let 'em visit now and then. I'm not suggesting even that all people live in enclaves all the time. But the availability of such places would be good for some people. There are ethnic districts in cities right now that provide ethnic shopping and ethnic eating facilities for people who don't live there, besides giving security to the people who do live there."

"Sure, but in those cases I could move in if I wanted to. You're proposing a system where they could pass a law to shut me out."

"They won't be preserved otherwise. Like the beautiful old Spanish parts of San Francisco. They're bought by other people when they get popular, and spoiled."

"Let me change the subject for a minute. My time is sort of limited. You know these people here. Is there anybody hot-tempered enough to strangle a child in some sudden rage? I mean, if the boy struck all the heads off somebody's zinnias?"

"If so, it wouldn't be the sort of temper they'd let show often, would it? I don't really know of any. Despite my lack of alibi, I can say for myself that I tend to be cold-tempered, not hot. Abner Milanowski, the prince of the pricklers up there, is a grumbler, rather than a volatile person. Pollyanna, whom you haven't met yet, judging from the way you were heading—"

"Who?"

"Pollyanna. Abby Francot. Never mind, you'll understand when you meet her. I wouldn't want to guess what's going on in her head. Maybe nothing is, but she certainly would never *show* temper. Then there's the great sufferer-in-silence."

"Who?"

"Becky Simmons. The blind one. So brave. Copes so beautifully. Ought to be called Miss Simmons Who Copes So Beautifully. And she's so proud of it, too, don't you think?"

Gerritt answered stiffly, "I couldn't say."

"You don't approve of me, but I call things as I see them. There's Grundler, of course. If the child had been dosed in weedkiller, she'd be the logical suspect. And there's that great gasping fish out of water, George Townshend. Just wasting for a piano bar or a confab with a bunch of pols at city hall. Now if the child were machine-gunned, or sunk in the lake with a basin of concrete about his feet, I'd say look to poor George."

With a sudden flash of revelation, DeGraaf realized what had been familiar about the way George Townshend had said, "Always glad to help the police." It was the exact tone of the mob man. His face must have showed his shock, too, for Nash said, "What's the matter?"

"Nothing. Just that you came very close to something I'd been thinking."

"At any rate, the wretched child was not machine-gunned. Let's see. You haven't met the oh-so-particular Charles Chide. Young Lake's answer to Truman Capote. No, that's not fair. Not fair to Capote. Then there's Ellen Norris Brown, who is never called Ellen or Ellen Brown. I leave her to you. And Angelo DiLeonardi, the impressario of the whole place. He might have a temper. So might Ellen Norris Brown, but she's too well-bred to show it, and he, being profession-ally optimistic whenever he stands on a square foot of Young Lake soil, simply can't. You'll see them as you tour around. If I had to plump for anybody, I guess it would be Sara Carini."

"Somebody mentioned her already. The Barkus boy used to ride his bike over her lawn?"

"Bicycle? Yes, he'd use his bicycle. He'd ride over it with roller skates. In a real pinch he'd use his feet. But the main reason I single her out is that she does have a temper. And she is the only one here I know of who is really *hiding* her feelings about children. Everybody else is either clearly beneficent toward the little monsters or definitely opposed. It's partly because of her official position, of course. She is the paid social director of Young Lake. And she certainly is trying hard to look ever-so-reasonable. But I've seen her glance at those children when she thought she wasn't being watched. Talk about pure venom!"

"Peter Pelham seems quite even-handed about the children."

"Well, he's for them, really. Mayors have that sort of personality, though. They're for everybody and against nobody. He's not exactly a cipher, but he's close."

"Why do you stay here with all these people you can't stand?"

"Look at the place. It's warm, clean, and usually fairly quiet. Where else outside of a tropical coun-try could I find that? Secondly, while I may give you the idea that I don't like these people, I like them as well as I like anyone. They're just about as flawed as the rest of mankind. That's all."

They stood on Nash's porch, looking out toward the street.

"Your lawn's like a putting green," DeGraaf remarked.

"Except for a place over there between the houses where the kids manage to run it bare."

DeGraaf looked around the side, between Nash's and the next house north. There was a path all right, worn to bare dirt. "The rest of it looks as perfect as the top of a pool table."

"I have Quirk do it. I don't enjoy mucking about in the hot sun myself, looking for dandelions."

DeGraaf studied the soldierly row of petunias, marching down to the curb in an orderly but hardly inspired column. "Does he plan the beds, too?"

Nash laughed. "Are you a naturalized-setting person? Yes, he does. Buys the stuff by the flat and puts 'em in. Regular production line. I suspect that this sort of arrangement makes it easier for him to weed, too."

"Does he work for a lot of people around here?"

"Abby next door, for one. I imagine he has about seven or eight houses on the two Loops. Some in the rest of the town. He's got a good thing here. I notice he just bought a new power mower. He's making money, that's for certain."

Gerritt's grandmother came striding up the walk. "So there you are," she said.

"Gran!"

"Come on home for lunch. Joe Cornish wants you to call him back, too. How are you, John? I'm sorry to interrupt, but this child ought to eat. Why don't you come, too? I have egg salad sandwiches."

"I have a left-over can of chicken spread I ought to use. Your grandson will probably tell you it ought to be crab."

"I'll start back, Gerritt. Come when you can."

"I think we're done," DeGraaf said.

Nash nodded. "We've decided I have no alibi. Otherwise, nothing much."

Leaving Nash still standing on his porch, Gerritt and Adelaide strolled along the sidewalk, taking the long way. Adelaide said quietly that they were certainly not going to cut through the back yards. "Nash doesn't approve of cutting through."

"I don't suppose the others do, either. Fond of their lawns, aren't they?"

"Like suburbs everywhere. They don't like their territory trampled. You can't entirely blame them. It comes from the same inner springs that makes them keep the place clean."

"I've heard that this morning, too, in a way."

"Getting tired of us?"

"Lord, no! I'm baffled, though. If I ever saw a less likely place for a murder, feud or no feud, I don't know where. I can see Tim Barkus getting spanked, but not killed. It's very puzzling."

"You need lunch. Maybe that will clear your head."

"I *love* children," said Abby Francot, a sweet smile playing over her wrinkled face.

Joe Cornish and DeGraaf glanced at each other.

"From the people I've talked with today," said DeGraaf, "you must be the only person around here who does. Except their parents, of course."

"Oh, heavens, no," said Miss Francot. "You

misunderstand them. The old people get irritated, then they act grouchy. But they really love children. We all do."

DeGraaf, in an act of will, prevented himself from saying, "Somebody doesn't." Miss Francot put her hand to the silver pot and poured a little hot herb tea into their half-full cups. "Sugar? Lemon?" she asked.

"No, thank you," said Cornish. "Don't the children run through your yard quite a bit?"

"Oh, yes. Because I'm right behind Mrs. Lane's house, and she has two children, of course." She patted her cottony hair. "I think I'm so lucky to hear all that life going on."

"Uh, doesn't it wake you up?"

"Oh, but wake me from what, Chief?"

"A nap, or sleeping late."

"You will find, Chief, that old people do not sleep as long as they did when they were younger. I only nap, when I nap at all, right after lunch. And then they're in school. And of course at night they go to bed." Her voice, a delicate fluting, rose slightly at the end of the sentence, as if it were all so obvious.

"Still, to have the traffic right across your lawn—"

"Well, you know, there's a place they come through quite often. And John Nash next door— it's right between the two houses, you see—makes such a fuss about it. I was so naughty, I got so every time I saw him in the morning, I'd say, 'John, how's your bare spot today?' Wasn't that awful?"

"He was angry?"

"A little petulant. He doesn't mean anything by it. But I was saying, there was a little bare spot.

Not that it hurt anybody. After all, there must be lots of places in the world where grass doesn't grow." She laughed a silvery laugh. "So I said to Quirk that he should find a nice large stepping stone in Tucson, and put it in for me, and he did. So now, of course, there's no bare spot there at all, and it looks quite nice. So you see, the children are no trouble really."

"It does seem," said DeGraaf, "that you found a more sensible solution than most people bother to think of."

"Well, John said—" she hesitated.

"Go on."

"I can't quite tell you in his *words*. He said, um, he would be darned if he was going to pay three dollars for a stone and labor to put a rock where he wanted grass just because some, uh, blank children trespassed. But he lets off steam that way. Excuse me just a minute; that's the kettle."

In the kitchen, its voice as light as its mistress's, the singing teakettle announced it was on the boil. She expertly spun her wheelchair and sped to the kitchen.

"She sure gets around in that thing," Cornish said.

"Mmm."

"Has a motor, too. Uses it to go to the stores. Or out for 'exercise.' "

"Air."

"What?"

"She says she goes out for air."

"So she does."

Carrying the teakettle and spinning the wheel of the chair with the other hand, Miss Francot returned.

"Are you admiring my chair?" she asked. "People do. I was so lucky to get it. And the power attachment is just lovely. It goes up and down the ramps at the streetcorners without even seeming to work at it."

"I've seen it," DeGraaf said. "It's really very powerful."

"It's a rechargeable battery, you know. Of course, I'm very lucky also to be able to live here, instead of an ordinary city where they don't have ramps at street crossings. I can go up a curb by hand if it's low, but it frightens me to tip like that. I'd be so helpless if I fell over."

"You can't walk even short distances?"

"Oh, heavens, no. There's no feeling, even. A spinal injury. Actually, it happened during an operation for a slipped disk, but I'm sure the doctor was doing his best."

"Did this end up in a medical malpractice suit?"

"Yes, but I'm not criticising your profession, Dr. DeGraaf. Poor Dr. Leeds was quite chagrined about it. It was several years ago, and he's died since. I didn't like to sue, but I couldn't very well work after that, and one does have to eat. I don't feel any anger toward him. Really I don't. Things are not always perfect in the world, but we owe it to ourselves to be cheerful. Don't you think so?"

"As a matter of fact, I do, Miss Francot."

"And as I was saying, I'm so fortunate to have this place to live. I'd be lost in a big city. I was one of the early residents of Young Lake. I was over on the east side of town then. But when they started building the two Loops, and they were so pretty with the curving streets and of course a little nearer the new supermarket they were building, I just knew I would be even happier over here. Since I was building, I could have them make the doorways extra wide for the wheelchair, too. So I sold the other place and moved. Isn't it lovely?"

"It certainly is."

"And never having to worry about the weather! Why, I haven't been caught in the rain three times since I've been here. And Quirk keeps a lovely lawn. Flowers the year 'round. It's just perfect."

"Were you out yesterday afternoon?"

"Oh, dear. That poor child. But such a mercy that he didn't suffer. I went to the grocery and got back around three, but I don't think I was out after that until evening. I often go out just before sunset. To watch the sunset, you know."

"How nice."

"You ought to try it. If you're going to live in a place like this, you should take advantage of its special beauties."

"I think we should talk with Sara Carini before much longer," Cornish said.

"She's the social director or whatever?"

"Right. It's a paid village position here."

"The only thing I know about her is that the Barkus boy used to ride over the point of her lawn."

"Well, there's the lawn. See for yourself."

They stopped walking at the point of the East Loop, where Prickly Pear Drive and Joshua Tree Path came together. The house on the point, occupying a diamond-shaped lot, was a Spanish-inspired tan brick with arches. The front of the lawn was worn bare and a curved groove ran across the center of the bare space. A bicycle speeding down

Joshua Tree and turning across the front of the lawn to speed up into Prickly Pear would make just such a rut.

"I'll bet," Cornish said, "she would have loved to lay a trap but didn't dare."

"I've heard she may have tried one. Do we go up and ring?"

"No. She'll be at work. We hoof it over to the community house."

At the lake a couple of men and a woman, all in their late sixties, were wading. They waved at Cornish. In front of the half-begun bath house a tablecloth was spread with lunch and towels. Past Young Lake the shuffleboard courts were all in use, and the benches lined with a mixture of observers and people waiting for courts. At the roadblock where Tucson Road joined Mesquite, policemen were still turning away cars.

"What do they think they're going to see?" Cornish muttered in the direction of the sightseers. "Bodies all over?"

Behind the shuffleboard courts was the village hall. The building was done in a mixture of faux-Spanish and American Functional. Dagger plants and celosias stood in front. The lawn was green and recently mowed.

"Does Quirk do this lawn, too?" DeGraaf asked.

"No. There's a village maintenance man. He does the hall, the fire and police station, and the whole area around the shuffleboard and tennis courts. Also the village sign, which naturally has to be kept planted.

"Naturally."

Sara Carini had an office, a white plastic pedestal desk, a white telephone, and a green and white ivy plant. She wore white high heeled shoes and a green linen dress. She looked between fifty-five and sixty, might have been older, and had the pared-down efficiency of the professional organizer. At Cornish's introductions she nodded and then sniffed as if she had read the first page of a report and hoped the rest would be brief.

"Sara, I hate to go around asking everybody these questions," Cornish said. "I have to. This isn't a town for crime. I hope you won't be offended, but you know how it is."

"The sooner you find out who did it the better, as far as I'm concerned. It isn't a nice thing to have happened here."

"Well, let me wade in. Can you tell me what you did yesterday afternoon?"

"Certainly." She flipped her daily desk calendar back one page. "Lunch with the bridge group. They want to use the hall facilities. They're too big now to meet in a house. I've OK'd it. Left them at one-thirty. One of them grabbed me to complain about the celosias on the hall lawn. She said she was promised last year it would be zinnias. Put her off until council meeting. The contractor for the bath house came in at two. Couldn't get rid of him until two-thirty. I had to see about some disputes at the shuffleboard courts. One couple said they were done out of their turn, even though they had properly signed up. Party of four men cut in ahead and wouldn't give up the court. I was supposed to call on the couple, but they weren't home when I got there. I called on one of the men at three-fifteen, and he claimed the couple hadn't arrived on time, so the four men took the space. In view of the fact that they missed the appointment with me, it seems possible. Dropped back to the couple's house, but they still weren't there. I stopped at the courts to ask the maintenance man to keep an eye on the sign-up books. Not really fair. He has enough to do. He wasn't there. Found him at a leak in the water main at the police station. Appointment with Peter Pelham at four. I was about five minutes late, which was all right, since he was too. Then I had to be back in my office by four-thirty to call the caterer in Tucson about the awards banquet. Best Floral Display in a Garden. Next Wednesday. Chicken croquettes. At four-forty-five, no, closer to five, I went out to catch the paper boy. He is employed by us, you know, to distribute the community paper, Dr. DeGraaf. The *Sunray*. But he hasn't been entirely satisfactory lately. I didn't catch him at the paper office, but I cruised around until I caught up with him at Mesquite and Butte Road. Talked about fifteen minutes. Then I went over to pick up some flyers at the printing shop. That must have been five-thirty, though I have it here on the calendar for five-fifteen, because I distinctly remember being afraid they had closed. Then I went back to check the office and close up. That brings us to six p.m. or so."

"Thanks, Sara. That's good enough."

"You have quite a day," DeGraaf said. "You've done this kind of work before, I think."

"I used to be a social director on cruise ships. This is more stable and less wearing, I think. In some ways. On the other hand, you get the same people over and over with the same complaints."

"Like what?"

"Like why don't we have a cribbage tournament? Or why can't we have zinnias on the hall lawn where we have celosias? Or celosias instead of zinnias. Or who's going to stop the townhouse people from parking in the supermarket parking lot?"

"That last one wound up with us," Cornish said.

"Certainly. It should. Half the things that come through here aren't social matters at all. And the ones that are! There are people who want every last moment of their social life planned for them. It's a wonder they don't ask me over to set their television sets and choose their programs. Oh, well. That's not your problem. I hope I've told you whatever you need." Her tone indicated dismissal.

"Not entirely. I wonder, while you were driving yesterday, whether you noticed anybody out. Say between three and four-thirty."

"I noticed quite a few residents. I'd like to say I noticed a dangerous-looking stranger, too, because I'd prefer that this crime didn't reflect on Young Lake. But I didn't. The residents themselves were on pretty usual rounds. Nobody out of place, you might say."

"Did you notice the children?" DeGraaf asked.

"Let's see. I didn't see the bus pull in. I did see a couple of children at about five, playing on the shuffleboard court. I probably saw other children, since most of them play out after school, but I didn't notice any, especially."

"Do you like the children?"

"Of course."

"People always say of course they like children. When often they don't. One doesn't have to, after all. Did you care for Timothy Barkus especially?"

"I know what you're getting at, Dr. DeGraaf. Timothy was not a well-behaved child. Not like the

Lane children, for example. Children vary in temperaments as do adults, I believe."

"Touché."

"However, I did not dislike him. I hoped he would soon mature."

"How do you view the situation between the children and the old people here, Miss Carini?"

"I don't. It's not as big a problem as the papers make out. After all, we have very few children here. And very few of our older people are worried about it."

"Would you like to see more people with children move in?"

"It's not my place to have opinions on matters of policy."

"As a home owner, you must have opinions."

"I live here because my work is here."

"As social director, do you plan social events for the children?"

"No."

"No Easter egg hunts? No Santa Claus?"

"That is their parents' responsibility."

"Anything at all for the children?"

"No."

"Are they non-persons in Young Lake?"

"Dr. DeGraaf, it's not a question of non-persons, but of non-budget. Young Lake and several other towns in the southwest are legally chartered retirement communities. The state of Arizona has passed a law permitting them to restrict their residents to older people. The children who have come here are living here in a possibly illegal status. For me to divert a part of my social events budget to their use could very well also be illegal. It would certainly be a misuse of my position. I do a job here. It's a job I don't want to lose. I don't make the law."

"Do their parents receive assessments for community fund dues?"

"Of course. And their *parents* may use the facilities all they want. Now, if there aren't any relevant questions left, I have a square dance for a hundred and twenty people coming up tonight, and I have to be sure there's going to be enough punch. Will you be so good as to excuse me?"

"You're going ahead with a dance right after a murder?" DeGraaf asked.

Thoroughly exasperated, she said, "Dr. De-Graaf. You are from Chicago. Would some ladies' club there call off a dance, even if a city councilman was gunned down in the streets? You have murders there on a daily basis. The rest of my community is not going to sit around and do nothing just because somebody died. And I suggest you get to work yourselves. In any case, the Barkus boy was not anybody special."

SIX

"You haven't made friends with Sara," Cornish said, crossing the parking lot.

"Better for me to make her an enemy than you. I don't have to live here."

"I may not have to either."

"What do you mean?"

"People are impatient. I get the idea that they're not going to take it lightly if I don't make an arrest in this business."

"You're worrying too soon."

"Probably. Carini was certainly cruising around town most of the afternoon. No alibi."

"What kind of car does she drive?"

"The white Toyota over there."

They peered in the window of the car. Inside, spotless white seats and a white carpet glared in the sunlight. In the middle of the front seat lay a white sweater and a green head scarf.

"What do you think, Joe?"

"I think the boy made her gnash her teeth several times a week."

"She's in the line of work where you gnash your teeth and smile at the same time."

"Sure. But still, the worm turns."

"She's no worm. Gets her way a lot of the time, I'll bet. Maybe I'm being too unsympathetic. After all, she's earning her way in a hostile world. Without help. Been working all her life, apparently. No time for fun. Providing fun for people who don't know what to do with the leisure they have."

"She gave herself away when you got her riled, I thought. Saying that Tim was nobody special."

"Maybe."

"Peter Pelham lives down there. On Tucson Road just opposite the tennis courts."

"You think he'd go out killing children?"

"No, not really. I'm just orienting you."

"I can't believe that anybody from down here would take a corpse all the way up to the Loop at the risk of being seen. Not unless they were desperate or panicked, anyway."

"What if it were in the back seat of a car? Or the trunk? It wouldn't *be* seen. Maybe whoever it was cruised around looking for a place to dump the body and there were people out walking every other place he went. That end of the West Loop is usually pretty quiet."

"A person with a car has a lot of choices, though. Like the whole desert."

"Maybe somebody wanted to throw suspicion on Abner Milanowski."

"Joe, I have just never been big on the idea of murdering with even the partial purpose of throwing suspicion on somebody else. It's too far-fetched. If you're saddled with a corpse and you have to get out from underneath, and somebody else happens to be handy, you might put it on him, maybe salt in some evidence, if you could do it without putting yourself in jeopardy. For instance, if you'd just drowned somebody and an excellent swimmer happened to be sleeping nearby, you might throw his snorkel near the body. But not if you had to leave footprints. And for sure you won't find a stranger and drown him just to throw suspicion on the swimmer. It's not certain enough. There are too many other ways to get back at somebody you hate. To drive over to Abner's place with a body involves risk. And then, it doesn't do more than cause Milanowski some inconvenience, like a few questions. The more likely significance of Milanowski is either that he killed Tim and dumped him near home because it was dangerous to carry him far, or, better, simply that he works all day and wasn't there to see anything."

"Well, that's nice, but which? It doesn't narrow the field at all. Everybody in the place knows Abner works on the paper."

"Except the dangerous stranger people hope we'll find," DeGraaf said.

"Yup. He's the only one who wouldn't know. That makes it all the better."

"Of course, Abner's is at the end of the Loop and there's desert beyond. An outsider could pick the spot for perfectly good reasons like that."

"Except that there wasn't any such outsider."

"Except for that. And general unlikeliness."

"Jeez."

"What should our schedule be, Joe? You have your press conference at five."

"There are sixteen houses inside or facing on the East Loop that you haven't hit. You did West Loop pretty thoroughly. I say we get George to survey East Loop first for alibis, while we figure out who has an axe to grind."

"Good enough."

"About ten of those sixteen are couples. And the

way things are in retirement situations, they usually spend more time together than ever before in
their married life."

"So you're saying the couples probably alibi
each other."

"Yes, although that doesn't necessarily make
them innocent. What it means is that you'd need a
motive big enough for both of them to kill, or for
one of them to kill and the other be willing to cover
it up."

"In other words, the probabilities are reduced."

"You bet."

"All right, let's let George see if he sniffs anything unusual among them. Meanwhile, I told Mrs.
Lane I'd be back around two-thirty. She gets home
from work then. And the kids get home at three. I
really want to talk with those children. I'll bet they
know more about Tim Barkus than his parents do.
At least they probably have a less prejudiced view
of him."

"I'll buy that."

"There's something funny about that Barkus
house set-up anyway. I think the Lanes will tell us
something."

"It's two-fifteen now. Let's stroll on over."

"There's Quirk and his wagon. And the brand
new lawn mower."

They approached Quirk's equipment wagon,
which was a large aluminum affair with fat wheels.
In length it was six feet, with three bins for loose
materials on the bottom and two layers of shelves
above. On the upper shelf were four flats of pansies. One of the bottom bins was full of manure.
Another, the center one, held black dirt. The front
one held only traces of peat moss. On the middle

shelf were trowels, two cans of insecticide, a slide sprayer, and a large bag of grass seed. Quirk himself was trying to hitch an empty fertilizer spreader to a clamp made for it on the side of the wagon.

"Hi, Quirk," said Cornish. "This is Dr. De-Graaf."

Quirk nodded his head. "I'm busy right now," he said.

"Oh, I can see that. You around here yesterday?"

"Are you kidding? I'm always around here."

"Where were you yesterday?"

"What do you mean? I was everyplace. I check everything. These people don't know how to do anything for themselves."

"Well, I mean, do you follow a schedule?" Cornish persisted.

"Don't be silly. I get here early, then I work all day. I get up early. I get here early. You can't do garden work when the sun gets low in the afternoon. You can't see."

"Can you give me an idea where you were at a given time? Say about mid-afternoon?"

"No, I can't. I go around. I keep track of what needs doing. Maybe Dr. Nash needs weeding; maybe he doesn't. Maybe Miss Francot needs bedding out; maybe not. These," he pointed at the pansies in the cart, "are for the bed in Miss Francot's back yard."

"What places did you go yesterday? If you keep track of what's needed—"

"Carini needed fertilising. Townshend needed watering. I go over there. I turn on the water. But do I just stand there and watch it water for two hours? No, of course not. I move around. I take the spreader to Carini. But after I spread it I like to water it in, so I turn on that water, too. While I'm watering Carini, I figure I can spade up the bed at Francot's for today, which I do. Then I cut over to Townshend and move the hose, and back to Carini to move *her* hose. Then Nash needs manure in the front bedding. Who knows exactly what time all this happens? Spading Francot yesterday was the big job. I was there more than anywhere else. I even had to go back after I turned the other hoses off. And besides that, I have to look at the other houses I do. You never know when something's drying out. And I stop for my money. They put it off."

"They put off paying you?"

"Sure they do. Nobody likes to pay. I have to go around and collect."

DeGraaf suddenly entered the conversation. "Don't they remember to water if something dries out?" he asked.

"Some do. Some don't have the sense. I have to watch 'em all the time. In this climate something can dry out overnight. You get wind and it can dry a bed out in a coupla hours."

"You from around here?" DeGraaf asked.

"Nope. Wisconsin."

"Too much snow?"

"Too much snow *shovelling*. You do people's yards in the summer, they want you to shovel their snow in the winter. I'm a gardener, not a snow-plow. I come down here."

"You have a truck?"

"Sure." He pointed down the block. There was a dusty blue pickup parked several houses away.

"Carry this in your truck?" DeGraaf indicated the cart.

"Yup. Rolls up into the back."

"Why bother with this? Why not just carry everything in your truck?"

Quirk looked at him pityingly. "Because this goes up paths, and this goes behind the houses, and this carries all my stuff without I have to climb into the truck all the time and move the truck all the time. That's why."

"Oh."

"*And* I've got work to do."

"Well, go right ahead. And thanks."

Quirk looked at the wagon for a split second, as if he did not want to leave it under their scrutiny. Then he scooped up some grass seed in a cup and set off to Sara Carini's pointed lawn, there to obliterate all traces of Timothy Barkus.

"Well," said DeGraaf.

"Well," said Cornish. They started toward West Loop. The postman was coming up Prickly Pear Drive in their direction, and Cornish called, "Greetings, Mr. Joyner."

"Good afternoon," said the man with an old-world graciousness, an air of courtesy that assorted strangely with the Arizona landscape.

"Hot uniform for this sun," DeGraaf said.

"Oh, it keeps up the appearances."

"Maintains the dignity of the postal services?" said Cornish. "This is Dr. DeGraaf. Postman Joyner."

"Thank you. Yes. I know of Dr. DeGraaf already, having had a chat with Mrs. Ross yesterday. Glad to have you among us, Dr. DeGraaf."

"Thank you, Mr. Joyner. I imagine this climate is better than taking the mail through rain and sleet," he said politely.

"Oh, yes. My arthritis is much happier here."

"Joyner lives in town, you know," said Cornish.

"When I reach retirement age, I guess I won't have to go anywhere," he chuckled. "Well, good day."

They had hardly taken two steps into Saguaro Drive when Miss Simmons with dog, tricycle, and cane, came up behind them. "I know you're here," she called, "but who is it?"

Cornish identified them both.

"How nice. I want to thank you, Joe, for keeping all those cars out of here. They told me all about it just now. I didn't realize how bad it was this morning when I went out. There was a lot of honking, but somehow I just didn't think." She looked directly at Cornish, but at his hairline, not his eyes. "It was difficult to cross streets. Tara is very cautious. He won't take me across as long as there are cars coming. He kept me there twenty minutes before Mrs. Brown came by and took us both across. He'll go on command, of course, but I don't like to do that."

"Been to the store?" DeGraaf asked.

"I'm afraid we practically make up reasons for trips around here. I've been to the drugstore for soap. I like the scented kind, and I buy it fresh when I need it."

DeGraaf pictured the sightless woman relying on scent for enjoyment where once it would have been color, perhaps. "Do you have Quirk do your lawn?" he asked suddenly.

"How you do jump around," she laughed, focussing on his left ear. "No, I can't really afford Quirk. Besides, I think I do pretty well, myself. I like the exercise, and after all, I'm not *crippled.* The

Lanes are very understanding if I mow part of their grass by mistake. And they help me. I have a small bed of flowers, which I weed by touch. Nothing complicated. But then," she added almost coyly, "I'm not as old as most people around here."

Cornish and DeGraaf strolled up Saguaro with her, until they turned off at the Lane house. Now that DeGraaf studied it, Miss Simmons had a much more ragged lawn than the ones Quirk seemed to produce. There was also an unmowed strip, just a couple of inches wide, down the middle of one side. In back she had a rectangular bed of zinnias and marigolds about two feet wide by five feet long. It was narrow enough to be weeded from either side.

The Lane's lawn was not Quirk's work either. It was dotted with a few weeds, but at least was all the same height.

"Come in," Mrs. Lane called. "I was expecting you. Hi, Joe."

"Hi, Amy."

"I just got home," she said, sweeping a doll and a child's sweater off the sofa in one lithe movement. DeGraaf realized with a small shock how accustomed he had become to seeing the stiff movements of older people. "Sit someplace," she said, snagging several crayons from the seat of the easy chair and a collapsed construction set windmill from the coffee table. "I can offer you coffee, milk, or orange juice. Also cookies. Come on. Tell me which."

"I'd have a cookie," said DeGraaf.

"And coffee," said Cornish. The young woman disappeared into the kitchen. The two men exchanged glances.

"Have you talked with her since she found the body, Joe?"

"Just last night."

Amy Lane came back with a steaming pot of coffee, cups rattling on a tray, and chocolate chip cookies. Plumping herself down on a pillow next to the coffee table, she waved at them to take what they wanted. "Why are you staring at me?" she asked DeGraaf. "Am I a suspect?"

"I'm sorry. No, I was just thinking what a blessing youth is."

She understood him immediately. "I think about that, too, sometimes, living here. It's pretty insistent, all the old age in one spot. And I'm not entirely convinced it's the kindest thing for them, either. Well, eat." She took a cookie.

"Look," she said after a few seconds. "I appreciate your getting here a little ahead of the kids so we can talk. It's one thing to be cheerful, but a friend of theirs has been killed. I suppose nobody else has said that. Called him a friend. Nobody—I mean among the older people—was a friend to him as far as I know."

"You're right. Nobody else has said that."

"I imagine it's all been 'I like children but.' "

"Right."

"Timmie liked these chocolate chip cookies, too. Don't worry; I'm not going all maudlin here. I even had some reservations about my children playing with Timmie. He was—he was not the sort of child who respects personal property."

"No, I've heard that."

"But he had a right to grow up, you know."

"For what it's worth, Mrs. Lane, two people who were speaking of Timmie's destructive behavior specifically said he was not like the Lane children."

"Oh, isn't that nice! I don't mean nice that Timmie was destructive, of course, but nice of people to speak well of Paul and Grub. Somehow you think no one ever notices." She played it down, but her eyes were glowing. Here was someone who cared fiercely for her children.

"They seem to think you have good kids."

She smiled. "All the same, I have rather disturbed kids right now. They know Timmie is dead; and he's dead in a nasty way, too. And they know about the feeling in town. I don't believe in hiding things from them, anyway, but even if I did they still couldn't miss the hostility. I don't like all this. I feel nervous for them. And pretty damn mad about poor Tim, besides."

"How did you happen to find the body?"

"Because of old Shep here. Shep! Where are you?"

A lump that DeGraaf had taken for a fur hassock raised its head and opened a pink mouth to yawn. Mrs. Lane said, "Oh, never mind. Shep wouldn't come home, Dr. DeGraaf. And that's not like him. He doesn't like being in the sun and he doesn't like things that hiss at him. He's your basic cowardly dog. Anyway, Grub went out to look for him and found him on the bank. He wouldn't come up, so she came to get me. And of course I went to look, and—well." She bit her lip.

"When you first got there, did you notice anything that might have been kicked or blown away or stepped on later? Any tracks? Scratches? Personal objects dropped on the ground?"

"Well, I don't know. I wasn't looking for anything like that at first. I wanted to find out what was down there. I was uneasy, like Grub, but I couldn't see until I climbed down. The sun had just set, and the light was bad. After I found him, I sent Grub to call. I don't think Shep carried anything off. I had the impression there were some weeds bent over, but not a very clear memory of where or how."

"Let me go back a bit then. When did you get home from work?"

"Two-thirty. Same as—oh, maybe more like a quarter of three. I had some groceries to get, myself."

"Did you see anybody on the way home?"

"I think I remember seeing Abby Francot. It's not easy to be sure, because those people come and go so much. It could have been the day before."

"Then when did the children get home?"

"Five after three, I should say. I'd just got the groceries put away and made some butter sandwiches. For some reason, they like bread and butter put together as sandwiches for an after school snack. And a glass of milk."

"Did they say anything special?"

"They have special things on their minds all the time. But yesterday it was about school, not about Timmie. Paul is giving his teacher used Valentines that he got last month and he's convinced she appreciates it. Maybe she does."

"Did they say anything about what happened between getting off the bus and getting home?"

"No." Suddenly she looked frightened. "Do you think somebody was waiting for the bus? Somebody waiting to hurt one of the children?"

"No. I have no reason to. I really wondered

whether Timmie had said or done anything out of the ordinary, or was going to meet them someplace later."

"They planned to go to the clubhouse later. In fact, they *did* go. But that wasn't unusual, and they didn't say anything about Timmie meeting them there, specifically."

"Where is the clubhouse?"

"I'm not supposed to know. Don't tell them. It's in the park space, dead space really, in the center of East Loop. It's their underground fort. I've always worried a little about snakes getting in there, but you have to let children do something secret, or they don't feel free."

"Yes, that's true. Did they give you any reason to think Timmie was going to meet them there?"

"No. But they were very secretive. It's always big doings in the clubhouse. It's become bigger lately, since the publicity about the feud between the older people and the children. They probably see themselves as an army of kids alone against the world when they're in their clubhouse."

DeGraaf let her be silent for a moment, and she finally said, "I'm not exactly frightened, you understand. But the whole thing makes me uneasy. I don't think children should see this kind of behavior coming from adults. And I don't think the type of response some of their friends make is a good thing, either."

"Does that mean you don't think the murder is connected with the feud?"

"Because I don't worry about actual violence but only the psychological effect of the feud? I guess that's right. I suppose I simply can't believe anybody would kill a child just for stepping on the lawn, or even for putting a scorpion in a mailbox."

"What about money as a motive?"

"I know some of the older people are terrified of the costs of having to build schools. And a lot of them really have *very* little money. They try to stretch their retirement benefits and so on over whatever they think the rest of their life is going to be."

"Yes, I know."

"But even at that! It's unbelievable to think of any one of them having enough of an individual financial motive to kill a child. And just that one child! Oh, it's just preposterous! All the people around here are nice in their own ways, too. I don't believe it."

But her voice had trailed off in strength at the end of the sentence, and DeGraaf asked, "What are you thinking of?"

"This fall. Somebody threw garbage all over our yard. At night. And I sat here and thought the same thing. Nobody would ever really do a thing like that. With all the garbage out on the lawn I thought nobody would do it. But they *had* done it, of course. And Timmie *is* dead."

There was a scuffle outside the door. Then, without appearing to have turned the knob, two children fell into the room, a blonde girl of about eight and a small boy, perhaps six. Their mother smiled and got up.

"This is Grub, whose real name is Esther, and this is Paul. This is Chief Cornish and Dr. DeGraaf to talk with you. And if you'll wash some of that dust off you can have cookies with us."

"Is he here about Timmie?" the girl asked.

"Yes, they both are."

"Can we give clues?" asked Paul.

"I hope so. Now wash."

"Me first," Paul shouted, and he raced for the bathroom, but Grub's legs were longer and she got there first.

"Well, they're sort of civilized," said Amy Lane.

The children were back in a few seconds, not much cleaner, but with very damp dust. Paul took three cookies, put two back when his sister ordered him to, and sat on the floor. Grub was much more serious. She studied Cornish and DeGraaf to the point of forgetting to eat.

"Can you think of anything to tell us about yesterday afternoon? Who you saw—that sort of thing."

Grub appeared to consider. Paul ate.

DeGraaf, who felt the question was far too general, started to talk. "We don't know Timmie like you. Can you tell us what he was up to lately? Is there any way, in your opinion, that he could have got himself into a mess?"

"He broke my airplane," said Paul.

"That was an accident," said his mother.

"No," Grub said, "it wasn't an accident. But it wasn't important, either. Paul, think of something important."

"I can't," said Paul, reaching for another cookie.

"We had the same driver on the school bus," said Grub, as if reliving the afternoon in her mind. "He ran over a snake. On the way home. But that's not important either. We came right home. We're supposed to."

"And we can eat," said Paul.

"After that, we went to the clubhouse. But only Fib was there. I didn't see Timmie after school, or after the bus, I mean, at all. I mean alive," she added, with the directness of children.

A shrill voice called in the back window. "Grub! Are you coming?"

"That's Libby," Grub said, and she went to the window. "I can't come now," she shouted. We've got company."

In the window was the thin face and the two aggressive pigtails DeGraaf had seen in his grandmother's back yard the afternoon before. "Come *on*," Libby demanded. "We've got work to do."

"No, I can't," said Grub. "We'll catch up with you later."

"Do you have to bring the *infant?*" asked Libby scornfully. Paul sucked in his breath to shout, and choked on a crumb.

"We'll be out later. Go away. We're busy."

"All right. If that's the way you want it." The face vanished from the window.

Grub came back and sat down. "Sorry," she said.

Amy threw up her hands in a gesture of good-natured resignation. Gerritt gave her a smile of sympathetic understanding, and then turned back to her brood.

"What kind of thing does Libby want to do?" he asked. "You know, Grub, I'm really serious. I'm trying to figure out what Timmie may have run into yesterday afternoon, and I have absolutely no way of knowing."

Grub folded her arms and pressed her lips together. After staring at DeGraaf a few seconds, she said, "I wonder if I might speak to you privately?"

"Certainly," DeGraaf said. "If you'll excuse us?" He rose.

"It's quite a walk," Grub said.

Betraying no surprise, DeGraaf simply followed. He noticed that Paul got up and followed too. Grub made no objection to this. Apparently 'privately' did not exclude Paul, but only the other adults. Amy started to protest, but then, apparently thinking better of it, simply sat and watched as DeGraaf and her children made their way out of the room.

They went out the back door, across the Lane's back yard, and took the path between Abby Francot's yard and Dr. Nash's. DeGraaf kept carefully to Miss Francot's side, and stepped on the stone she had had installed at the bare spot. He noticed that the children did also. They crossed the street in front of Miss Francot's house, and then detoured south two houses.

"Mr. Chide gets angry," was all Grub said about the abrupt detour.

The three passed Sara Carini's house at the point of East Loop and then found a path, rather unkempt, that appeared to be a public access into the center of the Loop. It led to the dead space behind the back yards of the houses on the teardrop-shaped block.

"Some day they're going to put up a park here," said Grub. "And then it will be too bad for us."

She led the way, DeGraaf following her and Paul trailing after, between some Joshua trees toward a pile of tumbleweed and sagebrush. Grub got down on her knees and, looking like the white rabbit in *Alice in Wonderland,* plunged down into the earth, through the thicket. DeGraaf was by no means convinced that a larger person could do this, and indeed he could not even see the opening from where he stood. But neither was he going to be left behind. He dropped down and pushed forward, on his hands and knees.

As soon as he got low to the ground, he saw the tunnel through the brush, and pushed on more confidently. There were twigs in his eyes and sharp dry leaves were getting imbedded in his jacket. The knees of his slacks did not bear thinking about. But there were no cacti, as one might have feared. The kids must have cleared them, and the hard mud underneath was smooth. When suddenly he came to a hole straight down, he stopped and peeped in.

"Feet first is best," came a voice up out of the hole. Did it have a triumphal 'I thought you could do it' note? DeGraaf pushed his feet in and, feeling nothing but hearing no cautions, let go.

He slid into a den. It was darkish but not black, with two holes for windows. "This is rather better than what I used to have," he said. "But where I lived we used to have a lot of rain."

"Oh, yes, if we had much rain, it would be all up with us."

A blow struck him on the back and bowled him over. Brushing dirt out of his face, he realized that he had not allowed for Paul's entrance.

"Sorry," said Paul. "We usually move out of the way of the door," and he sneezed.

"What's the matter?"

"Dust. Always stuffs up my nozzles."

"Nozzles? Oh. A lot of us call them nostrils, but I guess it's the same thing either way."

"I'm sure you won't tell anybody about this place," said Grub.

"Goes without saying."

"I thought so."

"That's the sign of the scorpion," said Paul, pointing to a board with a picture over the door. From the board also dangled, redundantly, a dead scorpion on a piece of twine. DeGraaf nodded.

"We trust Mom, you know," said Grub. "But parents get in funny positions sometimes when other parents ask them things."

"That's very true."

"And we don't want anybody to think—I don't know—it's hard to tell some things."

"You don't want to say anything bad about Timmie?"

Grub looked at him. "I think so. It seems nicer to talk to somebody with a fresh approach."

A fresh approach. Did children talk this way before they watched so much television? Recalling some extremely pompous moments as a child, he thought maybe they had. At the same time, Grub was not really being pompous. She was troubled, caught between some code that told her not to tell, and the conviction that she ought to help the investigation. She was feeling her way with a defensive formality.

"You go ahead," DeGraaf said. "I'll listen."

Paul settled down on a piece of wood and prepared to be serious. DeGraaf crossed his legs and sat, which gave him some headroom if he just tilted his head slightly sideways. Grub did not notice, but was searching inside herself for a proper way to begin without breaking any confidences.

"We've been having trouble here, you know," she said.

"You mean what they call the generation gap war?"

"Yes. It was pretty silly. Until the bugs. Then

everybody got excited. Mother doesn't want to be frightened." She came out with this last in a tolerant voice, understanding but not agreeing with her mother.

"Do you think she ought to be frightened, then?"

Grub thought a few more seconds, then said, "Well, Timmie's dead, isn't he?" To this unanswerable retort DeGraaf said nothing, and she proceeded. "It got worse when Fib had his arm broken. You see, we thought he knew who did it."

"You thought?"

"Well, Fib wouldn't say. I mean, he *said* he didn't know, but we thought he did know, if you know what I mean."

"Yes, but why shouldn't he have told you?"

"That's easy. Either he was scared, or it happened because he did something he shouldn't have."

"You're right, of course. That's possible."

"But then, everybody said we had to do something about it. The kids all said so, I mean. You know, when the adults were dumping garbage and all that, we did some pretty silly things, but not very serious."

"May I ask what?"

"We should have thought it over more, but it was so silly at first. We put the garbage back in people's mailboxes."

"That doesn't seem so very bad."

"Well, it got everybody upset. And you see, when I stopped to think about it, most of the mailboxes must have belonged to people who didn't dump the garbage. It's just reasonable. You understand?"

"Yes."

"So it was a sort of a mistake. But the kids—some of the kids were wanting to get back at them."

"Natural to feel that way."

"Yes, I guess so." She stopped. DeGraaf wondered whether it was better at this point to prompt or to wait. On the whole, he thought wait. After a few more moments, during which Paul showed admirable placidity, she spoke. "I think I'd better tell you."

"I wish you would."

"It would be easier if I knew exactly."

"Mmm."

"Well, after Fib got his arm broken, what we did was this. We started spying. At first we divided it. The three kids on West Loop did the people on West Loop and the two kids on East Loop did the East Loop. We wanted to find out who had tripped Fib. We figured the person would strike again."

"I see." What could be more natural, under the circumstances? There would have been little spies all over the place, and no telling what they had got into.

"But I didn't like it too much," Grub went on. "I mean, sometimes you'd see people doing things you knew they didn't want you to see. The rest of the time it was boring. And nobody tripped anybody, either. Nobody tried to get Fib, and besides that, his mother kept him home a lot after the accident. Timmie Barkus and Libby Potts were the only ones who really *liked* the spying."

"I wanted to make airplanes," Paul said. His sister looked at him and he went back to being quiet.

"I think they were still doing their spying by

Loops, but after we dropped out they didn't tell us. That's what I mean by not knowing exactly."

"Let me summarize, okay? You think that Timmie may have run into trouble because he was spying. You aren't sure it had anything directly to do with the Fib Levinson business. It could have, or it might have to do with the feud in general—like he might have found out who was throwing garbage on people's lawns. Or it might be that he ran into some completely unrelated problem while spying. Is that about it?"

"It doesn't sound like much when you put it that way."

"Oh, yes, it is. It's *really* important. Up to now we'd been thinking mostly about people who were upset with Timmie for some of the things he did, like running across their lawns. But you know, that sort of thing doesn't make a very good motive for murder."

"I guess *not.*"

"But if he was intentionally poking his nose into strange places, this does two things for us. One, it means there are a lot more people who might be involved, including people who didn't care much about lawns. And two, he had a chance to stumble on something really serious, that would make a compelling motive for murder. Now suppose he found out who put the scorpions in your mother's mailbox. That could be a federal offense. Not only are you supposed to put nothing but mail in a mailbox, but there must be some especially serious law about putting dangerous items in a mailbox." The kids were looking very serious. "Now look," DeGraaf said, "I know you kids put some garbage in mailboxes. And I know some kid must have put the scorpion in the mailbox of the woman who was bitten. Mrs. Grundler, I think. I'm not excusing that. In fact, I think you had better leave off the idea of personal revenge altogether." Both nodded, Grub with comprehension, and Paul because he got a general idea and because Grub had nodded. "I've got no idea who did the scorpion thing and I won't ask. But the point is, *you* wouldn't get into much trouble over it, while an adult would. The penalties are stiffer for adults and they're supposed to know better. So if Timmie saw something like that, he would have evidence that the person had committed a federal offense. And what's more, if it were a person in a responsible position, like an official around here, he could lose his job, besides. And his reputation. That wouldn't be true for you kids. So an adult could be terrified of being found out." He looked at the two serious, well-meaning faces. They were a little dusty and somewhat alarmed, but more open than the adult faces he'd seen that day.

"Look," he said, "this is no kidding. If somebody is frightened, there is still danger out there. Do you understand what I mean? Frightened people are dangerous. Frightened people can kill. I don't want to upset you, but I really wish you'd both kind of hang around the house for a few days. For God's sake, don't go spying."

"We'd decided we didn't like it anyway."

"What about Libby? Did she know what Timmie had found out?"

"I don't think so, because on the way home in the bus today she was talking about trying to find out what had happened to Timmie. As if she didn't know, and she wanted us to help."

"Do one thing for me. Please. I'll try to get hold of her to ask her to quit. But she might not listen to me. She'll figure I'm one of the grown-ups."

"She sure will," Grub giggled. "She's mad at grown-ups."

"But you can talk to her. Just ask her to lay off for a few days. Okay?"

"Yes. I'll tell her. I think you're right."

"Fine. Now is there anything else you can think of? Do you have any idea which people specifically Timmie was interested in?"

"There were a lot of them. Almost everybody. Miss Carini. And Dr. Nash. Mr. Milanowski and Miss Simmons. And Miss Grundler and Mr. and Mrs. Townshend and Miss Francot and Mrs. Brown and Mr. DiLeonardi, and Miss Perkins, but she's away on a trip right now so it can't be that, and Mr. and Mrs. Creel, but they're in Minnesota, I think. But the trouble is, Timmie was mad at us."

"Why?"

"Because we didn't like spying and quit. And because we didn't want to go on with the tricks."

"What kind of tricks?"

"Oh, he liked to do things to people. When somebody was taking a nap in the sun in the back yard, he would throw a stone into the yard and hit something near them that made a noise. Then they'd sit up and wonder what it was. Or he'd empty out somebody's birdbath. That kind of thing. He was so *silly* sometimes. But he said it was a war. He said if we weren't on the kids' side we were on the grown-ups' side. Anyway, he was mad. So he didn't tell us much. I guess he figured he'd find out what he could, and then he'd show us."

SEVEN

De Graaf left the Lanes' with Cornish in tow and headed immediately for the Pottses' house on the far side of the East Loop. They had a set of four plaster ducks on the lawn, one large and three small, all in a line. The house was pink stucco. There were no children's toys in front. Cornish rang. No answer, but somewhere inside a child cried. He rang again.

The door swung open, and at the same time, whoever opened it walked away, muttering, "Now you've done it. You've waked him up again."

DeGraaf and Cornish looked at each other wondering whether they were supposed to go in. They decided to go ahead, and stood inside in the vestibule. There was a glass table with bric-a-brac against the wall. Presently a woman returned, carrying a two-year-old boy.

"Oh, it's you, Joe," she said. "Stop that!" she told the child, who appeared to be doing nothing at all but wiggling his feet. She set the child down. He stood up immediately and staggered toward a coffee table laden with paperweights and small cigarette boxes. "Don't touch," said his mother.

"Mrs. Potts," Joe began, but she was telling the child to sit down and didn't hear him. He started over, introducing DeGraaf and explaining why they had come.

She waved at some chairs, and they sat. "Leave that alone," she said to the child, who was looking at a pedestal with a fern on top.

"Mrs. Potts," said DeGraaf. "We came over especially to see you and Libby. We think there may be some danger right now, in letting the children wander around—"

He stopped, for the boy was lurching toward him, and a split second later had grabbed his leg.

"Hello," said DeGraaf.

"Hello," said the child.

"Stop that," said his mother.

"I don't mind, Mrs. Potts."

"He'll wrinkle your suit."

"Oh, that's all right. Let me explain what I meant about danger," he continued. "We don't want to alarm you, but until we find out what really happened, we are quite uneasy about it." She looked entirely uninterested, as well as unalarmed. "We think the children may have been keeping an eye on the grownups, and Timmie may have seen something he shouldn't have." He stopped as Mrs. Potts rose, slapped the child's hand, which had been folding DeGraaf's pants leg, and plumped the child down in the center of the room, far from any object or person. The boy began to cry.

"Be quiet," his mother said.

DeGraaf sighed in frustration. "Is Libby home?"

"No, but she should be soon. She came in and

went right out again."

"Well, I wonder if you'd ask her to kind of hang around the house for—"

The child was coming back toward the coffee table and the mother was up again. She scooped the boy off the floor and took him to the dining room, where she deposited him in a playpen. He turned around in a circle once, confined, and then sat down in the middle and began to cry again.

"Be quiet," his mother said.

"Mrs. Potts?"

"Yes? I'm sorry he's so difficult."

"He's not difficult at all. They just need space at that age. Mrs. Potts, will you ask Libby to stay around the house for a few days? Or play at the Lanes? Do you have any idea what she's doing right now?"

"No, I don't know what she does after school."

"When you see her, have her play in your own yard, or have the Lane kids over here to play, or whatever. We'll clear this up soon, I'm sure. But meanwhile we don't want anybody getting into trouble."

"Oh, certainly. If you think it's important. But I don't know. I don't think she'll want to. Libby doesn't play in the house much."

The two men took the back door to Cornish's office, on the notion that the press would be hanging around in front. The number of cars in the parking lot was three times what it had been before the murder. And while there were fewer cars trying to get past the roadblock than there had been earlier in the day, a large number quietly parked along Yucca and Mesquite hinted of reporters somewhere, lying in wait. Since there were only three or four papers in Tucson, some of the national wire services had to be in on the story. And why not? If they thought the feud stories interesting, this development was compelling.

Having ducked into Cornish's office from the back hall, they opened the pebble-glass door a crack to look into the main room. Beyond the desk man, it was awash in reporters.

"Oh, lord," Cornish said. He went back to his desk, dropped into his swivel chair, and let his chin down into his hand.

"It's getting on to conference time," DeGraaf said.

"Yeah."

"Why so glum?"

"Jeez, can't you guess? I haven't got a damn thing to tell 'em."

"It isn't that bad. They can't really expect you to trip up a murderer in less than twenty-four hours."

"And to think I came here to get away from this kind of thing."

"I thought you came here to get away from high-sulfur fuels."

"Yes, but of all the places without the sulfur, I picked one that looked peaceful, didn't I?"

"Well, you've had several years of peace."

"The truth is, I picked a place that seemed to have less in the way of the sordid sorts of crime. It seemed cleaner here, somehow."

"I know. I can understand. Of course, the sordid can often be interesting. However. Why not tell these press people that you have reason to think the crime is an isolated incidence of violence, but you don't want to say more without further details?"

"And have the corporation and town on my neck for giving the place a bad name?"

"*You* didn't murder the child, after all. Somebody else did it. Reporters can smell evasiveness, and you have to give at least an impression of frankness. Give 'em two or three details from the autopsy results. Tell 'em your whole force is working overtime. You know the routine."

"It still boils down to not knowing who did it."

"When do we get the lab results back?"

"They'll trickle in, little by little." He picked up the desk phone. "Fish, did that stuff get back from the lab?" He listened a few seconds. "All right. But don't let anybody in here. And don't let anybody in the squad room, either. We've gotta get some work done around here." He put down the phone and after about twenty seconds a sergeant scuttled sideways through the main door and closed it after him. He stood leaning against the inside of the door, and breathed, "Gawd."

"I know, Fish. I know. Give me the stuff."

"Some of 'em aren't reporters, I don't think," said the sergeant. "Am I supposed to ask for credentials? Should we keep 'em all outdoors until five?"

"Let it ride for now. After the conference, I hope most of 'em will go away to write up their poison-pen stuff. After that, any civilians, or anybody who doesn't leave, we throw out."

"Okay."

The sergeant left the papers on the desk, squarely facing Cornish and right side up for him to read, and squeezed back out the door.

"This is still partial," said Cornish, glancing through the sheets. "Nothing we didn't expect. No skin or blood under the fingernails, worse luck. Just dirt, peanut butter, jelly, and paint."

"Thought so."

"Some of the tissue samples. Here, you take it. It's your sort of mumbo-jumbo."

"Let's see. You're right. Nothing exciting. Unless you consider being right exciting. No poison in the stomach. No long-term poison in the tissues. Well, that we hardly expected. Potassium concentration looks like he had been dead about four to five hours when the sample was drawn. So that checks. Okay, you still have a strangling."

"The school, by the way, says he did have peanut butter for lunch. The class went on a field trip to an orange grove. Took their own sandwiches and drank orange juice. His sandwich was peanut butter and jelly."

"So you can tell the boys of the fourth estate that everything possible is being done."

"Sure. And they'll still tear me apart."

"Why? Joe, what's the matter with you? You must have faced far more aggressive reporters on your job before you came down here. Why do you view these guys with this sort of anxiety?"

"I'll tell you why. It's because there's something going on here that I've never run into before and I don't like it. The reporters are after us. I mean they're out to get the town. I'm not kidding. I'm no great civic booster. I'd never heard of Young Lake before I started looking for a place to move to. But it just gets to me. Look at what happened here.

Other cities have muggings by the basket-load, rapes until you can't count and the reported ones are just the tip of the iceberg. Fires, kidnappings and killings of children, murders, every damn thing you can think of. But here—up to yesterday—all we had was a little garbage on a couple of lawns and some insects in mailboxes and a kid got tripped. And we've got stories on us from coast to coast. It's not that *I* don't take those incidents seriously. But for other people to headline them, in view of what's happening in the rest of the world— it's ridiculous! The reason is that basically we've got a clean safe town here. They resent it; they envy it, I guess. The eyes of the world are on us, unfortunately. And they're out to prove that there is no Utopia."

"Yes, I see."

"And this will do it."

"Sure. They'll blow it out of proportion."

"And that's why I say that no matter what I do or think or say at five o'clock, they're going to roast me and Young Lake."

Joe Cornish settled back in his chair with his weight on his neck and stared gloomily at the clock. DeGraaf started to thumb through the reports from the men who had surveyed the Loops and neighboring blocks. For now, he set aside everything outside the Loops, on the grounds that it was more probably a Loop murder and he could get around to the others when he had time. In the Loops themselves, there were several alibis that looked solid. One woman had a sister visiting from California and the two old people had never left each other's sight all afternoon. Two were husband

and wife. They claimed to have been picnicking from three to six and there was no reason to doubt it. One couple was in Europe. One man was proven to have been at work in Tucson all afternoon; his secretary confirmed it. One woman was at home with a nurse and a broken hip. Another had severe enough arthritis, with visibly enlarged joints, to make her unable to strangle anybody.

Those lacking alibis with whom DeGraaf had not yet talked included Charles Chide, who lived in East Loop across the street from Dr. Nash. Ellen Norris Brown, who lived next to Chide. Angelo DiLeonardi, who was president of Sunshine Corporation, which owned the development. Mrs. Levinson, whose son Fib, with his broken arm, had been playing in their backyard. Mr. Levinson was at work in Tucson at the time. DeGraaf's grandmother, Adelaide Ross, who claimed no alibi, since DeGraaf himself had been sunbathing most of the time and not watching her. And Popeye, who said he had been taking a nap.

There were too many possibilities in the Loops alone, and not enough real indications. And what about people outside the Loops? Less likely; not impossible. There was little reason at this point to think Cornish would ever solve the thing, he thought. Or himself either, the way things stood. He looked at Cornish, sunk in melancholy and ready to throw himself to the wolves of the press.

Suddenly, Gerritt's thoughts turned to the Townshends.

"Joe," he asked, "how well do you know the Townshends? How did they happen to wind up in Young Lake? Have they lived here long?"

Cornish glanced at DeGraaf in mild surprise. "What brings them up?"

"I don't really know. I guess it's just that when you're sifting through details any little thing that really seems out of the ordinary, sticks out. Have you ever seen the inside of their house?"

"No, now that you mention it, I haven't. I don't know them all that well. They've lived here for about a year. Just moved in like everybody else, as far as I know. What's the matter with their house?"

"It's all wrong; it's a hodgepodge. The furniture and household items are cheap and all thrown together without any thought at all. All their personal things, like their clothes, their car, and their scotch, are expensive and carefully chosen. It's as if they called somebody down here and asked him to furnish a house cheaply with enough stuff to make it look lived in. And then they just drove in the driveway and pretended to live here."

"They *are* gone a lot; that's for sure."

"Can you find out where they're from and what they are?"

"Sure. Take a couple of days."

Putting aside for the time being his curiosity about George and Leila, DeGraaf returned to the lab reports. Nothing. And he was willing to bet there'd be nothing unusual in the rest as they came in. Why should there be? A small child strangled. Nothing complicated. No weapon to trace. No obscure poison to track down. Just about everybody had hands. Nothing to look for.

And then it was five o'clock.

Cornish got up, smiled sourly at DeGraaf, and jerked his head towards the main door, meaning did DeGraaf want to come. DeGraaf got up and followed, thinking that Cornish could probably use another friendly body in the room.

"Did one of your old folks do it, Chief?"

Cornish had worked his way through a brief and rather complete statement of what they knew, including the cause of death, but omitting some details they wanted to keep to themselves. He had carefully explained that the investigation was still preliminary and there were no suspects. Then, as soon as he paused, this had to be their first question. He sighed.

"I told you we have no suspects. We're sifting everything and everyone. I have no particular reason to believe that an older person, or even a resident *must* have done this. But we did search the entire area thoroughly after the body was discovered and found no suspicious strangers. Naturally, that was a few hours after the killing, and there was plenty of time for escape. And I ought to add that by no means are all our people old. Most of them are retired, but many of them are under sixty-five. Of the rest, most are young in spirit."

"Young enough to strangle kids?"

"I have explained that the assault need not have required much strength. That fact doesn't imply that an older person must have done it either, though. A strong young person could have done it with ease."

"But you don't think so?"

"We don't operate on speculation. We are looking for facts."

A fat, balding little man with a briefcase between his feet and a thick note pad, said, "Haven't you found much in the way of facts on the scene, then?"

"We have some. But the fact that the ground around here is as hard as adobe causes a problem. The lack of witnesses also. As I say we have the time of death and the—"

"Times of death are *very* approximate, aren't they?" the bald man asked.

"There is good regularity except under unusual circumstances—"

"And it takes an expert even to make a good guess?"

"Yes, though we don't guess. We get a tight range from a number of facts—"

"And you don't have a regular coroner here? Do you think some local GP is equal to the job? Do you think the rights of the parents are being protected when you conduct the investigation with your own small local force and base it on a postmortem conducted by a local man who deals mostly in arthritis?"

"That would depend on his background and his ability. However, in this case we happened to have visiting here a well-known expert in forensic medicine from Chicago. Very generously, he has consented to work with us. This is making possible a number of observations which, rather soon I hope, may solve the case."

DeGraaf winced. "Rather soon." Cornish was rattled. DeGraaf could tell by the increasing formality of his sentences.

"Who is that, Chief?" the bald man asked.

"Dr. Gerritt DeGraaf. Cornish nodded at him. DeGraaf looked at Cornish. But now the bald man was on to him. Why did the other reporters let this one get in so many questions? He must be the dean of southern Arizona reporters.

"Dr. DeGraaf. Are you confident of finding the killer?"

How could he answer a question like that? It was too general for what his position here was supposed to be, and too speculative.

"That's a wrong question," he said. "It doesn't much matter what I predict, does it? We get all the data we can. We're working on several leads right now that may or may not pan out. This is standard procedure."

"Do you think the local authorities are able to give this case the expertise and sophistication that a big-city homicide department could?"

"Yes."

The bald man chuckled. "Oh, come on. You know we want a comment, not just an answer. What do you think? Are the boy's parents getting a fair shake?"

"The department here has all the expertise of a big-city force, since they were all trained in major cities. They have, also, several advantages over a city force. They know the residents far more intimately. You know how important it is to have a knowledge of the habits of the residents of the area, in terms of deciding what places are lonely and what are travelled, who watches the street and who doesn't, and so on. The local police know the area, and because it is limited, they can do an unusually good job of searching the place. And they have a concern about the case which a city force, dealing with several homicides a day, can never duplicate. There's no way for the case to get lost here, as it might in a major metropolitan area."

The bald man grinned. Two other reporters simultaneously began questions, looked at each other, and then one began on Cornish.

"Do you think your local feud is going to heat up because of this, Chief?"

"No. If anything, this has made people realize they were making a fuss when they should have been looking for peaceful solutions to their problems." Cornish, DeGraaf knew, privately hoped for this, but had little confidence in its coming true.

"You still having scorpions in mailboxes to deal with?" said the second reporter.

"No. And I hope it never starts again."

"What about the rumor that the ACLU is going to step in on the side of the parents?"

"I don't know about it."

"They're going to take the thing to court. And have the property restrictions declared unconstitutional."

"I'm sure that 'have it declared unconstitutional' is misleading. They might test the constitutionality of it. In which case it would be up to the court. Not to me. I don't make law."

"Whose side are you on, Chief? The old folks or the kids?"

"Now don't be silly. I enforce the law. I try to keep the peace. I don't take sides."

"There's a lot of talk in town that if you'd protected the kids as they came home from school this wouldn't have happened. That other kid had his arm broken. Wasn't that reason enough to be careful?"

"We have certainly been patrolling. However,"

said Cornish, measuring his words, "as I said earlier, the murder occurred after the boy had been home and then gone out to play. We had no reason to assign a patrolman to every child playing outdoors. You can protect people right out of their rights if you surround them constantly. I don't think the children would have liked it much if we had followed them all. Nor had any parents requested it."

"Have they now?" one asked.

Another interrupted, "Are you going to now?"

"What," asked the bald man, "are you doing to protect the kids now?"

"We have closed the Loops to the general public and asked the children in the immediate area to play at home. We still have no reason at all to think there is any danger to children in general. It seems likely that the Barkus boy got into something—we don't yet know what—and was killed because of it."

"But what about a homicidal child-hater?"

"We have no evidence of that at all. No messages. No special ferocity in the killing."

"But," said the bald man, "there is ferocity in any killing, isn't there?"

DeGraaf thought, "Touché." The bald man deserved the deference the others showed him.

Cornish said, "You have to go by the facts available. There are more and less violent murders."

"It seems to me," said the bald man, "that the murder of a child—by *whatever* means—is just about as brutal a crime as you'll ever come across. And you *know* you have people here who hate children."

"We have some who are annoyed by children. And we have some who are angry about the children. I hope we have nobody here who hates all children as a class."

"Breaking a child's arm goes beyond gentle pique, doesn't it?"

DeGraaf decided he had better step in. Cornish was running scared. He hoped he did not look as out of place as he felt.

"Look," he said, "you're making a semantic difficulty here, where there needn't be any. As Chief Cornish is pointing out, there are certain clues here, and we have to make what we can of them. Of course, this is a heinous crime we're dealing with, but there's lack of a particular *kind* of violence here. *Random* violence done to a body, particularly after death, is often associated with psychopathic murders. Lack of it suggests in most cases a more motivated, to our way of thinking, sort of killing. We take what is likely, after all, and work on it. We could run off in every direction, but that would hardly be systematic. At present we are conducting interviews with all the people in the area. This could produce a witness to the crime, additional information of a peripheral nature, or possibly the killer directly. This is uniquely possible here because of the limited area and the close acquaintance of the police force with the residents. I've never seen an investigation more wholeheartedly entered into. At the same time, one of our greatest problems today was the traffic situation caused by sightseers and the possible destruction of evidence by reporters trying to walk on the murder site. Chief Cornish has been forced to spend as much of his force on control of rubberneckers as on investigation. This ties up officers who could be working on the murders, as well as some who could be patrolling to protect the children you talked about. If you're really interested in the child's killer being caught, you can help us. Report the event, of course, but tell your readers that sightseers are not being allowed anywhere near the murder scene, so we won't have endless lines of cars to control. Chief Cornish realizes you have a job to do, also, but do it in a way that leaves him time to do his."

Cornish had his cue. "Let me set up a time for a conference tomorrow. Why not five again? We aren't trying to hide anything interesting, but we'd like to get a little work done in between."

There was a little laughter, a couple of grumbles, but Cornish went on.

"We're keeping the Loops sealed. It's better for everyone that way, but otherwise you can talk with the residents. I won't get in your way, if you'll try not to get in mine. See you tomorrow at five." He nodded, turned, and went into his office. DeGraaf followed quickly. He pulled the door closed, but they heard, and were happy to hear, a trampling on the stairs as if the herd was leaving.

"Bloodsuckers," said Cornish. "I suppose you're annoyed that I gave 'em your name."

"You had to, at that point."

"Bloodsuckers."

"I hope I didn't barge in."

"Jeez, no. I needed it. I run out of patience with things like that. I'd rather work than explain what I'm doing."

"I've been ignoring my old Gran all day, Joe. I'd better get home."

"Okay. I'll get to the paper work. Do you realize we don't know one more thing today than we knew last night?"

"Not quite true. We know a lot more about Timmie. And a few other things. Joe, we ought to call the Levinsons and ask them to keep Fib close to home for a few days."

"I already did it."

"Oh. Well, I'll leave the town in good hands and go have dinner. Bye."

EIGHT

Grub had thought she would just see whether Libby was hanging around the back yard. She wasn't, though, so Grub started down West Loop to see whether she was wandering around in search of excitement. Libby might do almost anything, Grub realized, rather than go home. Grub walked the whole Loop, counterclockwise, passing by Timmie's house before she got down to the point where the barricade could be seen. Timmie's house made her distinctly uneasy, with its look of barren watchfulness, and she hurried past. For some reason that she couldn't explain, she felt it would be wrong to let Timmie's parents see her out and about, apparently playing.

Grub checked out the red and white barricade at Mesquite from a few yards distance, not stopping to talk with the policemen on duty, as she might have done in more casual times. She turned up Prickly Pear Drive and circled it, up towards Potts's house. Once, opposite the access lane that led to their hideout, she stopped and called Libby several times. But in her heart she was quite convinced that Libby was not there. Libby would not go sit in an empty hideout when there was anything to do elsewhere, and since the feud started there was always something else to do.

A little more walking brought her to the Potts. She knew better, from long experience, than to ring the bell, so she ran around to the back and looked in the kitchen window. Mrs. Potts was drinking coffee at the kitchen table. Grub tapped on the window.

"What do you want? Don't wake the baby."

"Is Libby here?"

"No, she's out."

"Oh. Thank you very much," Grub said politely. And she ran back to the sidewalk.

She kept walking through the extreme north end of East Loop, heading down into Joshua Tree Path. For a second she thought of cutting home between the vacant lot and Abby Francot's house, which would take her into her back yard on Becky Simmons's side. But on second thought she felt going a little farther would give her a chance to look down the whole of Joshua Tree Path, and if she saw Libby she would call. She was a little confused, between her promise to DeGraaf to tell Libby to stay home and her other promise to him to stay home herself. She was not sure which was more important. And the block had a deserted quality which did not appeal to her. But she felt she owed it to Libby to go just a little farther.

She was now on the street between Charles Chide's house and John Nash's. But Libby was not visible. There was surely no point in going back down to the junction and the barricade. She gave it up. Libby was off on her own again, and that was like her. Grub turned back to take the short cut between Dr. Nash's house and Abby Francot's.

She carefully toed the line between, heading for the place where Abby Francot put the stone to cover the bare earth. And then, quite suddenly, she realized that she was afraid. Not that she had suddenly become afraid. She had been frightened for some time and just had become aware of it.

Grub broke into a run. She felt cold, and the sun seemed lower than it had been. She tore up the shortcut and leaped over the stone. Running into her own back yard, she jumped the vegetable patch in one leap, ran up the back steps and in the door.

"Grub! What's the matter?" her mother asked. Paul, playing on the kitchen floor, turned to stare.

"Nothing."

"Why were you running?"

"I just felt like it, all of a sudden."

At Gran Ross's, dinner was simmering in a pot. It smelled of red wine and onions and beef.

"Gran, do you ever go square dancing?" De-Graaf asked.

"Frankly, I loathe square dancing. And besides, you've gone off and left me unable to Watson all day."

"Is Watson a verb? In any case, I don't know what you'd Watson on. I'm spinning my wheels. All we've got is a welter of unrelated data."

"Well, relate it."

"That's the thing. But it doesn't all readily lend itself to relation. That's why I thought we might go over to the square dance. You could Watson there. Who gets invited?"

"Oh, everybody. It's a community thing, paid for by association dues."

"So we could just go."

"Yes. But I can't say I like to go dancing, with that child just killed. It isn't respectful."

"For the others it isn't respectful. We've got a reason."

"Do I have to dance?"

"You can think of some excuse."

The punch bowl, easily the size of a double sink, was a lime-green stagnant pool. DeGraaf stared at it for several seconds, dubious about its scummy surface. Around it, gabbling like ducks, the old people scooped the stuff into transparent plastic cups and backed away, their places taken immediately by other, identical old people. The vocal clacking was incessant. Somebody—probably Miss Carini—had had the sense to provide the punch bowl with two ladles. Even so, there was a crowd, and DeGraaf, standing near the table, was pushed by bony elbows whose owners disapproved of his standing in the way without either taking some punch or leaving.

"Gran, what is this stuff?" he asked, but she was not near enough to hear him.

He seized two of the ersatz glasses and filled them hurriedly. The green liquid had an odd, semi-effervescent look, and little bubbles seemed to be stuck in the greenish scum. He backed away with it from the punch bowl and the gabbling receded a little as he got out of the crowd. By comparison the general clatter of talk in the hall was quite bearable.

He found his grandmother standing near a woman who gave the impression of looking exactly as sleek and polished as she wished to look. In addition, she appeared familiar. DeGraaf studied the

pearls and natural color linen suit. She reminded
him, he decided, of his mother, and in addition he
had seen her at the meeting his first night in town.

"My grandson, Dr. Gerritt DeGraaf," his
grandmother pronounced. "This is Mrs. Brown.
Ellen Norris Brown."

"How do you do, Mrs. Brown? May I get you
some punch?"

"No, thank you. You two go ahead."

"May I get you something else?"

"No, no. I'm helping Miss Carini with the cater-
ing."

Why she felt that helping should exempt her
from eating or drinking, DeGraaf could not imagine, but he didn't press it. Meeting someone casually like this was just what he had hoped for in coming tonight, and his grandmother had singled out
one of the very people he had not yet contacted.
Mrs. Brown's slightly flushed face studied him and
the rest of the hall at the same time. She was the
sort of person who "never misses a thing."

"You are helping poor Mr. Cornish in his investigation," Ellen Norris Brown announced.

Since it had not been a question, several possible
responses went through DeGraaf's head. Perhaps
he should just repeat her statement, changing the
pronoun. But there was no point in being stupid
simply because she annoyed him. He said instead,
"Does everyone know that?"

"It's common knowledge," she said. "But I
knew before then."

Whenever she knew, she implied, it was before it
was common anything. "Why poor?" DeGraaf
asked.

. "I don't understand."

"You said 'poor Mr. Cornish.' I was wondering why."

She looked at him, ignoring the rest of the room for a moment, wondering how he managed this impertinence. DeGraaf, however, had a facial expression of extreme superiority which he used only on serious occasions, because he knew it worked. It worked now.

"I called him poor," she answered, "since I know he would rather not deal with something like this. In fact, I'm afraid he may not be equipped to deal with it."

"Mentally or in the sense of available resources?"

"Both."

DeGraaf knew she was accustomed to asking, not answering, so while he had her on the ropes he threw a couple more.

"Did his men visit you today to ask where you had been at the time of the murder?"

"Yes. They ought to have known better. At the same time," she added grandly, "I realize they have to ask everybody in the area. I certainly do not object."

"What did you tell them?"

"I was in and out. Like everyone, I suppose. Gardening. Shopping."

"Are those impressive marigolds yours?"

"Why, yes," she glowed.

"Tell me. Do you have trouble with the children getting into your garden?"

Her face closed down again. "Everyone has. It's totally insupportable. There is a state law affirming our right to have a retirement community here. It's inexcusable that they continue to get away with this."

"But the families concerned own their property."

"The law still says children can't live in town. It's up to the police or the development company to throw them out."

"Oh, come now, Mrs. Brown," Gerritt said good-humoredly. "Surely you don't really expect Joe and his men to take children away from their parents."

"Well, he should at least issue citations to the parents. Fine them. That would do it. They live here because they think it's less expensive than other places. Make it *more* expensive. That would do it."

"Mrs. Brown!" a voice called. "Would you give me a hand?"

"That's Sara Carini," said Ellen Norris Brown. "More people tonight than she expected. Excuse me." DeGraaf bowed.

"Gran, before I drink this stuff," he said, waving a cup that was still full, "tell me what it is. There's nothing that could be this light green color, with that funny fuzz on top, and carbonated at the same time."

"You coward. Look at all the older people drinking it and surviving."

"All right." He drank.

"It's made of ginger ale poured over mashed lime sherbet. It's no Pimm's cup, but it isn't too bad in small amounts."

"Let me dispose of our cups." With a basketball shot he got both cups into the bin near the wall.

"Now that you've tamed poor Mrs. Brown, what do we do?"

"Don't you start with 'poor' now. Possibly I find a partner, since you don't want to square dance and it would look odd if I didn't."

But it was not to be. Ellen Norris Brown and Sara Carini were bearing down on them. Sara's antipathy toward DeGraaf was for some reason forgotten.

"*Twice* as many people as we expected," Miss Carini said.

"*Easily* two hundred," said Ellen Norris Brown.

"There will never be enough cookies."

"I'll run over the the supermarket before it closes," said Mrs. Brown.

"But the reason we have come to you," said Miss Carini, "is that we didn't plan enough chairs."

"This is a dance, though," DeGraaf said.

"I'll leave you. I have to hurry," said Mrs. Brown.

"Oh, but we need a chair for practically everybody. The poor dears need to rest. Between dances. And then we have a long intermission. They need it. Though I'll have to cut it shorter than usual tonight, because we're low on food and they spend most of the intermission eating, of course. Anyway, the chairs are just inside the storeroom across the hall, and I can't get the janitor right now because he's trying to mop up where Ellen Norris Brown dropped the bottle of ginger ale. Oh, I hope she remembers to get more. Glass all over. I can't think what happened to her to drop it. She's so precise, really. And since you're the only man in the room at all *youngish,* I'd appreciate it if you'd help me get out fifty chairs or so."

When DeGraaf saw how it was, he took it like a man. "I'd be delighted," he said. "I'm feeling unusually youngish tonight. You sit someplace, Gran, and I'll be back. Talk with somebody."

"They're all here because they want to gossip, of course," said Miss Carini. "Why, we have people here tonight who *never* square dance." Her eye lit on Adelaide, who stared back at her with such an implacable smile that Miss Carini took DeGraaf's sleeve and hurried him away.

In fact, DeGraaf noticed as he hauled chairs—and discovered that moving chairs gave him excellent cover for watching people without appearing to be watching—there were people here tonight who not only did not dance but could not dance. He saw four with crutches and one with a walker. Two people were in wheelchairs. One of those was Abby Francot. Miss Simmons was here in spite of her blindness, and he saw another with a white-tipped cane. It was remarkable how readily accepted these people seemed to be. In a way, it made him warm to the place.

As the little rows of folding chairs grew, so did DeGraaf's impatience. Talking with Miss Carini as they worked was difficult. Every remark that might lead to some personal comment about herself she turned instead to a statistical description of Young Lake. What was going on under the surface of Sara Carini he could not guess. And he felt a sort of uneasiness, born no doubt of the sense that he was wasting time when there was probably something he should be noticing.

The square dance was supervised by a professional caller, who was now describing just how the couples were going to move in the Virginia reel. He wore bib levis and the most aggressive red and white plaid shirt that DeGraaf had ever seen. It was surprising, DeGraaf thought, that the man did not have a corncob pipe clamped in his teeth. And then he noticed that the second fiddler, who did not call, had a corncob pipe. DeGraaf smiled, then felt he had been condescending. Why shouldn't these people amuse themselves any way they wanted? What if it wasn't exactly authentic? The old men and women had worked their ways through long lives. Let them enjoy their later years.

Finding himself released by Miss Carini's effusive thanks, he went to see his grandmother. On the way he passed a group intent on doing a Virginia reel of their own. It consisted of the handicapped members. As he watched, Miss Francot and a man were attempting to do-si-do in wheelchairs. Miss Simmons at one side, was giggling, "Oh, I couldn't. I wouldn't know where I was." And a gentleman was saying, "I'll hold your arm. Nothing to it."

In a way, it was pleasant. There was an acceptance of age, and at the same time a feeling that they were not going to be defeated by it. DeGraaf felt again a sympathy for the retirement community. And yet his uneasiness did not go away. Nor was his grandmother relaxed when he found her.

"Where were you?" she asked.

"Gran, you never fret about me. What's the matter? Aren't you feeling well?"

"I feel perfectly all right. I don't know what's the matter. People look less human to me tonight than usual. It's stupid of me, I'm sure."

When the fiddles began screeching for the Virginia reel, they both winced. DeGraaf kept watching, nevertheless. He saw Ellen Norris Brown glide around the edge of the refreshment table, bump into a chair, and sit down as if exhausted and distressed. He saw Sara Carini scrutinize a small slip of white paper that might have been a cash register receipt. He saw Abby Francot do a neat figure eight in her wheelchair. He saw Miss Simmons skip straight into her partner in a do-see-do, bite her lip, apologize, and do the maneuver perfectly twice more. He saw Peter Pelham, the mayor, smoothly escort a winded old lady to a chair. And he saw that none of the children's parents had come to the dance.

There was a scraping of fiddles, a scratching of feet, the voice of the caller, amplified and metallic, the cackles and giggles of a hundred dancing older people. And as they had earlier in the evening, they began to look all alike to DeGraaf. He could not distinguish their wrinkled faces, their creaky motions. He could not tell whether one of them or another had killed the child. They were interchangeable. They were old, irritable, and resentful, and they had destroyed an outsider. And there was nothing he could do about it.

Suddenly, some people across the room stopped dancing. Was someone sick? Had somebody fainted? Now several little groups were standing still. With the quieting of the clumping, scraping feet, other groups turned to see what was happening. In a contagion, everybody stopped dancing and the caller, who had been staring at his assistant, looked up frozen, with his fiddle in his hand. The other fiddler, the last to catch the feeling, ended with a shriek of bow on strings.

At the far side of the room, just inside the door,

was Joe Cornish. He walked across the room, and
DeGraaf read on his face what was there for everyone else to see as well. There was only one reason for its grimness and trace of fear. There had
been another murder.

Cornish reached DeGraaf and they looked at
each other.

Cornish said, "Libby Potts," very quietly, but
the people nearby took it up, whispered it to neighbors, and the sibilant telegraph took it through the
hall. He turned and walked out the nearest exit
door, followed by DeGraaf and Adelaide.

"There's no hiding this," Cornish said on the
back stairs. "We've got the floodlights out. We'll
just have to seal the whole place off."

The body lay stiffly under the unnatural glare of
two large floodlights. They cast sharp, triangular,
double shadows from the girl's nose down across
her lip and from her chin down her shoulder. They
brought her eyesockets into sharp contrast and
threw her neck into such shadow that her head
seemed unconnected to her body. The cacti and
bits of brush in the area cast double forked images
of themselves that ran screaming out into the vast
blackness.

Abruptly DeGraaf became aware of his nails
digging into his palms. His arms and shoulders
were rigid, and he found, rather to his surprise,
that he was very angry.

He squatted down, studied the body, the ground,
the slope. There was no more to be seen than last
time, though perhaps that itself was something to
take note of. There was no scratch or mark on the
ground as far as he could see in this light. There
were no parents here this time, either.

Photoflashes were exploding, leaving pink after-images in his eyes.

And there was Cornish.

"Joe, wasn't there a guard on the spot?"

"Up to noon. We had every photograph we could think of by then, and we'd been over it and over it in daylight. Samples of the dirt, the whole bit. There was nothing left here to be seen. Once we closed off access from Tucson Road and found that residents weren't prowling about, I sent the men off to do interviews. Damn!"

"The same place! I suppose it doesn't matter. There are plenty of other places to put a body, if you're looking." DeGraaf said, "It's humiliating, though."

"Where would *you* put a body?"

"There are vacant lots in this block four plots wide. There are two foundations under construction. For that matter, there are a couple of empty houses."

"Okay. This is a hell of a thing, isn't it? You look like the wrath of God."

"I should have told that child to stay home."

"We told her friends. We told her mother."

"I should have *found* her. I could see her mother wasn't going to rush out to help."

"We didn't have any special reason. We thought we were making something out of nothing even to go to her mother. Oh, hell. I agree with you. We should have tracked her down and taken her home. But it's not your fault; it's mine. I'm the policeman around here."

"We certainly won't have to tell the rest of 'em," DeGraaf said grimly. "There won't be a child in town let out alone after this."

Finally he was alone with the body in the infirmary, and it was time to do another autopsy. From this infirmary Timothy Barkus had just that evening been released to a funeral home. And De-Graaf was cursing aloud as he worked.

It was eleven p.m. when he finished and pushed his rows of bottles over to the back of the counter to be collected and sent to the lab. He checked them once more for correct labelling. He pulled a sheet over the body. He washed up a second time. Then he lurched over to Cornish's office. There were lights everywhere around the building, and employees' cars, but no reporters yet. Had the previous crop gone home after the conference? If so, they wouldn't have heard the news yet. He hoped they didn't hear for a while. He had a lot to get off his mind before any outsiders started asking questions.

DeGraaf was surprised to find his grandmother in Cornish's office, pouring coffee while Cornish swore. She was explaining to Cornish why, under the circumstances, swearing would do him a lot of good, particularly if he pounded his desk with his fist at the same time. She stirred cream into the coffee as blue curses floated over her white head.

They hadn't heard DeGraaf open the door, but they heard him slam it. As he stared at his grandmother, she said mildly, "I didn't think I could sleep, dear."

By unspoken consent, they all sat down. De-Graaf opened the meeting.

"I'm afraid we have another one in almost every way," he said.

"As bleak as all that?" said Cornish.

"Libby was strangled, like Tim. The main difference was that she was definitely struck on the back of the head first."

"With what?"

"Something I can't quite identify. Round—that is, cylindrical. A little bigger around than a baseball bat, I should say. Possibly with a raised ridge around the end. A big pipe with a narrow edge at the end would do it. But I don't know just what any pipe like that would be used for."

"With all the construction going on around here, it wouldn't be hard to find dozens of different kinds of pipe."

"No. Somebody should take a look at the sites."

"Well, at least it gives us something concrete to look for."

"After she was knocked down, Libby was strangled in the same way as Tim—simply pressure over the whole front of her neck."

"Any reason to think it required medical knowledge?"

"No, but it was perfectly efficient. It wouldn't rule out a doctor. This method, by the way, gives the killer the advantage of not leaving bruises of a definite finger size. Now another thing: I think, from the lack of abrasions on the back of her head, that Libby was strangled in a different place from Tim. A softer or smoother surface. This isn't certain, for a simple reason. Tim *may* have been partly conscious and twisted around. Libby certainly wasn't. Therefore, cautious pressure on her neck, even if she was lying on concrete, might not have produced abrasions. Still, the odds are she was strangled indoors. On a rug or smooth floor like tile or polished wood. A rug might have left fibers in the hair, so the other surfaces are more likely."

"That isn't a hell of a lot."

"Oh, I don't know. It says we have the same killer. You may think that was obvious, just because this is a small town, but that doesn't make it certain. And very likely the *site* of the killing was different. Also, you have a pretty definite picture of the whole method now, if you should get a person coming in to confess and needed a check on whether the confession was a fake."

"We should be so lucky."

"You have a whole set of parallels between this and the first case. It's clear from the same things— abrasions on the elbows and ankle bones, and in this case the knee also because she was wearing a skirt and Tim had on pants—that she was carried to the dry wash in the same sort of boxlike carrier. She was probably left on her back a little while after she was strangled, but not long. Then she was folded up and put into the wagon or cart or whatever. I'll get back to that point in a minute. The trip was long enough to jiggle her some and make some surface abrasions on the skin over the bony parts that rubbed on the contraption. The roughening didn't go through more than the outer two layers of skin. From the microscopic look of the abrasions, it can't have been a shiny smooth surface, but it's not sandpapery, either. Unfinished wood or a matte-finished metal would do it, though a lot of other things are possible. Fiberboard. Burlap. Any coarse fabric. Because I can't find any fibers in these abrasions either, microscopically, I lean toward unvarnished wood or an unfinished sort of metal surface, of the coarseness of the underside of a bicycle fender. Not that a bicycle had anything to do with it, but the sort of metal that feels a bit rough to the touch. The absence of fibers isn't conclusive, you know. There are just so many variables in these things. For instance, if the jiggling should be in the direction of the fibers, the ends might run into the skin and get lodged there, but if the jiggling is crossways to the fibers, and the trip was short, none might. Anyhow, from the same facts, I'd say that the trip wasn't long, or at least the vehicle wasn't moving for long, which is the same thing. The abrasions would be worse. Between five and twenty minutes, at a guess."

"That much we guessed ourselves, dear," said Adelaide.

"Why?"

"Because Joe had the entrance to the two Loops blocked off. All day. It had to be done by somebody in the Loops. And that means he didn't have to travel far with the body."

"Fine, Gran. That reinforces everything. We have several facts that point to the same conclusion. On the first killing we had some physical facts, plus the less compelling reason that a person doesn't like to travel far with a body. But this is very strong now, that the killer is in the Loops. You could call it something like ninety-five per cent."

"Why ninety-five?" Cornish asked.

"I'm just talking. You can't set a figure. But I'm saying it's pretty certain."

"Then why not a hundred per cent?"

"You can never have a hundred per cent certainty on this sort of thing. You always have to take it with a grain of salt when some sleuth says *only* such-and-such a thing could have happened. There's no telling what he left out, or how many other possible explanations there might be. What he may mean is that it's eighty or ninety per cent certain. And that's a lot. Most court convictions are based on what I would estimate to be about sixty to seventy-five per cent probabilities. That seems to be what juries think is beyond all reasonable doubt."

"But, Gerritt, that's terrible," said his grandmother.

"I don't think the system would run otherwise. To get a ninety percent probability of guilt on something as complicated as most murder cases is pretty much impossible, unless you have both facts and a confession that explains previously unexplained facts, and is psychologically reasonable. And you tell me, Gran—what would you guess the truth value of most confessions to be?"

"Not high."

"I agree with her," said Cornish.

"Right," said DeGraaf. "Triangulation, where a couple of independent facts—or more—all point to the same conclusion, is the strongest kind of evidence you can have. And even that will never give you a hundred per cent certainty."

"But it *is* certain that nobody from outside the Loops could have put that body in the Loops," Cornish said. "We had the road barricaded and guarded and let only people from the Loops through. So the killer had to be somebody living in the Loops?"

"Oh, lord, Joe. Want some other scenarios? Listen. Number one. Libby was killed outside the Loops area by the policeman who, in a police car, went the rounds asking people for alibis for yesterday. He carried her into the Loops in his police car and dumped her body while he was interviewing West Loop residents, thus losing scarcely any time. Number two. A resident of the other part of Young Lake, cutting across the back yards, went into the Loops area to visit a friend. Libby saw him and accused him of killing Timmie, whereupon he killed Libby also, borrowed a cart and dumped her body where he dumped the first. Number three. A stranger, call it a madman, comes walking in from the desert on the north. He lies in wait for a child. Or maybe he sees Libby and beckons to her. She was a curious, actually nosy child. She'd approach him. He hits her on the head, and when she is knocked down, strangles her. Grabs a wheelbarrow in a back yard and trundles her to the dry wash. No problem."

"All right. All right. Enough. What about the fact that, according to you, she wasn't strangled on rough ground?"

"I said probably. But that's easy enough. Throw a jacket over her head so she won't be heard if she screams. Then hit her. She falls to the ground with the jacket over her head and he strangles her with her head on the jacket."

"But why would he *do* it?"

"Look, it's partly the lack of motive that makes us think it's improbable. But it isn't impossible. We certainly hear enough about killings without significant motive these days. One marauding madman would be enough."

"We searched the area yesterday. We are today, for that matter. Just in case."

"You can't pretend you could ever search the whole desert. For your peace of mind, though, you might try it with a good hound before your men track all over everywhere." He smiled as Cornish grabbed for the phone and issued an order. "I agree, Joe, that the killer is very probably in the Loops area. There's no need to get upset about not being able to comb the entire Mojave. I just said you could never be a hundred per cent certain. What we're doing right now, trying to relate a lot of facts to each other, produces the strongest fabric of guilt you can make, if you have enough pieces for it. What I really laugh at is the group of un-related guesses, all of which turn out to be a hun-dred per cent true. Sherlock Holmes, for instance, does this all the time."

"Like what?"

"Well, a man walks in the door and Holmes says, 'I see you are an asthmatic bachelor, a Ma-son, and have just bicycled here.' He's going by a very few facts, it turns out after the amazement subsides. The man is a bachelor to Holmes's eye because his suit is unpressed, asthmatic because he is wheezing, a Mason because he is wearing a Ma-sonic watch fob, and has bicycled over because there are clip marks on his cuffs. This ignores the fact that he may be a manufacturer of watch fobs whose wife is visiting her mother, who bicycles only on weekends, and is wheezing because he ran all the way to Holmes's to present him with an im-portant case."

"But how likely is that?"

"So-so. My point is that the likelihood of all the guesses in either case being right is small, since they are independent. They don't triangulate."

"What chance do you ever have of being right, then?"

"That's my point. Let's imagine that the man

had been out of breath, had bicycle clip marks, had grease on the inside of one shoe, and his palms were creased and red. There we have four possibly *related* facts. They all point, of course, to recent bicycle riding. Independently, they could be explained by other things, but taken together they are immensely strong. The probability that he had just been bicycle riding would be immensely high."

"Yes, I see."

"What I'm saying is that we have to hit on a person or scenario that all our facts triangulate on. Deduce what we can from any given fact, but collect more. We're not in as bad shape as you seem to think."

"Prove it. What other facts do we have to go on here?"

"Time of death," said DeGraaf, and only his grandmother noticed the grimness in his voice. "Libby was killed sometime between three-fifteen and five or five-thirty at the latest."

"A little after we were talking with the Lane girl."

"Around the time I was talking with Grub in the hideout at the earliest. And asked her to ask Libby to stay home, if she saw her. Then we talked with Libby's mother and asked her to keep Libby home when she came back. And then we came back and hung around here waiting for the press conference instead of going out and finding the kid."

The coldness in his voice was unmistakable now. Cornish looked at Adelaide, who shrugged. Then he glanced at DeGraaf, who was balancing a pencil between his two index fingers, methodically, as if he were being careful not to seize it and break it in half. For a few moments there was complete silence.

"I would like to make one simple remark," Gran Ross said. "Aside from the fact that Libby was probably dead by the time you would have gone looking for her, the fact is that, even if you had warned her to stay home, it wouldn't have done any good unless you set a policeman to trail her every minute."

"Why do you say that, Gran?"

"When any child is outdoors as much as that one is—was—there's a problem in the house. Libby has poked around my place, and no place on earth could be duller for a child. She will sit, and I've seen her do it, in front of the Lanes' house for two hours waiting for them to come home from a shopping trip. Anything rather than go to her house. I've met the mother briefly, and she's a picker. The child would have stayed away unless she was chained."

"Yes. She was horrible with her two-year-old. She's the same way with adults. I saw her in action at a coffee we both went to at Becky Simmons. She was making a big production of helping Becky, who you could just see didn't like it. And giving the other guests suggestions on how *they* could help. I've never seen her with the children, but that type is unstoppable. What they do with strangers they do ten times as much with their families. God forgive me for talking this way about a woman whose daughter's just been killed, but she *is* a relentless scold. Any child would be miserable with it. And as a matter of fact, I think Libby would have got away from any policeman. She must have been good at slipping away."

"Okay, okay," DeGraaf said.

Cornish said, "You mentioned a little while ago that Mrs. Ross should estimate the reliability of a confession for you. Now you have her as an expert on Mrs. Potts. What are you really, Mrs. Ross?"

"I'm a retired old lady," she said.

"I think we ought to tell him, Gran."

"If it doesn't go any farther."

"Gran is a retired psychiatrist, Joe. She is pretty well known for a number of books. Her field was the development of nonverbal communications theory. It makes some sense, you see, to ask her about people's personalities as communicated by their gestures and so on, especially since they're unaware of a lot of the feelings they're expressing that way. But she doesn't want it known."

Adelaide said, "People talk with you in a very constricted manner if they know about this."

Cornish laughed. "As a matter of fact, while Gerritt was talking I was straightening up my posture and I stopped bending these damn paper clips. I see what you mean. I certainly won't tell anybody."

"All right," DeGraaf said, "what have we got, as the probabilities go? We have a killer who lives in the Loops, an adult with access to some sort of small, enclosed transport, someone strong enough to lift a child weighing about fifty pounds, though a person can move a body in stages. You can put it in a sitting position and lean the shoulders into the container, then boost up the back, slide the body forward, and then lift the legs in. You could do it without lifting more than maybe twenty pounds at any time. It lets out any severely arthritic person and likely eliminates the heart patients too. Even

Becky Simmons or Abby Francot could do it."

"And of course Dr. Nash could do it easily," Cornish said.

"Why are you mentioning him especially?"

"I don't know why, exactly."

"I do," said Mrs. Ross.

"Oh, why?"

"Because you sense his vicious streak. Look at the way he pulls his shoulders together when he watches people. He oozes misanthropy."

"Well, you know, I think you might be right. He bothers me; that's for sure."

"Gran, what about Abby Francot?"

"Pollyanna? What about her? That woman never says what she thinks. She leans back when she talks. Everything is always lovely, to hear her describe it, but she's not giving any of her personality away. I don't know why, though. You have to realize that I don't socialize much."

"What do you think of Becky Simmons?"

"Heavens! I never talk with her. I met her when I first moved in, before the house was settled or anything. And she was just so proud of her own bravery that I couldn't stand it. I shouldn't feel this way, I'm sure, but people who get a lot of mileage out of their handicaps bother me. I admire quiet stoicism as much as anybody, I think. But this aggressive, self-satisfied *coping* gets my goat. Simmons and Francot both."

"You really don't have to be so defensive about it," DeGraaf said, smiling.

His grandmother only said, "Well!"

"What about Cora Grundler?"

"She's a griper. Lots of people are like that. It gives them a feeling that they know where they stand. And they have a fear of being taken, too, I suppose. Grouchy. Everything is wrong; inefficiency everywhere. It also gives her a clear line on something to say in any conversational situation. I chat with her now and then. On the street. I don't entertain."

"I know. Have you formed any impression of the Townshends? They live across the street from you. You must see them come and go."

"And come and go, and come and go. They hate it here. You ought to look into those two."

"Say! That's what I meant to tell you, before Libby drove it out of my mind," Cornish said.

"What's the trouble?"

"I was looking into who owned the land outside the development."

"Yes?"

"Three large parcels of land around town are owned by an organization out of Chicago called Green Acres Development. They hold one parcel that is seven hundred acres and two much smaller ones."

"So?"

"Tracing the ownership, it turns out that the sole owner of record is George Townshend."

"Aha."

"And Fish, who was tracing Townshend's connections back for you, found out the same thing."

"That gives Townshend a pretty decent reason to stay around."

"Or at least to come and go. Green Acres apparently bought up a little more land last month at a fairly low price. Not as low as they must have paid for the original parcels, though. The land was nearly worthless before Young Lake was opened to development."

"Why didn't the Young Lake developers buy the land?"

"The Sunshine Corporation? Well, their money was tied up already in the development. They have loans outstanding. They have heavy equipment to maintain and they are still building some of the community facilities as well as houses. The bath house, for instance, has been promised for three years and they're just getting to it. I'd say they're stretched pretty thin."

"They can't be happy that somebody is systematically buying up the land around them. It cuts down their ability to expand after they've got themselves clear on this lot."

"Right. They couldn't expect to buy up the whole country, naturally, but they might expect to pick up more land as they made profits."

"Any connection between the two companies?"

"None known. They're both out of Chicago, but that doesn't mean anything. This area has had a lot of development from the midwest, 'way back. People escaping midwestern winters discovered it a long time ago."

"Any evidence of bad feeling between the two companies?"

"I don't know of any. I'm not sure how you'd find out. You could ask Townshend and then ask DiLeonardi, of course, but I don't suppose they'd admit it if there were. There might be gossip in the Chicago investment community. I could see who we know there who might give us a line."

"It couldn't hurt. So now—we have a feud brew-

ing up over the last several months between the retired people in town and the children. It hits all the
papers through the good offices of the national
press services. What, I wonder, does this do to
housing prices in Young Lake?" Gerritt asked.

"Down," said Cornish, laconically.

"So I would imagine. Now, what effect would
this have? The Sunshine Company would be
stretched tighter, no doubt, with houses not moving as fast. Anybody wanting to buy land nearby
could get it for less, probably, since he would have
no competition from Sunshine and outsiders would
value it at a lower price because of the depreciation
of the only town nearby."

"Right."

"It is therefore to Sunshine's great interest to
end the feud. And without it getting in the papers,
certainly. For it to simply peter out would be the
best thing. Or, perhaps they could bite the bullet
and have the children thrown out of town. There's
no evidence that they have tried that, is there?"

"No. And I'd know, if anyone did. I'd have to
do the throwing out. In fact, DiLeonardi would be
likely to ask me about it if he were thinking of it.
Wondering how feasible it was, you know."

"If they did have the children out, they would be
betting on the publicity hitting briefly—it would be
big, I think they would have to realize that—but
once it was over and the thing settled, presumably
housing prices would go up again. Especially if the
children were gone once and for all and retirees
could be certain that here they would not have to
pay for bond issues for schools and so on."

"No," said Adelaide.

"No?"

"No. You'd no sooner get the children thrown out—why, you'd have barely threatened to—when the ACLU would step in, take it to court with the parents, and you'd be tied up for years. That would leave them in financial limbo. It would be the worst thing they could do."

"Then what," DeGraaf asked, "if they decided to frighten people with children away?"

They were silent. It was past midnight, and abruptly the three of them felt tired and cold. The pause went on, while each of them waited for one of the others to say, "Nobody would do that." None did.

Finally DeGraaf spoke. "I don't mean they'd go in for murder as a policy, of course. But what if somebody rather official played pranks on the children to frighten them. And what if the prank of tripping Fib Levinson overreached itself and his arm was broken. It all depends on how you fall, you know. And what if Tim knew who did it? Or found out? And *that* threatened scandal."

"Why hasn't Fib been attacked then, as well as Tim?"

"Presumably either because he didn't see who tripped him—Tim may have seen more than Fib or found something out later—or because his parents have been keeping him close to home. They have been keeping an eye on him."

"I'd say we had better talk with that boy."

"And his parents. Speaking of parents, where are the girl's parents? The Pottses?"

"At home. I stopped by while you were at the lab. They're distraught."

"Did they report her missing this evening, or did somebody just find her dead?"

"They reported her missing, but not until seven."

"Why so late? We'd warned them there might be danger."

"She usually stayed out late. They wouldn't normally expect her in until six at the earliest, they said. So she was just an hour late when they called."

"How'd you find her?"

"I sent half the force out. By that time you were at the square dance. We were ringing doorbells, but George said something like, 'Wouldn't we hate ourselves if she were in the dry wash?' And he went to check. And sure enough, damn it."

"Mmm."

"I sent over an officer who knew them fairly well to let them know. They didn't come to the station. Just waited there, stunned, for more information, so I went over later myself."

"People react in their own ways to crisis."

"When I saw them Mrs. Potts looked numb, but Potts looked like he was getting angry."

"When the parents in general get really angry around here, you're going to have trouble."

"Don't I know it."

NINE

DeGraaf got up very quietly at six o'clock the next morning. He tiptoed out of the house without waking his grandmother, for he felt that people in their eighties who had been up past one a.m. should be allowed some rest. But he left his bedroom door open so that she would see he had gone and not start him a breakfast.

In the grey light he walked to the cafe, which opened at six-thirty for breakfast. The walk cleared his head, for the air was cold with the cold of a desert night not yet shaken off. It was Thursday.

At seven-thirty, with several cups of coffee, a slice of ham, a Danish, and two rather hard fried eggs inside him, he wandered out to the corner of Mesquite Lane and Tucson Road to watch the children get on the school bus.

The sun was fully up now, though low on the horizon and blinding orange when he looked east. The land was striped with long purple shadows of buildings. There was a scent of cactus in the air, and bacon from the cafe. Along the sidewalks, very subdued, came nine children, each one accompanied by a parent and by enormously long shad-

ows that seemed because of their size to move the
figure, rather than the other way around.

The parents must have some kind of communication system, DeGraaf thought, for all of
them to know of the murder so soon. It had not
been on the late television news, and papers from
Tucson would not be delivered for a couple of
hours.

If the children were quiet, the parents were grim.
The bus, rudely yellow and cheerful, was standing,
its motor running. But the driver looked
embarrassed. He nodded to each child as the group
boarded, as if the children had gained in some
manner more status than he. When the children
were aboard, the parents continued to watch. They
waited, not talking, not interfering, while the bus
started up, and they did not start to talk away until
it had hummed down the Tucson Road and passed
the sign that read "Young Lake, the most peaceful
town in the world."

At this point, three of the six mothers joined together and walked away. The two fathers nodded
at each other and walked off separate ways. Three
mothers stood staring after the bus. One was Amy
Lane. When she was fully satisfied that the bus was
gone, she approached DeGraaf, seized his sleeve
with a lack of grace that was foreign to her, and
said, "Please come and talk."

So urgent was her voice that he merely followed
her.

Amy Lane sat on the sofa with her hands folded
in her lap. Her posture was rigid, and when De-
Graaf said, "Shall we talk?" she jumped.

"I haven't offered you coffee," she said, and before he answered ran out to get the pot. Returning,

she said, "I'm sorry," but she didn't specify what she was sorry about. DeGraaf watched her pour coffee and knew that she was terrified.

"Should I move?" she asked.

"You mean move out of Young Lake?"

"Yes."

"No, I don't see any reason for that. I would say you'd do well to meet the bus after school and have the children play indoors."

"Oh, I can do *that*. I would anyway, after this. But I can't do it forever. That is, I could walk them to the bus and back home indefinitely, but if I kept them in the house, so they couldn't play outdoors, half our reason for living here would be gone."

"I don't think it will be for long. Sooner or later we'll find out who's doing this."

"Too late for those two children."

"I know." Something in his voice made her look again.

"I'm sorry," she said. "I didn't mean to make it sound like an accusation. It isn't your fault. You didn't make it happen. It's just that I'm so frightened."

"Grub says you were frightened before."

"Does she? She notices things. Grub is very sensible, and I don't think she'd walk into trouble. But Paul is so little still." Suddenly she began crying. DeGraaf walked over and, sitting on the arm of the sofa, draped his own arm over her shoulders.

"Let me give you a suggestion. Plan to keep them inside, or at least within sight for one week. If we haven't caught the killer by then, do you have any friends or family you could stay with until we *do* get him?"

"Well, I have a cousin in Phoenix. I guess we

could stay with her for a while, but not indefinitely. But I'll certainly call her." She looked somewhat relieved and DeGraaf moved back to his own chair.

"Who could be doing this?" she asked.

"I don't know. What do you see in the people around here?"

"They're ordinary. They're really very nice, as a matter of fact. Of course they're old, and some of them are a little crochety because of it. Some of them feel useless. They have their aches and pains, too. But I have asked the children to respect their age. I can't imagine anybody so deranged as to kill a child." She thought a moment and then shivered. "I suppose that's partly what frightens me. Somebody is hiding. Inside himself."

The Lane house was next to Miss Simmons's, and, sighting the lady in the back yard weeding, DeGraaf went to talk with her. He had left Amy Lane shaken but determined to protect her children. He found Miss Simmons totally placid.

"It's Dr. DeGraaf," he called. "May I come over?"

"Oh, of course."

The dog, Tara, raised her head and looked at him. Apparently she recognized him, for she put her head back down again and went to sleep.

"You do very well with those flowers," DeGraaf said. Becky Simmons was patting the ground around one of the zinnias. Her thumb on its thick stem, she explored the ground for a hand's breadth around the plant. She found a weed about two inches high, and pulled it. She encountered a small tuft of grass where it should not be and grubbed that out too. Both went into a brown paper bag next to her.

"I've often wished I could have portulacas like your grandmother. But I need something tall and straight, so that I can feel the stems. Zinnias can be spaced evenly and laid out in a row, and they don't sprawl. I can keep it up quite well this way."

"Do you do the grass too?"

"Oh, yes. I have a mower and Mrs. Lane has a fertilizer spreader and we loan back and forth."

"But how do you do the edges?"

"Well, I can feel the edge of the flower bed with the wheel of the mower. It's not so very difficult. I run along the grass until I feel the wheels drop into the spaded-up part. That's why I have so much space between the grass and the flowers. Otherwise, I'd mow the flowers."

"It looks very nice."

"Sometimes I miss a strip of grass between two runs with the mower. I think I'm going in a straight line, but I veer off a little. That's the hard part."

"Then what do you do?"

"Oh, sooner or later Grub tells me."

"Have you ever thought of having Quirk do your lawn? He seems to do half the people in the Loops."

"No, I can't afford it. Besides—" she stopped. "It's something I *can* do. If not perfectly. I don't like to give up doing more and more, if you see what I mean."

"Yes."

"Besides," she added more brightly, "I think everybody needs outdoor exercise, don't you? I'm nor the sort of person who can just lie around in the sun and get a tan and do nothing. But this way I get air and sun and exercise."

"You're not afraid to be out here?"

"Afraid?"

"There have been two murders. Maybe I shouldn't bring it up. You heard about Libby? I don't want to frighten you."

"Yes, I saw Amy Lane this morning. Talked to her, I mean. I suppose I don't feel personally endangered. We were talking, Amy and I, about what those two children could have blundered into. Maybe I'm expressing it badly. But my feeling is that they saw something they weren't meant to see. It's Amy's idea also. And that led to their being killed. It's a horrible thought. But if they did see something, well, frankly, that isn't going to happen to me." She looked squarely at his left ear, with a smile that was extremely sad. Whether for herself or for the children he could not tell.

"Do you and Mrs. Lane chat much?"

"Some. She works, of course, and she has the children to care for, too, so she hasn't as much time as I have. I make cookies now and then for the children. And now and then when something complicated comes up, she helps me."

"Like what?"

"Oh, dear. Well, like the time a bird came down the chimney. I didn't know what it was at first. It sounded so much *larger*. And then she came over and she said it was a bird, and I wanted to get it out without hurting it. Actually in the end it was Grub who got a fish net or a butterfly net or something and caught the bird. Little Paul helped the time I spilled the dry peas. All over everywhere. I could pick them up, of course, but I just couldn't *find* them all. And I was afraid of slipping and falling on one if they were all over like that."

Between Miss Simmons and Abner Milanowski's cactus patch lay a lot that was sold and beginning construction. There was a trench for the sewer line and a square pit smaller than a basement, with some sagebrush blown into it. By comparison, Milanowski's prickly terrain looked like a garden spot.

It was now nine o'clock and DeGraaf found Milanowski having orange juice and a cold enchilada for breakfast.

"You back again?" said Milanowski.

"As you see me."

"Well, I've got no more alibi than last time."

DeGraaf thought, last time was only yesterday. "You had a description of your day last time, anyhow."

"And a lot of good it did you, I'm sure. You can have the same thing this time. I'll type it up when I get to the office. You going to come around every time we have a murder?"

"We going to have murders every day?"

"How should I know, DeGraaf? I don't do 'em. Somebody just puts 'em on my doorstep."

"Why is it that I never hear any sympathy for the victims?"

"Look, I'm as shocked and sorry about these killings as anyone else. But don't expect me to pretend love for the children of Young Lake. You have to understand that they're a nuisance and an intrusion. Children aren't welcome here. They have no right to live here."

"But you do grant, I hope," Gerritt retorted, "that they have the right to live."

Slowly Milanowski answered, "It's not easy for people here. They've really resented, maybe hated, having those kids around, and it's not easy for them to suddenly tell you they're sorry those kids are dead. They'd be sorry if kids somewhere else got killed. Or their own grandchildren. But they can't scream at a child one minute and then carry on to some stranger about their regret or sorrow. Even if you actually feel like it."

"I see."

"I'd feel like a hypocrite, see."

"I suppose so." He didn't comment on Milanowski's change of pronouns.

DeGraaf cut through the vacant lot between Milanowski and Miss Simmons's. He waved at Miss Simmons, who was feeding her dog in back. There was no response, though she stood up abruptly at the sound of feet on the dried earth. Was she more frightened than she admitted? He called out to her and she recognized his voice at once and waved. He cut through the next lot too, to get to the East Loop, and saw Abby Francot outdoors. She was deep in conversation with Quirk and did not see DeGraaf. He walked toward them and was surprised to see them jump apart as they, like Miss Simmons, heard his feet on the clay. By the time he reached them, Miss Francot was placid and Quirk was gone, pushing his cart down the walk.

"How are you, Miss Francot?" DeGraaf asked.

"Oh, very well indeed. See what Quirk has done for my door."

Swinging the wheelchair deftly around, she led him over to a newly planted rose bush. "Now isn't that nice?" she asked. "Quirk is so thoughtful. He found it in town at half price, and I hadn't even asked for one. And it's so fragrant."

"Miss Francot, what I'm going to ask is a terrible imposition, but may I see the rest of the inside of your house? The part that I didn't see yesterday?"

She hesitated only a second, then said, "Surely. Two children have been killed, Dr. DeGraaf. I don't think it would be appropriate for me to be obstructive."

She wheeled up the ramp that led to her back door. The door was unlocked and the doorway wider than usual.

"I think I told you," she said pleasantly, "that I had the house built with special modifications to accommodate the wheelchair."

"Yes, you did. You were already living in Young Lake at the time. May I show myself around?"

"Please do. I'll wait here so that you're not disturbed."

Starting in the kitchen, DeGraaf noted the handle over the sink. She could pull herself up by it to reach things on the back of the counter. The dinette table had no chair near it at all, suggesting that she just pulled up to it in her wheelchair to eat. The absence of chairs also provided a great deal of space in the room. He walked into the hall. In the bathroom he found two handles over the tub and one near the toilet. The room itself was square, providing ample turning room for the chair. He checked the bedroom. There was a high and low handle near the bed. In the living room there were none. Perhaps she used none of the low furniture herself, or perhaps she kept the room entirely for company. Except for the large arches where the other houses had doors, and the specific alterations he had seen, the house was very much like the other homes of its kind in Young Lake. In the small dining room there were four chairs at the table. The room did not look used. Off the dining room was a utility room, containing a water heater, fuse box, and tiny furnace. Its door also was oversize. There was no basement, no upper floor. Of course, no stairs.

Suddenly he heard a scream from the kitchen and swung around, expecting to find that Miss Francot had either been attacked or had gone mad. As he looked through the door in to the kitchen, she laughed.

"That's the teakettle. I thought we could have some tea."

Now that he thought about it, the sound was more a whistle than a scream. What was happening to his nerves? Miss Francot was already pouring boiling water into the pot. A large tray with milk and sugar stood on the counter.

"May I help you?" he asked.

"No, thank you. I'm good at this. If you would just move a chair away from the table for me. We'll have it in there, since there's no place for you to sit in here. I usually eat at the dinette."

She was right behind him as he moved the chair. She carried the entire tray balanced on the palm of the right hand, cups, pot, sugar and milk all steady, as she wheeled her chair with the left.

"I've had to get quite strong in the arms," she said.

"I should think so, to get along without help."

"Yes, most people don't realize, but a person with non-functioning legs has to practically chin herself to get up out of bed in the morning." She poured tea. "Milk? Sugar? And I do all my own housework. Actually, the vacuuming is quite easy. And mopping isn't bad, either. But I don't get the corners very well. Every few months Quirk comes in and scrubs corners for me. He doesn't want anyone to know, because he says he's a gardener, not a cleaning man." She laughed.

"Quirk is just about everyplace around here."

She looked at DeGraaf. Then she went back to the previous sentence. "Living alone, of course," she said, "things don't get very dirty. So the cleaning isn't much of a problem. I find bedmaking much more frustrating, because I have to keep running back and forth from one side to the other to pull the sheet smooth."

As he left Abby Francot's, DeGraaf saw Quirk's cart in front of Dr. Nash's next door. Quirk himself was not to be seen, either in Nash's back or front yards, but through Nash's front window he saw two figures in outline. One was dapper and thin, surely Dr. Nash. The other, large but somewhat slouched, with a cap on its head, could only be Quirk. Quickly DeGraaf advanced upon Quirk's cart. Still Quirk did not come out of the house. That was odd. It was quite a long session just for telling a man to cut the grass more often, or even for making out a paycheck for the month.

The manure in the cart was fresher than the day before, but still properly aged. The grass seed was almost gone. In the bottom of the grass seed bin, exposed by the low level of the seed, was a glass tube, about six inches long by an inch wide. It had a plastic stopper, and the stopper had a label reading "Becton-Dickson." DeGraaf snooped without touching anything. Presently, under a group of large bulbs that as far as he knew might be tuberoses, he saw a discarded cap, brown in color. On the side were the words "Warner/Chillcott."

"Hey! What are you doing there?" Quirk yelled from the walk.

Nash was not with him.

DeGraaf, secure in the knowledge that he was looking without touching—indeed, he had his hands clasped behind his back—merely said cheerfully, "Admiring the efficiency."

"What?"

"A place for everything and everything in its place. Very nice."

"Oh." Quirk seemed disarmed.

"You do sort of get manure and black dirt all over the shelves. But the plants can't mind of course." He pointed at some bagged rootstock. "Very nice roses."

"Blaze," said Quirk with an effort. "Old-fashioned but dependable. And they'll climb."

"So they will. Special purchase?"

Quirk was struggling not to show impatience. "Half price in Tucson."

"You live in Tucson?"

"Sure. Can't afford it out here."

"Well, I didn't mean to keep you. Many thanks."

"Sure." Quirk watched DeGraaf cross the street.

* * *

Across the street lived Charles Chide, whom De-Graaf had not met. He was home. He was delighted to meet DeGraaf.

"Oh, come in," he said. Curly grey hair, left quite long, bobbed as he nodded his head. He fluttered. "Come through here. I was just working, but I'm glad to talk at the same time, if you don't mind."

"Certainly not."

The house was entirely furnished in white wicker and wallpapered in a design of white trellises twined over with green ivy. It was cool but looked insubstantial. Chide had converted the dining room into a studio with several windows. It faced north and west and had a very good light this time of the morning. Here he had a drafting board, placed in a horizontal position, and watercolors. The subject he was working on was a cactus in full bloom, which stood in a pot on a tiny wicker table near the table.

"You'll be amazed, of course, but magazines will pay for these," Chide said, flapping his hand at the painting. It was a good, delicate likeness of the plant, but very pale.

"Do you sell them also?"

"You mean as original paintings? Yes, I have a little outlet in Tucson. It caters to the tourist trade, don't you know." He sank back into his chair.

"Is that your only work?"

"Oh, dear, yes. It is now. I used to do scenic design. In Chicago. But I've retired. And, really, I make as much as I ever did before. I had contacts because I used to produce watercolors of mid-western wildflowers. But, my goodness, these sell even better. It is really remarkable what magazines will pay. And the occasional advertising thing, you know."

"Do you paint outdoors at all, or only in the studio?"

"Oh, I love to work outdoors. It depends on what I'm working on, of course. If you're wondering whether I was out overlooking the scene of the crime the last two days, however, the answer is no. I've been doing a series on opuntia for an Arizona state magazine and I've been in the house all the time. Except to go to the grocery store. I suppose that doesn't give me much of an alibi, either." He laughed happily.

"Well, no need to worry about it. That seems to apply to nearly everyone I meet."

"Awful for you. You know, Doctor, it's to be expected, really. When people are retired they tend to rather while away their time. Most of them just wouldn't have alibis for any extended period of time."

"That's for certain. Tell me something. Do you have Quirk do your lawn?"

"What? You surprise me. Do you recognize his work? Yes, he does the lawn and the flower beds too. You may find that odd," he said uneasily, "but you see, I paint them. I don't grow them."

"And they say medicine is overspecialized. Well, thanks."

On the way out he looked in Chide's garage. A Mercedes, beautifully kept, with red upholstery and red carpeting. No garden tools. No wheelbarrows. Several portable aluminum easels hanging on hooks. A shovel. To dig specimens? De-Graaf left.

* * *

DeGraaf turned south when he left Chide's, and, passing a house whose owners were in Europe, came to the point of East Loop, where Sara Carini's house stood. She was at work, of course, but he did not intend to ring the bell in any case. Instead he walked to the point of the lawn and studied the rut Tim had made there with his bike.

It was evident that Quirk had been at work. The rut had been flattened considerably, probably with a roller. Then the bare earth had been scored, according to proper grass-planting procedure, and grass seed sown and watered in. There was a cross-hatching of the shovel marks. He looked at the ground close-up and could actually distinguish some of the seed. Over it all, Quirk had thrown a small covering of straw.

The run itself had extended over a length of twelve to fifteen feet, depending on how he measured the widest part of the curve. Tim's rut ran between these bushes and the house. Stepping back from contemplation of the rut, DeGraaf turned to the bushes near the sidewalk. They were part of the town planting, but were, as were many such clumps about town, on the house side of the sidewalk. Another grouping was on the street side of the sidewalk, but DeGraaf did not concern himself with those.

He squatted near his clump of bushes and began inspecting them. He pushed back leaves, ducked down to look up into stems, and ran his hand along interior parts of the small trunks. Painstakingly, he worked his way down the line.

"Hum," he said presently and sat up. He checked again. There, on one thick stem, just eighteen inches from the ground, was a deep gash in the bark. It covered three-quarters of the stem, including all but the side that faced Miss Carini's house. It was quite fine, only thick enough to have been made by a very dull knife or something of the same width.

From the same spot, DeGraaf looked toward Carini's house. His eye picked out two trees on the lawn, one ten and one about twelve feet away. He stood and crossed to them. The bark of the lemon tree was unscathed. On the far side of the orange tree, however, was a mark in the hard bark. Not a cut, it went around the three-quarters of the tree that faced the house, and was the width of the cut in the bush. This was some twenty inches from the ground.

After one good look, DeGraaf stood, brushed his knees, and, as if the thing held no more interest, strode away eastward toward the Levinson's home.

It was nearly eleven when he hit Fib Levinson's. The house was on Prickly Pear Drive, facing East Loop from the bottom. To find the place, he asked directions from an old couple who were sitting contentedly on a porch in an old fashioned porch swing. They told him Levinson's was right next door.

Mrs. Levinson was decisive and clear.

"Someone injured my son," she said. "I would like to sue the man; people should not get away with things like that. But I don't know who it was and Fib doesn't know."

"Can you tell me what Fib said he noticed, if anything? He must have seen something."

"We've been over it and over it. You can imagine. There are bushes at the corner of Mesquite and Prickly Pear—"

"Wait, just a second. Let me get everything straight. When exactly did this happen?"

"Well, a little more than three weeks ago. He was just coming home from school. He got off the bus, and on the way he passed the bushes. He was carrying a library book, so maybe he wasn't watching his feet. I don't know. And something like a pole or a rake handle or a stick came out of the bushes and tripped him."

"You mean it was just minutes after the bus pulled in? Someone could have watched for the bus to arrive and been ready with the rake handle or whatever?"

"Not quite. He had stayed talking with the Lane children for quite a while after the bus got in. They were going to work on their clubhouse and were planning to get some things at home, some pieces of wood or something, to hold up part of the roof in a new section. So after they talked he started running home."

"Oh. So a person who had seen the bus arrive could have gone home and got a rake and come back to the spot on the chance that Fib hadn't left yet?"

"Yes, I think so."

"Then what?"

"Let's see. Miss Carini was coming along the sidewalk behind him when he fell. She had seen him running and she saw him fall down. She says she thinks she saw something like a stick, but she wasn't sure. She hurried up to see whether he was hurt. Well, he had caught himself on his arm, not the one that was holding the book. And the way he landed, he broke a bone."

"It can happen like that. You can break a bone on a little fall and come out of a big fall with hardly a bruise."

"Yes, that's what happened."

"Didn't Miss Carini look behind the bushes?"

"Not at first. They're fairly thick but besides, she didn't realize there might be anything there. I asked her about it later, of course, and you could, too. But she thought at the moment that he had tripped over something on the sidewalk. It didn't occur to her until later that there was nothing *on* the sidewalk. You see?"

"Yes."

"And Fib was moaning and couldn't tell her at first. He says, and she says, that they think they heard a rustle in the bushes, but it stopped right away. He must have run away immediately, of course. And by the time Miss Carini went into her house to get a blanket to put over Fib and to call me, there was nobody there. Miss Carini was really very helpful."

"Yes, I'm sure she was. Miss Carini is a very efficient person. Does Fib have any reason to think somebody might have it in for him?"

"No, not at all. Fib hasn't got into this feud thing much. If it had been the Barkus boy who was tripped, I wouldn't have been surprised. He was always into everything. But Fib is rather quiet. He's seven, just between the ages of the Lane kids, and he plays with them most of the time."

"But not lately?"

"I've been keeping him in the house. I don't know what's going on around here, and I don't want him out until this thing is cleared up."

"I'm not amused at being asked whether I'm running around killing children in my development," said Angelo DiLeonardi.

DeGraaf said mildly, "I only asked what you had been doing the last two afternoons, Mr. DiLeonardi. Everybody else in the Loops is being asked the same thing." He studied DiLeonardi, a big man with iron-grey hair and a dominant, aquiline nose.

"That doesn't help much. Of all the people around here, I have the least reason to mess up property values in Young Lake. That may sound callous, but as a fact, it's true."

"Actually, I'd just as soon eliminate you, for that very reason. But it would help to know where you were."

"It still means suspicion, and I resent it."

"I don't think that trying to eliminate you because of your improbability is the same as suspecting you as a significant possibility."

"All right, all right. I'm not opposed to a quick resolution of this disaster, God knows. It's about the only thing that could help right now. But my job here is the sort that makes an alibi impossible. I have to be everywhere. We have six houses going up in one street alone, on the west side of town. There are two under construction here in the Loops. In addition, I take prospects out to see the town. I show people model homes. My God, my day is so broken up you'd need a computer and a stopwatch to find whether I had enough of a break anywhere for a murder. And even that would depend on a lot of people remembering exactly when I was with them, if you want confirmation. *I* say I haven't had two minutes of time to spare in the last month. But I can't prove it to you."

"I'm eager to be convinced."

"I'll give you my appointment book. It's only partially helpful, though. People wander into my office through the day and want to see the town with an eye to buying. So I drop everything and take them. They might or might not leave a name, depending on how interested they are. These days people often won't give an address for fear you'll send them a lot of junk mail. So you couldn't find them to confirm it. There was one of those early yesterday afternoon."

"You do just about every job around, then."

"Just about. A full-time employee costs money, one way or the other, commission or salary. And they all want to specialize, just sell, usually, when we need a jack-of-all-trades. I have another full-time man and a secretary, and that's overhead enough, given what costs are."

"And what are costs?"

"Are you kidding? The cost of pouring a slab of concrete—never mind pouring a foundation for a basement, which is much more labor—has tripled in two years. Plastering! Used to be everything down here was plaster. Bug-proof, you know. But there are three steps in plastering—the under-layment, the rough coat, and the smooth coat, and the costs have gone out of sight. Now we use plasterboard. And that gives you seams and the customers complain about the seams. Ever tried to explain to a customer about labor costs? Only specialists do plaster. The customer will talk to somebody here and find out his house cost him $35,000. Seven years ago, but does he think about that? He comes to me and says he wants one like it. I tell him it's going to run $50,000 and no plaster. The screaming? The only thing I can do is sit back and wait while he goes to a few other developments and prices houses. Then he sees we're in the ball park."

"But he does come back? You're doing well then?"

"Listen we're carrying so much heavy equipment it'll be ten years before we find out whether we're doing well. In spite of all the years we've been here, we're still hocked up to our neck. Putting together a place like this takes half a lifetime. When I get through with the retirement community business, *I'm* gonna have to retire."

"Well, let me ask it this way. How badly was the feud hurting you? To say nothing of the murders."

"Are you kidding? Sales are off and of course it's the feud. Right now we're in the middle, in different stages, of building several houses. Construction workers we hire by the job, we don't carry. And as long as our heavy equipment is in use we're okay. But I've only got just so much sales backlog. There are a dozen lots around town, three of 'em in the Loops, that are sold but not built yet. Now, people pay for the lot, then they pay for construction, in installments, as we build. If they back out now, we keep their lot payment, but we're still stuck, because we can't build. And now suddenly, in the last two days, what I've seen is this. People who have signed for a lot, but not paid for it yet— two of them—have backed out. What am I gonna do? Sue 'em for the lot cost? Also, we've had a couple here in the last day or so who were pretending to be interested but really just wanted a conducted tour of Murderville. I can smell a real customer a mile off. Down payments slowed up over the feud business and in the last three days, since the murders started, we haven't had a single new buyer. The ones under contract are getting antsy, too. But I guess they can't quite make up their minds to lose what they've put into it so far, so we haven't had a mass runout."

"Who would benefit by your failing?"

"Oh, don't say that word. There are a few land companies in the southwest who are doing retire-ment communities. They'd all have to benefit some. But I can't see them sneaking in here and killing kids just to split a few extra customers with their other competitors."

"What about people who own land nearby?"

"Near here? Some of the land just outside is owned by a single company. If they wanted to buy up adjoining land cheap, a drop in our property values would help. On the other hand, the land they already own would go down in value, too. And there is no certainty it would come back up soon. If they had plenty of cash and no time limit, it might not matter. But whichever way you look at it, I think it would be in their interest for us to become totally developed, so that we had no more land to build. Then they, holding the only available land around here, could start developing parcels. Slowing us down could put off their cashing in un-til it was too late for them to see the profits in their lifetimes. I told you, it takes time to get the benefit of this sort of development."

"Under what circumstances would a person in that position benefit?"

"Well, if he were trying to buy a large parcel nearby that was just too expensive for him currently, I guess."

"Do you have partners who would like to see you in personal trouble? Partners with money who would like to buy you out, cheap?"

"I have no partners at all!" DiLeonardi said harshly. He caught himself and added more quietly, "My wife works in the office also. I was able to start here because I was able to buy the land for next to nothing and happened to find a spring of water on it. The profits have all been put back into further development. I don't have any partners and I don't want any partners."

DeGraaf spent two hours more wandering around the Loops. He borrowed several large bath towels from his grandmother, rolled them into a large cylinder, and tied them with string. He carried the cylinder up to the dry wash. Taking a thermometer from his pocket, he put it on the bare earth not far from where Tim's body had been found. The officer on duty simply stared. DeGraaf himself sat down for three minutes, then read the thermometer. Next he placed his roll of toweling on top of the thermometer and walked away, waving to the officer.

He visited Cora Grundler, across from his grandmother, and found that she had not been exaggerating when she said she did not buy food lavishly. She threw open her refrigerator, which held nothing but a dry piece of cheddar cheese, a fresher piece of Swiss, four apples and a box of English muffins. A walk to Dr. Nash's office in town, just past the supermarket, produced Nash's statement that he did not own a car, bicycle, tricycle, wheelbarrow, or wagon of any sort. Back to Nash's garage, alone, to confirm it. The garage contained three Victorian sofas. Ellen Norris Brown owned a car and a two-wheeled garden cart and admitted to them readily, but would not let DeGraaf in her garage to check. Libby Potts's grandmother had arrived to take care of the baby while the mother stayed in bed. DeGraaf then turned back up West Loop to the dry wash, read the thermometer again, and took the towels back to his grandmother's house. Popeye, finding that Adelaide had been deserted by her grandson, had taken the old lady to lunch, but she was home when DeGraaf returned with her towels. DeGraaf called Joe Cornish from the house and gave him a list of a few things he'd like to know. Cornish groaned, and by that time Gran had made DeGraaf a cup of coffee and a grilled cheese sandwich. He needed it.

TEN

Gerritt sat eating, listening to his grandmother and Popeye talk. He suspected her of chatting with Popeye because she knew DeGraaf was in a gloomy frame of mind and would rather not make small talk.

He was feeling useless. He felt there was pressure on him to hurry, but he could not rush his ideas. At least all the children in the Loops would be well watched today. Certainly they would be watched, because two in a row had been killed. They'd be watched because any parent could see the danger, not because DeGraaf himself had been a help. If he had reached Libby earlier—surely she had an idea what Timmie had been up to. And she had kept it to herself. The Lane kids didn't know anything special, did they? Hadn't they told him all they knew? How could he be sure? An adult must always find the world of a young child partially inaccessible, even if the child isn't intentionally hiding anything.

And what if neither child had known a damn thing? DeGraaf found himself looking speculatively at Popeye. His grandmother was talking with Popeye in a way that DeGraaf now perceived as kindly, for Popeye's conversation wandered. His mind broke loose easily from the subject and went

241

meandering. A typical part of aging? Well, but not
a necessary part. Gran Ross, who was older
showed none of it. Popeye was a character in his
own right. Which was a polite way of saying he was
odd. What if DeGraaf's calculations were far afield
and neither child had known anything damaging
and had been killed by somebody more than a little
odd, for odd reasons that were sufficient to him?

Popeye and Adelaide were smiling at him. He
must have been staring. Now what?

"I'm feeling a little frustrated," he said.

"Don't blame yourself," said Popeye. "You're
trying," and he laughed.

Was that an odd laugh? What did anybody know
about these people? What were their families like?
By the nature of things in Young Lake, everyone
arrived with what was a sort of clean slate, coming
from a place unknown, with a history unknown
into a town that a few years before had itself been
nonexistent.

"Gran, I've got to go out and walk. I won't be
long."

He hurried out, thinking that his grandmother
knew what he was thinking. Thinking it was bad to
start suspecting friends. There was no doubt
Popeye had been nice to his grandmother. And
however independent she was, she needed an occasional friend.

A block away was the barrier. The officer was
patiently turning still another car around, while
several more behind him honked their horns. One
in an open car, and the one who was turning, expressed their opinions through open windows.

"You call this a free country?"

"Sorry, sir. We can't let anybody through."

"It's the people who pay the highway taxes."

"I'm not allowed to let anybody through."

"What right do you have to close streets?"

"This is a police investigation."

"I'm not doing any harm, anyway."

"Sorry, sir. We can't let anybody through."

"What kind of a police state is this?"

"Sorry, sir, but we can't let anybody through."

"What if I get out and walk?"

"Sorry, sir. We can't let anybody through."

"The kid's a goddamn parrot."

Joyner, the postman, approached the barricade.

"Hello, Mr. Joyner," the officer said, waving him through. Joyner nodded pleasantly.

"What *is* this?"

"How come *he* gets in?"

"He's the mailman, sir. Government business."

"Listen, I just want to drive through once with my girl."

"Sorry, sir. I can't let anybody through."

"And he isn't anybody, I suppose?"

"Sorry, sir."

Joyner walked crisply toward DeGraaf, pushing his big canvas mail carrier along on its rubber wheels. He nodded politely to DeGraaf.

"Hi, Mr. Joyner."

"You would think, wouldn't you, that those sightseers would feel guilty. Tying up police officers who might be out doing their duties?"

"Yes, you'd think so."

"Things go better when people have a sense of responsibility, Dr. DeGraaf. But that's rare these days."

"I know. Well, that is a very proper attitude for the carrier of the mail, Mr. Joyner."

"I do what I'm paid for, you know. I've never been late to work, doctor. Never in thirty-four years, if you can believe that."

"I certainly do. I just wish you'd seen something that could help us."

"I figure I just get to the Loops too late. I do this block facing on Prickly Pear, then up into the Loops. I usually start on them at four."

How did Joyner know the times in question? Did the newspaper carry it?

"Anyway, I'm on the alert now," Joyner said.

"What do you mean?"

"I run into most of the people here every day. I'm watching to see whether any of them are behaving peculiarly."

"Please—either don't do it or don't let them see you watching."

"Don't worry, Doctor. I'm not a child."

DeGraaf said, "What order do you do the Loops in?"

"Well, you know, I could start with either one, because they both end at the same point. The distance would be the same. But I always do the East Loop first, up Prickly Pear and down Joshua Tree. Then I do into West Loop up Canyon Trail and down Saguaro Drive."

"Always?"

"Always. I've found that if you once start a route, you're stuck with it. Try to make a change for variety and you get all kinds of complaints from people who are getting mail later and feel shortchanged. You know how people are. If they want to make complaints they ought to do it through channels. But instead, they'll lie in wait for you. And then hold you there talking while your schedule is being set back."

"I can imagine. I'm sorry. I've been doing that myself, holding you here talking. Go along. I don't want to make you late."

"Good heavens, no. I wasn't hinting about you, Doctor. I really wish you wouldn't think it. You have a reason to talk. It's official business."

"Thanks, Mr. Joyner. Go ahead, though. Don't be late."

The upright little figure nodded and moved off, pushing his mail cart before him.

Joe Cornish had been out some of the day and was just back; his office was in an uproar. So was his stomach. So was his theory of the case, about which he said that calling it a theory was throwing roses at it. It was a salad, he said, more than a theory. He favored Dr. Nash as killer, but threw in the rest of the population for safety. He had been out talking with people. He said he wished he could say he had been talking with suspects, but since you had to have reasons to think of people as suspects, honesty forced him to call them people. He kept lowering his head and blinking his eyes like a bull that didn't know which way to charge.

Lunch for Cornish had been three beers, to judge from the cans that still stood on his desk.

"I'm going to hand this desk over to you and leave," he said to DeGraaf.

"Oh, sure. I'm doing just great." DeGraaf flopped in a plastic swivel chair.

"All right, what do you suggest, then?"

"If I had a suggestion, I'd be following it."

"That's a point."

"Get any answers to those questions yet?"

"Yes for yesterday's questions. Very few fo today's except a couple of phone calls. Three hundred and twenty dollars worth of telegrams and phone calls already for the department to pay for."

"Can I help it if you're trying to solve a murde on a budget that only permits you to ticket bi cycles? When you have your annual budget con ference, remind them that you had murders to solve."

"Remind them? The murders'll still be going on We'll be lucky if there's a soul in town left alive by then."

"Okay. Okay. What did you get for your three hundred and twenty bucks, Joe?"

"A lot of junk, if you ask me. Popeye, who, by the way, also has a name, which is James Masters worked at the pottery he says he worked at, retired at sixty-five as he said, and has no criminal recor in Chicago or with the FBI. The Levinsons in herited their house from Levinson's father Levinson himself was a chiropodist in Akron and i now a chiropodist in Tucson. No record. Both hi bank and Popeye's show reasonable savings and normal transactions. Becky Simmons was a lega secretary as she says and was burned in a stean pipe explosion as she says. The doctors claim ther was evident damage to one cornea, less to the oth er, a blow to the head whose effects are hard to predict, and possibly some psychological trauma They can't prove she's really stone blind, but he report of seeing nothing in one eye and fogg bright light in the other is perfectly possible i those circumstances. The insurance compan looked into it, of course, before paying the claim

"Same, roughly, with Abby Francot. There wa

damage to the spinal nerves during surgery. Apparently the doctor panicked a little and just closed up the incision before trying to find out how extensive the damage was. It might have been a partial or total severing of some nerves, and possibly just bruising. They tell me severe bruising sometimes repairs itself and sometimes doesn't. The doctor paid, anyway. He practiced for several more years, and then died.

"There isn't any easy way to check whether the Townshends are buying any more land around here or negotiating to, except for getting a plat book, finding the owners of all the land, calling them and asking whether anybody has been making them offers. I have somebody doing exactly that. As for Sunshine Company, DiLeonardi may have told you he has no partners, but in fact he has two. Maybe he wants to forget about them. It's an Illinois corporation and lists a Tony Savocci and Edward Levine besides DiLeonardi."

"Ah. Did you check what business they're in up that way?"

"Construction."

"Can we find out whether Savocci or Levine are in financial trouble?"

"Maybe. I can call a guy I know."

"Anyway, without rushing into hasty conclusions, sometimes the mob converts greyish money to clean money by investing in perfectly legitimate businesses."

"I know. But DiLeonardi seems really strapped for cash. According to sources around here."

"Not impossible to set up a man to run a legitimate company with a given amount of money and let him try to make it. We don't know what would happen if the thing started to fail, because it hasn't yet. Anyhow, we're guessing."

"So where are we? That kind of group doesn't go around killing kids for the public relations advantages."

"No. It isn't professional. Sounds as if they're out of it."

"Next—Abner Milanowski was a newspaperman as he said. A managing editor. The money he saved is reasonable given his salary, and he supplements it by working on the paper here. Ellen Norris Brown moved here with her husband, who has since died. They had money which they had inherited years before. She still has it. No known problems, except that she has a reputation of behaving oddly at times. Probably nothing to it.

"Amy Lane, as you knew, is a widow. She inherited the house and a little money from her grandfather, and at a time when she needed it badly. Working at the supermarket, she can just about make ends meet. The Pottses—um, Potts was a stockbroker. Moved to a Tucson office when Mrs. Potts inherited the house."

"You have a lot of inheritances here."

"What would you expect? Let's see. It's practically the same story with the Barkuses. He was a produce manager in Indiana and was pretty lucky to get the same post here when he inherited the house."

"Find anything out from hospital records? Or marriage licenses?"

"Yeah, yeah. Tim was the child of Mrs. Barkus's first marriage. She and Barkus were married only four years ago. It puts a new light on his reaction to the boy's death. He gave a fine performance of somebody who didn't know what to say to a sick friend," DeGraaf said.

"Sara Carini was a social chairman on cruise ships. She applied directly to DiLeonardi when she heard of the post here through the grapevine. Got it because of her experience. No other reason. No connection with the company as investor or anything else that we can find. No evidence of excessive savings or hanky-panky."

"I'm not surprised."

"But Dr. Nash, now! Here's a funny thing. He has a very large bank account in Chicago and a smaller one here, plus a broker who won't reveal how much stock he owns. We can put some pressure on, but it looks like he's very well off. And that's funny for two reasons. First, because he was in general practice before he retired, which is not your big money-making field in medicine."

"No. Specialties are. Especially the ones that require a procedure. Surgery. That kind of thing."

"And second because he seems to be making big deposits still. And what can he possibly make around here? I don't mean he's salting away a fortune, but it's more than I would expect. Outside of that, nothing shady, and no malpractice claims. Cora Grundler. She's on tight money; she gets an allowance from a fund.But she's not quite as poor as she thinks—or says—she is."

"Lot of people have a poverty psychology."

"Charles Chide has a few modest investments. He has a gallery in Tucson that sells his paintings as well as some other people's. Joyner, the postman, has a good record and lives quietly. In fact, he has a spotless record."

"He tells me he's never missed a day."

"Right. He has a house on the corner of Yucca and Mesquite. The least expensive model. Not spending an unusual amount of money."

"Okay."

"You certainly go in for money questions, don't you?"

"I tend to think money problems cause more passion, hatred and fear than do normal passion, hatred and fear."

"Well, you've hit another strange case."

"Quirk?"

"Right on the button. He lives in Tucson, as he told you. But he lives in a six room split level, drives an MG when he's home, and has a yard that must be half an acre. By the way, he doesn't raise flowers in his yard."

"Wife work?"

"Nope."

"Curiouser and curiouser. Actually, I think I have a glimmer about Quirk. But whether it ties into the killings, I couldn't say."

"Whatever—he isn't making that kind of money by mowing lawns. My wife would divorce me if she could marry that kind of house."

"You're married?"

"Sure. Didn't you know?"

"Well, it doesn *show,* after all."

"You thought I had more sense? Now that I've ruined my reputation, what are we going to do with all this data?"

"What you usually do with data."

"What?"

"File it."

Cornish stood up disgustedly and flapped the

papers. "By the way," he said, "the dog didn't pick up any trail."

"But think of the feeling of thoroughness you have."

"Sure."

"Actually, I think I can see a few possibilities here. I'm going to go home and think about it."

"Think about what?"

"Oh, come on, Cornish. Don't press me. I haven't got anything, just suspicions. Anyway, Popeye tells me I've been neglecting my dear old Gran. I'm going to go home and offer to take her out on the town."

"At her age?"

"Listen, at eighty-two she has a lot more life than some of these exotic young things you see around. Oh, I'm sorry. I forgot you were a married man."

DeGraaf opened the back door, to sneak out the side of the office where there were no reporters. As he closed the door, Cornish called after him.

"You're just trying to get out of the press conference."

For a while it seemed so pleasant. DeGraaf had the murders briefly out of his mind and told himself that such a procedure would mean he was fresher when he came back to it. At seven Gran Ross had put on a blue pants suit that did good things with her silver hair. DeGraaf thought he looked nicely non-medical in denim. He had said, "Gran, I'm going to take you out for a big steak and salad and a piece of apple pie, assuming you can get that kind of meal in Tucson."

"Would you consider guacamole, enchiladas, frijoles refritos, chiles rellenos, and a custard?" she asked. And so it was decided.

"I wish I could take you in my car, my dear," he said, "but it's several hundred miles away. May I drive you in yours?"

"You may."

At seven-fifty they backed out of the driveway and headed down Saguaro. At the barricade they saw George standing guard and they waved at him. Joe Cornish was coming up the sidewalk on foot. "Where do you think you're going?" he asked.

"Tucson. Food," said DeGraaf.

"Oh, no you're not. Let me in and I'll explain while you're turning around. You can back up into Canyon Trail."

"What's happened?" DeGraaf felt his mouth go dry.

"We've got another one. I just heard. Fish and Eddie are up there trying to set up the lights."

DeGraaf turned cold. He pictured Grub or Paul lying dead in the wash. He was afraid to ask or move. He pictured their mother.

Then he burst out, from fear, "We can't have. All the children are under lock and key!"

"I know, but it wasn't a child this time."

"Who?"

"It's Joyner, the mailman."

DeGraaf heard his grandmother gasp. He felt sick. "I'd better drop you home, Gran," he said.

"I'll go home, but come there when you're done and bring Joe. I'll make some stew and we can talk. You won't have eaten, either of you."

"I'm sorry about your evening, Mrs. Ross," Cornish said. "My wife isn't too happy about it, either. I was going to go home tonight for a change."

ELEVEN

"Joe, it can't have happened in the same spot again. You were guarding the dry wash tonight, weren't you?"

"Yup. He—whoever—found a clever way around that. Put the body someplace else. In the lot where the new construction is starting between Abner Milanowski's and Becky Simmons's."

"There's a sewer ditch open there."

"You've got it."

"I suppose the guard in the wash never saw anything?"

"Right again. There are bushes along the road there. And the front of the vacant lot is full of sage brush. Besides that, Abner Milanowski's stand of Joshua trees is in the line of sight there, also. And if that weren't enough, the guard stayed down in the wash where the bodies were found, not up on the sidewalk."

"And I imagine that anybody who lives in the Loops could have walked past the wash today and easily discovered that the guard couldn't see far."

"Right."

The body lay in the ditch, recently dug for the sewer line, and was invisible from the sidewalk. In fact, it was invisible from a few feet away. The ditch was narrow, eighteen to twenty inches wide, but over three feet deep. Joyner lay somewhat bunched up in the bottom. But it was what stood on the ground near the ditch that startled DeGraaf. It was Paul Lane's red wagon.

"Transportation," said Cornish, pointing at it.

"How'd you find him so soon? The body is pretty well hidden. Were you looking for him?"

"Cora Grundler hadn't got her mail by five-thirty. So she called the post office. Which was closed, of course. So she called us. Our first idea was just that Cora hadn't been sent any mail today. But she said it was the day her magazine came, and it was an expense and she wanted it. So we rang up Popeye, who's across the street from her, and he hadn't got any either, although he usually gets a hometown paper on Fridays. Called Joyner to see if he was home and he wasn't. That was odd. He was a stickler for doing a job and a stickler for routine. He'd go home and make his dinner every evening. Then he'd go out and play shuffleboard under the lights. But it wasn't late enough at that time for him to be at the courts. And lord help me, my first idea was that he'd killed the kids and made a run for it. I suddenly realized that he was one person outside the Loops who was allowed inside every day."

"I thought of that today when I saw him go through the barricade. Don't worry about it. You're supposed to be suspicious."

"So we started calling people to see who had got mail and who hadn't."

"And then you went out looking. But why look right here?"

"Mr. Milanowski, Miss Simmons, Mrs. Lane, and the lady next to Lane's with the heart attack and the nurse all had received mail. The houses past that hadn't, so he must have left off somewhere around Townshend's. We looked in the dry wash first, although the guard hadn't seen a thing. Checked the wash in both directions, and then started on the vacant lots. As soon as we hit this one, the ditch was a natural."

"You must have barely missed the killer."

"How do you figure that?"

"If he brought the body here in the red wagon, it's pretty obvious, isn't it?"

"Tell me."

"The wagon is shallow and open. He's not going to run around town with a body in an open wagon in the light. After he killed Joyner, which probably was around four-thirty or quarter to five, he had to keep the body somewhere until dusk or dark and then wheel it over here. Cora Grundler had called you well before then. You were still phoning, I suppose, but the killer may have had a number of details to take care of. Anyway, it gets dark about seven and right around then he sets out with the body. By seven-thirty—is that about right?— you're out in force surveying the place to see where Joyner left off and so on. I'm sure the killer didn't have to travel far with the body. It's not five minutes from anywhere to anywhere else in the Loops, but he cut it close all the same. He must have finished about ten minutes before you hit the area."

"And maybe twenty minutes before we found the body. All times approximate. Damn! If we'd taken Grundler more seriously we could have caught him."

"Maybe not. He would likely have seen you

coming—and *if* he did, and he's smart, which he is, then he would simply have dropped the handle of the red wagon and walked away. If you'd seen him then, he'd have been a citizen out for a stroll."

"Damn it anyway."

"But to be safe, you need a photograph and then a cast of the tire tracks of the wagon in this loose dirt. I wish he'd been stupid enough to step in the dirt when he dumped Joyner from the wagon, but no such luck from the looks of things. I suppose he backed the wagon up to the ditch, let the back wheels tip and Joyner's weight carry him over into the hole. It's so simple."

"Those tracks can't be anything but the wagon."

"I think you're right, but it's important to be sure," DeGraaf said.

"It's thorough, and it's necessary, especially if we ever get to court. But what's the specific importance?"

"Because it suggests that whatever he carried the children in was too small to carry Joyner. It makes a lot of difference to us. It tells us what to look for. Unless it's a double deception. If he brought the body here earlier, in his regular carrier, then it's a bigger carrier. So we not only need to know that those tracks belong to the wagon, but that their depth is the same that the wagon would make if it were loaded with, say, a hundred and forty pounds. See?"

"I see."

Cornish occupied himself for the next twenty-five minutes giving minute instructions. He had lights set and the tracks photographed from several directions. Fish came in with plaster and took castings of the tracks in four different places. Cornish himself measured the distance between the wheels and between the tracks. George finger-printed the wagon. They photographed the body in its resting place, then put plastic bags over the hands and at last lifted it from the ditch. Two officers placed the body on a stretcher and the stretcher moved away. Where the body had lain was a triangle of red and blue.

Cornish stood at the edge of the ditch.

"What's that?"

"It looks," said DeGraaf, "like part of one of Paul Lane's airplanes."

The car with the body rolled off to the infirmary.

"Well," said Cornish uneasily. Then he stopped.

"Shall I get a shot of it, sir?" asked Fish.

"Oh, sure. Then pack it up and take it to the station with the rest of the exhibits."

"You mean the wagon, sir?"

"Of course, Fish! Get moving, will you?" Cornish snapped. He looked absently out over the desert. DeGraaf was looking vacantly out toward the center of the Loop.

"When you went around looking for Joyner, did you call on people? What were they doing in the Loops at that time?"

"*I* didn't. I was in the office. I'd just headed this way when I met you leaving. George had taken my car to go looking. From what the boys were reporting, half the people were eating and the other half were just done eating. The whole place eats earlier than people do in big cities."

"What were the Lanes doing?"

"Washing dishes, as I remember. We can check with the boys."

"So we can. I imagine you're searching the Loops."

"I've called in everybody we've got. They're interviewing every damn soul in the Loops, married or single, heart attack or arthritis, eighty-five or five. I want to know where everybody was every hour of this evening, and I want to know it before they've forgotten a single detail. And every officer is going to ask to enter the house and talk there, in case someone has been careless and left an odd detail lying around. I don't have reason for a warrant for any house. And of course it would look like an obvious shotgun, desperation move if I asked for warrants for all of them. I wouldn't get them. But I just don't think anybody is going to refuse."

"It's a remote chance that they see it, but ask 'em to keep an eye out for something that could be used to strike a man on the head from behind. It needn't be long-handled; Joyner was short. Also blood on any floor or rug; but he only bled a little and I can't imagine our killer being that careless. Not this guy."

"Unless, of course, it's not the same guy. Or it's a separate person who's—um, inexperienced."

"Listen, why don't we come right out and say it?"

"You go first."

"You think the children, maybe the Lane children, could have killed Joyner."

"If you know what I'm thinking, then you're thinking it, too."

"It makes no sense."

"Look, Gerritt. We know from your autopsy data that the children couldn't have killed the two kids. They're not heavy enough. But imagine how they'd feel. One after another of their friends gets bumped off. They're angry. Why not? They decide to get revenge. They lie in wait for a handy adult. Joyner comes along. His route takes him right by their house. He delivers the mail to their house, and they see him. Then he goes to Becky Simmons. Meanwhile they're getting the baseball bat. By this time he's at Milanowski's. Along come the kids, one pulling the wagon, and the other carrying the bat. Joyner is circling past the dry wash area now— by the way, was that the direction he went?"

"Yes."

"They walk along until they're sure they're out of sight of the guard in the wash. That wouldn't be difficult, since he was so far down the slope. The top of the Loop is undeveloped and there's nobody around. Maybe one of the kids tells him their dog is down in the brush, stuck, and asks him to help get the dog out. He leans down to look and blam! Grub smacks him in the head with the bat and Paul pushes the wagon under the body as he falls. Simple. They simply turn around now and head back to the vacant lot near Abner's. They *know* Abner isn't home. Everybody knows that. They know Becky Simmons is on the other side of the vacant lot, and *she's* certainly not going to see them. All they have to keep watch for is cars. If they'd seen one coming all they need to do is push the wagon down one of the vacant slopes, body and all. But no cars come along. Which isn't surprising. Few of the residents need cars and no outsiders were being allowed in. They get to the lot between Simmons and Milanowski without any trouble. Pull the wagon over to the ditch, push it until it tips part way in, and there you are. Go home to dinner. That's the reason he was tipped in and not lifted. They weren't strong enough to lift him."

"Why pull him back to the lot at all, then? Why not send the wagon down the bank wherever they killed him and avoid risk?"

"Because they figured in the ditch he'd be hidden. As he was. They figured it would be longer before he was found, and the times would become confused and they'd be safer."

"A six-year-old and an eight-year-old are supposed to have figured all this?"

"In a general sort of way. Older people who get trickier also point themselves out. Grub could figure it."

"The motive isn't strong enough."

"Is any motive strong enough for risking murder? But remember they'd found the body of a friend. That's going to have affected them pretty strongly. They may know, too, that the law is not the same for children."

With a sinking sensation, DeGraaf remembered telling Grub somewhat the same thing. What had he said? Almost that very thing, that the penalties were stiffer for adults.

"There's no clear evidence that the killer is different from the one we've been looking for."

"Oh, no. Except that the method is different: no strangulation. The category of victim is different: not a child. And the place the body was disposed of was different: no more dry wash. I know there may be reasons for this, even if it is the same killer. But I'll tell you something, Gerritt."

"What?"

"You'd better look carefully at that head

wound. Tell me whether the weapon could be a baseball bat.''

Cornish had gone to his office to co-ordinate the house-to-house inquiry, and DeGraaf was alone in the infirmary with the body. He recorded the temperature of the air and the body at the site of discovery. Now he turned his attention to detailed close-up photographs of the wound to the head. On close study, he found it to be a large curved depression, like the one on Libby's head, but deeper, as if it had been struck by a harder blow. If, as he believed, it was struck by the same hand that killed Libby, what would be more likely than to hit an adult harder than a child? And then find out the victim was dead and there was no need to strangle him. He had to be certain—

The skull was of normal thickness. The depression showed no unusual softness or fragility. Generally, DeGraaf thought that a person of normal strength, swinging a heavy weapon like a baseball bat or a metal pipe would have made a much more crushing blow. What did that tell him? A person of below normal strength could have done it with such a weapon. An old or sick person, or a child perhaps. There was no way to rule it out. Another possibility was that a person of normal or above normal strength swung the weapon, but swung it in a confined space, where it could not travel through a normally wide arc. He might have been the wrong height or in the wrong position for a good swing. Or, perhaps, a person in a wheelchair, who would be in a low position and where the momentum of the blow might be dissipated by the countermotion of the wheelchair moving backward.

The other possibility was that the weapon had been short and not very heavy. In that case a child or an ill person couldn't have produced this damage. It would take moderate power to kill a man with such a meager weapon. Not unusual strength, but normal, healthy adult strength.

There was another category of events that might fit. Joyner could have been knocked down onto a cylindrical sort of object. Or the killer could have banged his head into a lamppost or a pole. If he had been knocked down, there would be a second bruise where he was hit first. But there was no such bruise. Had he been held by the hair and the head banged into a post? No. The hair was not pulled out anywhere, nor even much displaced. Had he been tripped so as to fall backwards and had he then struck his head on a pipe lying on the ground? Possibly. The backs of his shoes, however, were as polished as the front. Joyner must have polished them each morning when he was ready to set out to work. Somehow, it was very Joyner-like to do so. There were no cuts, bruises, wire marks or abrasions on the lower backs of his legs or on his ankles. Not conclusive. Pretty indicative, though.

What would make just that sort of depression? Something cylindrical, about three or four inches in diameter. Once again there was a slightly deeper part at the end. He immediately thought of a baseball bat with a coarse wire wound once around it near the end. That was silly. It could be anything and there was no more reason to keep coming back to a child suspect than anybody else. That was just worry showing itself. It could be a fender of a car. Or a bicycle. Could he have been run down by a car or bike? DeGraaf thought not, on the whole. He had never seen a case of either without some other noticeable abrasions with bleeding. The only other injuries here, however, were made after death.

DeGraaf parted the man's thin hair. There was very little blood in the hair. The skin was hardly broken, though badly bruised. The murderer would have no blood on himself at all, and the weapon would have very little. It would have some skin cells, though, and possibly hair, if they could only find it. The weapon was smooth; that was clear from the fact that the skin was not broken, except over a few bone fragments. Therefore, it was readily washable. You could still find traces of the blood, even so, but you couldn't make expensive tests on every cylindrical or semi-cylindrical object in Young Lake. Perhaps the coming of dawn would reveal the weapon in the vacant lot. If not, barring luck, it would be almost untraceable.

DeGraaf shaved an area over the wound, and the appearance of the skin confirmed what he had thought. He took samples, hoping that there might be traces of material from the weapon in the wound. A magnifying glass revealed none, however. He got out the microtome and made three slides. He did not see any foreign substances. Well, the sample could go to the lab. An NAA test might come up with something.

He wheeled the body to the X-ray machine and made four exposures of the skull. They would have to be developed in town.

And then he faced the body. What could it tell him? Bloodless abrasions of the knuckles of the right hand. There were traces of brownish powder ground into them. The chances were the abrasions had been made by the bottom or sides of the rusty wagon. He bottled a sample for testing. Dirt in the hair, on the left side of the face, and on the hands. There had been dirt on the clothes, also, before they were removed. It was probably the earth from the ditch, but he took a sample from the hair, from the hand, and cut two samples from the clothing. On thing was certain: Joyner had been the model of the clean, pressed mail carrier this afternoon.

There were spots where the body had been bumped, presumably when it was tipped into the ditch. But there were no bruises made before death except for the one on the skull. There was a tiny cut on the chin, very likely made by a razor blade while shaving.

Why couldn't the body tell him more?

DeGraaf went ahead with the incision. He found a man of late middle age with no organic disease except moderate fatty deposits in the arteries, including the coronary arteries, and some evidence of arthritis. There was no evidence of poison or of strangulation. The cerebral fluid, however, was bright with blood, and the brain under the parieta deeply depressed, hemorrhaging, and pierced with fragments of bone. The arcus parieto-occipitali was virtually obliterated.

Everything was clear about how the man had died. Nothing was clear about why. DeGraa cleaned up and put the room to rights slowly, turning over what he now knew, sifting it for additiona help. He couldn't see any. He put his bottles in a row for collection, figured up the time of death from the usual signs, and marked the wound, th abrasions, and the patches of postmortem lividit on sheets of prepared autopsy paper that had from and back outlines of the human body.

Joyner had died between three and five-thirty, most likely nearer four-thirty. The lividity evidence was not at all clear. It looked very much as if he had lain in almost the same position in the ditch as he had when he fell from the blow. If he had been left lying, perhaps in a house, until he was moved in the wagon, then both in the house and in the ditch he lay slightly bunched up and on his left side. In the wagon he must have been on his back. There was rust on the back of his jacket. But the trip had not been long. The problem was that De-Graaf could not distinguish, from this evidence, between two scenarios: first, that he was killed, lay on his side for a time, was carried in the wagon too briefly to affect the pooling of blood, then was dumped on his side and left to be found, or second, that he was killed, immediately but briefly carried in the wagon, then dumped on his side and left permanently. And what was bothering DeGraaf was simply that this uncertainty would make it possible for a child to have killed Joyner.

Gran Ross, Joe Cornish, and Gerritt DeGraaf sat around Adelaide's fireplace and watched the fire burn mesquite wood. They had managed to talk generalities during a late and somber meal of good stew and red wine. Now they were silent. Outside, the night had the particular void quality of the desert, where there was no moisture in the air to diffuse light and warm the objects it shone on with a glow. There was a breeze that came from one side of the void with a smell of dust and went off onto the other side without meeting much resistance.

"Found the bag," said Cornish suddenly.

"What?" Gran and DeGraaf asked together.

"The mailbag. And the cart it was on. George found it. In the vacant lot."

"Oh. Did he photograph it before he moved it?" DeGraaf asked.

"Naturally."

"Anything interesting?"

"Nope."

"Great."

"The guys who were paying calls around the Loops tonight came on one interesting thing. There was a little dirt on Abby Francot's floor. She says she broke a flower pot—dropped a pot of Boston ivy while she was taking it to the kitchen to water it. She was going around the corner, she says, and the wheel of her wheelchair caught the wall and she lost her grip on the pot. She had swept most of the dirt up but the man noticed it and asked."

"Get a sample of the dirt?"

"Yup."

"Would somebody take the plant to the water, I wonder, or would you get a pitcher and take water to the plants?"

Adelaide said, "If you had a lot of plants you'd carry the water to the plants. Otherwise, you might take the plant to the water."

DeGraaf said, "I think that sounds reasonable. I have a sample of the dirt from Joyner's hair and clothes. We can have it checked to see if it matches."

"I'll get it taken in tonight."

"You'll have to have samples of the sides of the pot, too, to check for skin and hair."

"We've got the pot. The plant's in a bowl in he

kitchen. She wants to get a pot from Quirk tomorrow to repot it.''

They were silent again. After a while Cornish said, "Don't you think it's about time now to give us your autopsy report? Or did you find something you didn't want to find?"

"Not exactly. It was like this." He gave them a full run-down, leaving nothing out. Cornish listened without interrupting, and sat for a minute after he finished, just thinking.

"Well, Joe," said Gran, "what would you tell a person who demanded you fit a scenario to these facts? One killer or more than one?"

"If somebody demanded an explanation, and it was somebody I couldn't tell to go to hell?"

"Yes."

"Okay. You have to see this in the context of the feud. There's just too much coincidence if you try to take the feud on the one hand and a clutch on unrelated murders happening right in the middle of it on the other hand. The feud between the old folks and the children was both the cause and the setting.

"Somebody here really hated children. But it had not become obvious, maybe he wasn't really aware of it himself, until the feud began. Then the feud brought everything into stark relief. For one thing, the discussion of the problems of having children around began to worry him on financial grounds. What if they had to build a school? What if there were teenagers around, and vandalism? And then the feud did another thing. It caused tempers to run high, on both sides. Possibly the children began to taunt him. Especially Tim Barkus.

One day, annoyed beyond endurance, he hides behind a bunch of bushes and trips Fib Levinson with a stick. And Tim, as luck would have it, sees him. This is bad enough, but it is not only a matter of tripping the child. He has a rather official position around here, and not only does he fear being liable for the injury, and possibly guilty of assault, but he may lose his job as well. Who was it? Mr. Joyner."

"Ah," said DeGraaf, and as Cornish looked at him he cast his eyes at the fire.

"So it was Joyner. Joyner, who is a government employee and could lose his job over this. Joyner who owned the least expensive of the Young Lake housing models and lived very modestly. On a postman's salary, he *would* live modestly, and he would fear the expense of schools. Joyner, who would be in trouble even if he did some trivial thing, like tossing a little garbage on the children's lawns, and lord knows we had enough of that. Joyner, who had unlimited access to the Loops, and what's more, who would be least suspicious at the very time of day both children were killed, because that was the very time of day when he was always there.

"Tim told him that he knew, maybe blackmailed him, and Joyner watched for an opportunity. He had by far the best information, as letter carrier, about exactly who was home and who away, who was sick and who was nosy, about every single person in the area. He knew where it was safe to kill and when it was safe. We can bet he made use of the bushes that the community carefully planted everywhere to conceal himself from view from the houses, but he would know which houses were safer than others. He simply caught Tim one day on the sidewalk, spoke with him, very suddenly grabbed his neck and squeezed. When Tim was on the sidewalk unconscious, Joyner leaned his hand on him and in a minute he was dead. Now Joyner, who was near the end of his run and low on letters anyway, bundled Tim into the wheeled mailbag. No problem. Joyner was smallish but wiry and Tim was a child. He trundled Tim over to the dry wash —for all we know dropping mail off along the way to disarm suspicion. The rough canvas inside of the bag rubbed Tim in several places, because it was very tight fit.

"Abner, of course, wasn't home to see anything. Joyner dumped Tim out of the mailbag into the dry wash. And that, of course, explains why we didn't find any tracks or scratches on the ground. Those mail carriers have fat rubber wheels. Then he turned around and was back on the sidewalk in a second. Traffic is so light there at the end of the Loop that the chances of meeting a pedestrian or car are very remote, and if he had, he could pretend to have lost something. A letter that had blown away, maybe. And the mailbag, remember, is deep enough so the body wouldn't show while it was inside.

"He left the spot and went on delivering mail. There was no blood on the mail, because there was no bleeding. He had lost, I should think, not more than five minutes, and not even these picky customers will notice five minutes. But he was unaware of one thing.

"Tim had told the other children. As soon as Tim was found dead, the other children knew. They were all afraid to do anything at first. All except Libby, who either had not much sense or not much fear. The next day she confronted Joyner. He panicked and struck her with a package from his bag. It was something cylindrical, in one of those tube packages. And while she was down, he strangled her. He dumped her, the same as he did Tim, in the dry wash. And Joyner, who was growing old, old and taunted, in a world where youth is king, felt a sense of satisfaction. The disturbing elements were gone. His dry, ordered world could go on."

"And then?" said DeGraaf.

"And then comes the twist. Grub and Paul have had too much. They'd seen two of their friends killed, and not far from where they live. They've seen television; they know all about violent revenge. They didn't tell anybody because they were afraid. As far as they knew all the adults might be in it together. So this afternoon they caught up with Joyner on his rounds, bringing the wagon for transportation and the baseball bat to kill him. Grub hit him; Paul caught him in the wagon as he fell. They took him to the vacant lot and dumped him. Then they went home, watched the *Three Stooges,* and ate dinner."

"Do you really think the children capable of that violence?" Gran asked incredulously.

"Why not? They've lived in a climate here where the adults have been resorting to violence. That's what I meant about the feud being a setting. With the adults acting the way they have been, are the children supposed to be more mature?"

"But I think they are," said the old lady.

"What?"

"More mature. The adults have been thinking finances, by and large, and then they get excited and irrational. The children have been thinking in terms of personal relationships and that, to my mind, shows a less simplistic and less crisis-oriented value system."

"Does that mean you think they're innocent?"

"I can't really tell about that, Joe. It means I think their motives are more respectable."

"What do you think, Gerritt?" Cornish looked aggressively at his colleague.

"I? Oh, it's clever and pretty subtle. It misses a few facts, or items we take to be facts, but that's all right. You can always allow for a couple of mistakes in gathering or interpreting facts. I just don't believe it."

"Why not?"

"I don't think it's reasonable. I'm working along different lines myself."

"Like what?"

"Let me work it out first."

"I would like to know where those children were this afternoon. Do you agree that may be important?"

"Yes, I guess it may be."

"Do you want to call Mrs. Lane, Gerritt, or shall I?"

"At this hour?"

"Yup. Very few people around here will be asleep tonight anyway."

"I'd better do it."

Within a few seconds it was evident that Cornish had been right about one thing: Mrs. Lane was awake. She answered the phone in one ring.

DeGraaf, with a face that looked as if he'd eaten a spoiled oyster, began to talk.

"Mrs. Lane? This is Gerritt DeGraaf. Did I

wake you? Good. Well, I understand. May I ask
you a couple of questions?" Here he winced so badly that both observers knew Mrs. Lane must have
said something friendly and helpful.

"Thanks. No, I'm at my grandmother's. Yes,
I'm afraid he was. Hit on the head. Well, I don't
know. Uh—I was wondering whether Paul and
Grub were all right. Yes, I know you would have,
but I was wondering whether they'd seen anything.
Oh. Well, were they there all afternoon? Do you
remember when that was? Did you get your mail?
What time was it then? Where were the children
while you were doing that? Good lord, no. I wish I
knew *what* to think. Yes, it's safer that way, or at
least it'll make you feel more secure. Thanks, I will
if I can get free of this. Good night."

DeGraaf returned and sat down.

"All right," said Cornish. "What about it?"

"The children wanted to play outdoors, but she
didn't want them wandering around, so she asked
them to play in the back yard. At one point she
took a picnic snack out to them. She had promised
them the picnic to give them a good reason to stay
there. She ate a sandwich with them. That was at
four. But she didn't keep looking at them every second because she had a chicken to put in the oven
and two loads of wash to do. After all, she works."

"Don't be so defensive; just tell us."

"She says this is the day she does towels and
sheets. The laundry room has a vent but no window, so she couldn't see them while she was actually washing. She didn't see the mailman, either, but
the mail was there when she remembered to check.
That was five o'clock. She checked because she realized it was late for the mail. Anyway, she never

saw the children leave the yard, or the yard empty of children, and she had told them not to set one foot outside their property. She says they do what she says when they know she really means it. Also, she has the impression that even Grub was frightened by what happened to Libby and wouldn't go out of the yard anyway. I can believe that. She was a little angry that I seemed to think they might slip out, but she doesn't know about the wagon and airplane, so she wasn't very upset. And she wants me to come to dinner sometime. Does all that tell us anything?"

"Why didn't you ask whether they owned a baseball bat?"

This remark effectively dried up conversation for several minutes. The flames died and Gran Ross heaved two more chunks of mesquite onto the fire, stirring up the previous pieces and bringing the blaze to life. After a time Cornish said, "I suppose it doesn't matter. They could borrow one, even if they didn't own one."

"Did you get any more information on the stuff you were checking?" DeGraaf asked mildly.

"Townshend *is* buying up land. We found two five-acre parcels that had been sold to him last month."

"What about last *week?*"

"Nothing."

"What do you think, Gran?"

"About what? Who the killer is? Oh, Gerritt, I'm afraid I think everybody could have done it. That is, I think they mostly have the psychological capacity, if they were frightened enough. I do know one person who's a fake."

"Who?"

"I don't think I should say right now. It might be misleading. There's a complete absence of any evidence that would be condemning. A lot of people put on some kind of front. If I connect it with anything, I'll let you know." She saw DeGraaf's serious face and added, "I really will, you know."

"Gran, don't say anything like that outside of this room. There's a killer out there and you would be dead in an instant if he or she thought you had anything. I mean it."

"I believe you, Gerritt. Don't look so fierce. After all, whoever it is hasn't been playing games up to now."

"You're my favorite relative, you know, dear."

"Gerritt!" she said severly. "What about your mother?" But he knew she was pleased.

"Mother's a fluff-headed darling, but you've got the character."

"She's actually quite bright, Gerritt. It runs in the family. But she has devoted it all to the development of social graces and social contacts. It's my fault, of course. I always totally neglected that side of life. And so do you. It's no wonder alternate generations resemble each other. Simple rebellion."

"Listen," said Cornish. "If you two can cut the family gossip, we've got a small problem in front of us. Triple murder."

"I want Gran to keep herself safe until tomorrow," said DeGraaf. "Then we should be all set. I hope."

"Why will we be all set?"

"Because by then we'll know who did it."

Cornish jumped up, spilling his drink in the process. "You mean you know who it is?"

"No."

"Well, what the hell *do* you mean?"

"Joe, settle down. You'll pull a tendon. What I mean is this. I've narrowed it down. Way, way down. But to tell who it is in a way that will satisfy me, we're going to have to run a little experiment. If we're lucky, it might even get us a confession."

"What do you know that I don't?"

"Nothing. You have my notes on every interview I conducted without you. I even explained about Miss Carini's tree and bush with the grooves cut in them. From a chronological point of view, Fib Levinson's accident is the most important factor. Straw-in-the-wind sort of thing. The rest are just details you have to put together. Quirk's work cart, the use of the red wagon, the milk on Tim's elbow, the relationship that existed between Grub Lane and Tim just before Tim was killed—she was very accurate about that, by the way—even the afternoon soap operas on television. They produce probabilities."

"You sound giddy," said his grandmother.

"I am. I've stopped being worried."

"Wonderful," said Cornish.

"In a way the marks on Carini's tree and bush are as important as Fib's accident. That's putting the whole order back a few days. But I think the Carini business marks the opening salvo." Noticing that his glass was empty, DeGraaf picked up his drink and Cornish's and went out to the kitchen to refill them.

Cornish turned to Adelaide.

"Uh, I shouldn't ask you—" he said in a low voice.

"Go right ahead, my dear Joe."

"Tell me—is Gerritt any good at this sort of thing?"

With a faint smile, she said, "He's very highly thought of in some circles."

"Do we go along with him?"

"I think we do."

DeGraaf entered with the glasses. "Gran, it is time for you to Watson. In fact, rather more than Watson. In the morning, you call up a couple of the neighbors. You need two or three large electric coffee pots. Your own is too small."

"Gotcha."

"Have you been watching television?"

"No."

"Joe, Gran will be having a coffee here at ten-thirty tomorrow. I realize it's Friday, but we'll have to convince the people who work, like Sara, Abner, and Amy Lane, to take an hour off. I'll call people and make sure they come, but if they call you to check, back me up."

"Sure."

"We'll have all our so-called suspects, plus Mayor Pelham and Quirk. Now what I want you to do is this. We'll need two officers inside the house. In Gran's bedroom, I think. We'll have the party in here, and there's no way out of the living room except through the hall, and the bedroom door faces on the hall and looks this way. They shouldn't be seen of course."

"George for one. He's discreet."

"Good. Anybody watching from that position should be able to intercept a person who tried to leave in a hurry. We'll need two men outside as well, back of the house. You never know."

"If you say so. You going to tell me why?"

"No. We don't want any amateur acting jobs, do we? Now we also need two men in the front. They could sit in a car on the street quite nicely. They don't have to be hidden. There's a person who ought to notice them."

"Okay."

"And a pound or two of dry ice. Better make it three. Send a man to Tucson for it first thing in the morning if you have to. We'll keep it in the freezer here. Don't get it too early, or it'll evaporate, but I want it well ahead of the guests. Say about nine-thirty."

"Roger, Boss."

"Spare me. After the guests arrive, you will need to go to an office in town and seal it. I'll give you the information then in a note. I don't mean you personally. One of your men. You should stay here. For the drama."

"Thanks a lot."

"You probably wouldn't be convinced otherwise."

"Don't explain. If I sound grumpy, it's just because I damn well hope it will work. Whatever it is."

"That makes two of us."

"Three," said Adelaide.

TWELVE

As Cornish later reconstructed it, in the peace of a time several days later, the riot really started with early morning shuffleboard. Some of the old people were in the habit of playing shuffleboard very early in the day, starting, this time of the year, around seven. But on the particular Friday in question, they played for half an hour, and then, because of a chance remark, started instead to talk about the situation in Young Lake. A few more old people, out for their morning constitutionals, noticed the knot of men and women on the courts and stopped to join in the debate. A few more sauntering by on their way to work or to breakfast at the cafe joined in. And just at quarter to eight the bus drew up at the corner of Mesquite and Tucson, only a few yards away, to ferry the children to the school in the city.

This produced silence on the courts. Along the streets came parents, guarding their children. The children filed into the bus; the parents stood sullenly and watched; the old people stood and watched. And then somebody threw a shuffleboard quoit. It struck the front right window of the bus. The glass did not break, but a spiderwork pattern appeared on it and some slivers of glass fell on two children getting ready to board. The quoit itself ricocheted and hit the father of one of the children. The eight parents turned to face forty old people, the father yelling, "Who threw that? Show me the bastard who threw that!"

Amy Lane pushed the rest of the children onto the bus immediately. The old people were screaming and the parents were screaming. The old people, advancing toward the bus, may have looked menacing only because some of them were still carrying shuffleboard sticks, but they were angry, too. One asked whether the children had killed Joyner in revenge. Amy shouted, "Police!" and pushed the parents onto the bus as well. She had to seize the father by the arm and shout in his ear, but when his foot hit the second step of the bus, the driver, with some aptness of thought, put the vehicle in gear and moved off.

"Police station," Amy yelled at the driver. He appeared to agree, for he turned into the station driveway. It was not fifty yards from the shuffleboard courts, being across the street and just a little south, but the old people were slow. The parents piled off the bus into the police station and the bus driver, seeing his cue, took Yucca Drive around the block and went off to Tucson with his load of children.

The desk sergeant heard them coming. He rushed to the front steps in time to be run down by the irate father, who by now was in the lead. The sergeant sprawled on the step while the father stood over him yelling, "When are you going to protect our kids!" at his upturned shoes.

"You gonna sit here and watch our kids all get killed?"

"What are we paying for?"

"We have to watch our children like hawks because you don't protect them."

"Call Cornish," the sergeant yelled to the young man at the switchboard.

The sergeant scrambled to his feet. Now he also heard the roar on the grounds just below him. The crowd of old people had caught up, and it had swelled in size. There were people who had been heading for the supermarket, people who were leaving for work, and people who had heard the ruckus from their homes and had run out to investigate. The noise brought more, and some people came out of the public buildings also to see what was happening.

The rumor had run through the crowd that children had killed Joyner. This meant it was war. A second rumor was that the parents were in the police station and the police were on their side. Seeing the sergeant and parents on the steps seemed to confirm this, and, by some sort of contiguity, to confirm the other rumor as well.

If the old people had been cowed yesterday by the deaths of two children, that was now forgotten. The old people, shunted aside by a society where youth counted for everything, still could stick together. They roared favoritism at the sergeant, and the parents shouted back. Then a voice from the crowd of old people made a comment about the sergeant's children.

"You don't care what happens to our places

you people with a houseful of brats!"

The sergeant meant to keep cool, but he was angry and he phrased it badly. "You ought to be ashamed of yourselves," he yelled. "You're old enough to know better."

That did it. Screaming, shrieking, cackling that Young Lake didn't take care of its own, that Sunshine broke its promises, the whole crowd surged forward. There was a law against children in Young Lake, they yelled. Children were illegal here. If the company didn't stand behind its word, they'd make it see the light. Quoits went shooting through the air. The sergeant ducked. Mrs. Levinson was hit. The window of the station behind Amy Lane broke in a thousand pieces. Old women in support hose and Red Cross shoes went screeching through the flower beds with shuffleboard sticks, lopping the heads off the celosias. Old men on canes reared back and pounded their canes through the windows of city hall. People peered through their bifocals, taking aim at the light globes in front of the police station with rocks they had found lining the edge of the flower bed. Old men and women pulled and trampled and pushed. The urn of petunias, a big concrete casting, went over and rolled down the length of the steps with cracking thuds, scattering old people and policemen like geese. The policemen, reinforcements, scattered through the crowd, but gaped instead of acting, because of a total lack of training in geriatric riot control. They felt if they grabbed a man, he might break. And in any case, they reminded the policemen of their grandfathers and grandmothers. A newspaper photographer was pushed over backwards into the goldfish pool, camera and all. Two old men stood near a police car, methodically squirting linament from a tube into its gas tank.

Then, quite suddenly, it was over. The mob had worn itself out.

People looked about sheepishly. Arthritis reasserted itself. Men picked up their canes. Women dusted their clothes. Quietly, each one hoping not to be noticed, a couple of hundred people simply turned around and went home quietly. The sergeant, still standing on the steps thinking vaguely that he was guarding the police station, gaped but didn't move. It had taken just one hundred and fifty seconds.

Cornish, who had really hurried, pulled up in front of the station in his car. Most of the windows on the ground floor of the police station were broken. Petunias sprawled down the steps in their dirt. Heads of flowers lay everywhere on torn, muddy lawns. The celosia beds looked like salads.

In the goldfish pool a soaked newspaperman stood up and without a word walked away, trailing his wet jacket and carrying a camera that left a string of water drops behind it.

Cornish said, "Gawd."

By nine a.m. Young Lake was in a ferment. Mayor Pelham had taken to walking up and down the streets, calming the people as he went, a sort of perambulating fireside chat. Cornish, calling on all his men yet another time, wasn't afraid of another riot. He thought everybody was rather shamefaced about it, though there was talk among the town' parents of forming a vigilante committee to find the person who was killing the children and deal with him themselves. Henry Potts was holding a meeting of parents in the gym.

What Cornish was afraid of was publicity. He was informed that shots of the town were being rushed to the stations for news broadcasts, and they should make interesting viewing. Radio news had it already. He was afraid of hordes of sightseers. They were turning up already, though that was because the early morning news had carried the fact of Joyner's murder. What would it be when this hit?

He asked the state troopers to block the road from Tucson to Young Lake entirely, and to let through only those people who could prove they were actual residents. Even this turned out to be a problem, for relatives of residents were starting to arrive, to protect their parents or to take them away from the scene of danger. Finally Cornish worked out a system. If someone wanted to get through the troopers' barricade on the highway, he was to give his name and the name of the person he was going to visit. The troopers would radio the name to Cornish. Cornish would contact the Young Lake resident in question to confirm. Then Cornish would give the troopers the go-ahead to let the car through.

All this took some time to work out with the state police captain on duty. The man kept asking whether Cornish wouldn't prefer to have the troopers just come in and "clean things up." Keeping his temper, Cornish said no, his people were too old for tear gas.

Having worked it all out, he was suddenly fearful that the system might keep Quirk out. But a quick check found that Quirk was already on the job.

Reporters got through, somehow. Cornish was uncertain whether they had bribed the guards or whether the guards had decided they did not count as sightseers. On the whole, Cornish decided to let them prowl around. They came with sleeping bags in their cars, plenty of beer and granola bars, prepared for a long stay. Cornish told them to stay out of the Loops and they appeared contented to look for town officials to interview, or prowl around town looking for local color stories.

Cornish had some uniformed men out conspicuously pacing the streets, to warn reporters in a gentlemanly way that sneaking into the Loops would not be tolerated. He also put out the information that a major press conference was called for two o'clock. Then he went back into his office to pray over a bottle of beer.

The lab sent in the information that the dirt from Joyner's hair and the dirt from Abby Francot's broken pot were the same type.

The dry ice, oddly enough, got through the trooper guard easily. Cornish had called an ice cream company to deliver it, the boy driving the truck claimed official business, and the equipment came through without even a radio call.

DeGraaf had very little trouble getting people to agree to attend the ten-thirty coffee. His aguments ranged from social appeals, to claims that the public welfare required attendance. Most were attracted by the idea of getting the most recent news, though Abner Milanowski said they could do that without him. He was needed at the paper, he said, today of all days. DeGraaf said he could make it to the paper by noon and if he didn't come Cornish would pick him up. At that, Abner said it sounded interesting if it were so important, and agreed to come. Dr. Nash was planning to see two patients in the morning, but agreed to cancel them. "For all I know, they'll be afraid to go out, anyway."

The town as a whole was divided between those who felt a great need to stand on street corners talking about what was happening and those who were afraid to go out of their houses at all. Seven people called the drugstore, which delivered, to have their insulin sent to them, saying they were afraid to leave home. The supermarket, which never delivered, got so many requests to send food that Mr. Ambrose was seriously considering hiring a temporary boy.

The Loops were isolated from all this. Blocked off from normal traffic for three days, and well aware that the problem was in their midst, they talked very little. They puttered about their gardens, giving a fine performance of carrying on under enemy fire. And they suspected each other. They stayed out of isolated places and stared around for help when confronted by a neighbor. Their lack of conversation was due to the fact that they did not know who to trust.

THIRTEEN

"Gran, do you know your cue?"

"Well, dear, it isn't very difficult. When you ask for the coffee, I bring it."

"You have to prepare it, too. It has to be the right one, you know."

"Gerritt, I have *some* sense, after all. I'm not gaga yet."

"You're right, Gran. I'm acting nervous. I may be a little worried."

"You may." It sounded as if she were giving permission.

At nine-twenty Cornish phoned to say that the dry ice was on the way.

"Shall I get a warrant for the office you want us to search?" he asked.

"Now, it's no good pumping me for which office it is. I'll give you the address while you're here. You can perfectly well keep it guarded without entering until you get the warrant."

"All right, all right."

"Hey, Joe! When is garbage collection in the Loops?"

"Tomorrow, I think. Wednesday and Saturday."

"Can you check, and if it happens to be today, tell them not to start?"

"Okay. See you in half an hour, and I'll bring the boys."

Miss Simmons was the first to arrive, carrying her white-tipped cane in one hand and a large coffee urn in the crook of the other arm. DeGraaf watched with admiration as she crossed the street in front of her house. She had left the dog home. There was no traffic in the Loop, of course, and when she reached their side of the street she felt for the pavement of the sidewalk with her toe. She turned south, letting her cane feel the dirt of the undeveloped lots, while she walked along the sidewalk. DeGraaf knew she was feeling for the grass of his grandmother's lawn since it was the first lawn south of the vacant lots. She found it and continued, feeling for the first pavement to go off from the sidewalk, which would be their front walk. Should he go out and offer her his arm? On the whole, he thought not. In a moment she was moving up the walk with some confidence, the cane now moving in wide sweeps. On the steps Adelaide met her.

"I know I'm a little early," she said breathlessly, "but you wanted the pot, and I assumed that you might want to get the coffee started."

"I do. Thanks, Becky. Gerritt is arranging chairs and everything. I'll let him seat you."

DeGraaf seated Miss Simmons among a couple of dozen folding chairs, near the table. He turned and bumped into Popeye, who had entered without knocking.

"Hello, youngster," said Popeye. "And Miss Simmons."

"Why don't you sit next to Miss Simmons, Popeye, and keep her company? I want this open space here for Abby Francot's wheelchair."

Abby herself came in only seconds later, singing out to Gran that she loved her house. "It's grand of you to have us, Adelaide," she said. "I just wish I understood what it's all about. Your grandson sounded so serious."

Ellen Norris Brown brought a large silver teapot, some Earl Grey tea, and Charles Chide. Leaving Chide, she repaired to the kitchen. Mrs. Grundler, who had come in the door just after her, stood in the vestibule waiting for somebody to pay her the proper attention.

"Mrs. Grundler!" said DeGraaf graciously. "Good of you to come. Will you sit here, next to Miss Francot and Mr. Chide?"

Cornish had slipped out the back door and around to the front of the house to effect a natural entrance. Quirk came up behind Cornish, and was squashing his hat in his hands. He was partly relieved of his embarrassment by the arrival of Abner Milanowski, who shouted, "Well, get on in, you two. Don't block the door. If we're all going to miss a morning's work for nothing, let's get started."

"Come in. That's absolutely right. Mr. Quirk, how about over here?" And DeGraaf put him on the far side of the room, facing the door but farthest away from it. "Abner, thanks for coming." Abner was put near the door. DeGraaf placed Cornish in the only seat next to Quirk.

Dr. Nash arrived the next minute, which DeGraaf had rather expected.

"Dr. Nash. I'm glad you could take the time."

"We have nothing but time around here. Retirement Acres."

"Yes, but you keep busy. Would you sit next to Mrs. Brown? Let's distribute the men around, shall we? Thank you."

George and Leila Townshend came in with Amy Lane. All three looked pale under their Arizona tans. George slapped DeGraaf on the back and allowed how they wouldn't be serving any hard stuff, but he and Gerritt would bear up. Amy Lane winced for DeGraaf and took a seat near Milanowski, to which DeGraaf did not object. He put Leila Townshend near Dr. Nash and George Townshend on her other side.

Angelo DiLeonardi, owner of Sunshine Corporation, came in a little late with Mayor Pelham and Sara Carini. It had the look of an official delegation. DiLeonardi immediately asked for a glass of water and swallowed two aspirins from a packet in his shirt. He started to hand the glass back, reconsidered, and took two more. Sara Carini held a shiny white purse on her lap like a shield and sat quite still.

George and the other officer were in the bedroom. The sergeant was outdoors with Fish in the car. Two patrolmen waited outside the back door. All were eating peanut butter cookies and drinking coffee, which Adelaide had supplied them in spite of their being on duty. All except George in the bedroom, who refused the cookies on the grounds that he had to hear what was going on.

"Well, this does it," said DeGraaf. "We're all here."

"We're not all here," said Nash. "There must be twenty more people who live in the Loops."

"Yes, but they are twenty we don't want. No room. No chairs. No coffee. No need."

"Does that mean you know something?" Sara Carini asked, and then raised two fingers to her mouth as if she had not meant to speak at all.

"Yes, actually it does. Now, I'm sure everybody wants to get rid of this burden we've been carrying. The strain is terrible for everybody. With one or two exceptions, perhaps."

He studied the people in the room. Blankly innocent faces, interested faces, nobody shifty-eyed or furtively looking for doors to escape through. A well-behaved group.

"We have noticed a few facts about the murders and surmised a few more. One is that the victims are not connected in any simple way. They are not, for example, members of a family being wiped out for an inheritance. Nor are they all children. What we do know is that both Tim and Libby had reacted very strongly to the town feud. They had, in fact, taken it upon themselves to spy on the older inhabitants. In the course of this spying they may have stumbled on something bigger than they bargained for. And died because of it. The death of Mr. Joyner reinforces this supposition from a different angle, since a mailman, visiting every house in the normal course of his day, is ideally situated to see somebody doing something he shouldn't be doing. And in fact, he told me he was keeping his eyes open."

"Of course," said Dr. Nash, "that is complete supposition."

"Naturally. Short of finding eyewitnesses, that is what facts are used for, to construct a supposition."

"Well, show us some facts that construct it, then."

"I'm planning to. Now—we know from certain abrasions made after death and some other physical facts about the bodies, which I will leave out so as to avoid upsetting the ladies, that the two children were transported in a comparatively small container, closed at least on the sides. This container was neither very smooth nor very rough, nor carpeted. In other words, the sort of thing that, jiggling along, would produce light abrasions but not sandpaper the skin. Unpolished and unenamelled metal would fit the case nicely. But unfortunately, a large number of people around here have such a container. Miss Francot's bin on the back of her wheelchair, Miss Simmon's box on the back of her tricycle, Mr. Milanowski's deep wheelbarrow, most automobile trunks, even Mr. Joyner's mail bag because of its rough fabric—all would be quite appropriate."

"Well, I never!" said Abby Francot.

"So that line of thinking produces too many possibilities, though it does eliminate a few people. But ask yourselves this. What could cause murder? There were a number of transporting devices, but how many motives serious enough for triple killing? We're concerned here with the deaths of two children and an old man. I'll admit I considered possibilities as far-fetched as you, Mr. Townshend. You might gain from the murders because the price of surrounding land would go down as a result of the scandal and the fear that Young Lake might be unsafe to live in. Then you could buy land cheaply. However, this was a desperation theory. The result was too small for the risk you would have to take,

and there was no real certainty that the value of th
land would go back up. As a probability it wasn'
worth bothering with, and beyond checking you
company to see whether any illegal business wa
going on that the kids might have fallen into,
washed you out.''

Townshend, very red in the face, said, "Thanks
lot.''

"So what was there? After a great deal of frustra
tion, I uncovered a scheme that has been going o
under your very noses and *is* a crime. It first raise
its head when I found part of a medical compan
vial and part of a tube for pills in Quirk's garde
wagon. Quirk had an excuse, through his yar
maintenance and landscaping business, to be any
where in Young Lake, and to be seen talking wit
anyone. But more than once I found him in ver
close, very long conversation with people, whic
was odd, since he was hardly chummy or ga
rulous. And then suddenly I tumbled to it. Yo
have here old people with a variety of ailments, c
aches and pains. For them, many of whom don
drive, Tucson is a long trip. We've heard them sa
often, haven't we, how nice it is that everythir
they need is right here? So you have a perfect ma
ket for a man to bring in drugs and distribute the
under cover of a perfectly legitimate gardenir
business.

"But how did Quirk know who wanted the stuf
Where would he find out who needed drugs wit
out actually asking questions and arousing susp
cion? The answer to that is near at hand. There
one doctor, and only one, who practices in Youn
Lake. Had there been another doctor in town, wi
ing to prescribe a fair number of legitimate dru

available at the pharmacy here, this would never have happened. And of course no one but the pharmacist would have made any money.

"But Young Lakes has one and only one doctor and he, as he'd be the first to insist, dislikes to *prescribe* amphetamines, barbiturates, and the whole range of tranquilizers and pep pills we all know and love and people incessantly ask for. His attitude was quite admirable, except that he used it both as a screen and a gimmick. A gimmick because it forced people to consider going to a doctor twenty miles away if they wanted their pills. And that set up a large demand. A screen because nobody who knew his attitude would be likely to suspect what he was actually doing. He was giving Quirk the names of people who wanted drugs and the type of drug they wanted: whether it was tranquilizers, painkillers, or whatever. Then Quirk, while gardening or calling to offer garden service, could casually mention that he was stuck with a large bottle of tranquilizers that had been prescribed for him which he no longer needed. Did Miss X or Mr. Y know of anybody who might want them? And they did. I'm sure he became quite smooth at it. It was profitable because they could buy wholesale and charge above market. And as income it was even more lucrative because many of the drugs people wanted were either illegal or very carefully controlled, or in some cases considered dangerous by most physicians and rarely prescribed by anybody. Naturally, they could charge a whopping price for illegal drugs. Of the legal drugs, imagine Nash ordered them and Quirk picked them up and delivered them. Quirk and Nash must have developed a thriving business."

"You're heading for a slander suit, DeGraaf," said Nash softly.

"That's all right. I have all my money tied up in hula hoops. Now—in this explosive situation, all we had to have happen was this: one of the children in the kid's spy ring had to see a transaction. Had to see the pills passed over and the money paid and tumble to what was going on. And nobody who watches television could fail to understand what was going on. It could have been, for instance, Tim Barkus. Perhaps he taunts Nash and Quirk with what he knows. Quirk ambushes the child. He strangles him on the street, in a place where the bushes screen him from observation, not a difficult site to find around here. Then he bundles him into his garden wagon under a tarpaulin or a piece of burlap. Of course, strangling the child on the street explains the abrasion we noticed on the back of the head. Now he trundles along up West Loop until he gets to the undeveloped lots. Quirk's wagon is always around. Nobody would notice. He dumps the child out down the slope of the dry wash. He knows, of course, that Abner Milanowski is gone all day. Everybody knew it. As an additional check, his car would be gone. It was a perfect place to dispose of a body.

"It was Quirk, not Nash, who did the actual killing, because Quirk, not Nash, had the wagon and could be seen with it. Nash couldn't be seen with the garden wagon without being very conspicuous. He was such a fastidious person and so scornful of working in the yard. And Nash has no other transporting device—no car, no wheelbarrow, no nothing.

"Libby Potts, however, knew who Tim w

going to be spying on that day. The next afternoon she confronted Quirk, and she, too, was killed."

Quirk leaped to his feet. "That's a lie," he shouted. "I never killed any kid."

"You have an expensive house in Tucson. You live beyond any possible reach of your claimed income. And with what we know now it will be easy to find somebody, somewhere in town, who will admit to buying drugs from you."

"I never killed anybody! I was—I wasn't even in the Loops at four that afternoon. I was in town."

"What town?"

"Young Lake. The other side of Young Lake."

"Can you prove it?" DeGraaf asked.

"Be quiet, Quirk!" Nash barked.

"Yes, I can prove it! All right. I'll tell you, but you won't set me up for any murder. I *was* distributing some amphetamines. Two women there —they say they need them to stay awake at work. But they're such proper little bitches otherwise, they'll tell. They'll talk."

"They'd better."

"You idiot," Nash muttered.

"But never any killing," Quirk said. "And I'm not taking any responsibility for what he did. He ran the whole thing and he got me into it. Told me how to approach people. It wasn't my doing."

"You have no proof of this man's ravings. You've frightened him into making foolish remarks," said Nash, with a face that looked merely disgusted.

"No, I don't think so, Dr. Nash. I believe we can find people who will testify that Quirk came to them soon after they visited you. You can't have left them too much time—they might have actually gone to see a doctor in Tucson, and liked him. Once we start looking, the pharmaceutical companies will probably show excessive orders for the size of your practice, and, I'm betting some rather strange substances were ordered as well."

"That won't prove anything; legal medicines!"

"In addition, Mr. Cornish is going to take you into custody. Meanwhile, he will obtain a warrant to search your home and office. I'm betting we find records of some of your illegal suppliers there as well."

At this Nash leaned back in his chair. His skin took on a tight, waxed paper look and his mouth froze in the remainder of his superior smile.

Cornish stood up and called, "George!" The two officers came out of the bedroom. "Take them in."

Quirk made a move as if to jump away, but Cornish was standing next to him and seized his wrist. Quirk saw he was at the back of the room, and to reach the door would have had to leap over several folding chairs, two elderly women, and dodge two police officers. He gave up and he and Nash marched out, Nash urged along in a daze by George.

Miss Simmons, who had been swivelling her head more blindly than she usually did, suddenly said, "I can't *believe* it!" and burst into tears. Startled by an outburst from such a controlled woman, Adelaide hurried to her and gave her a tissue. Blowing her nose, Miss Simmons sobbed and said, "I thought he was so *nice!*"

"Who, Dr. Nash?" DeGraaf asked.

"No, Quirk. He kept asking to help. Oh, dear. Maybe that was why."

"I don't doubt it," DeGraaf said. "He'd assume

there would be some drug you wanted and that
would be difficult for you to get because of your
disability."

The door slammed and Cornish returned. He sat
down and folded his hands. "A drug problem in
paradise," he said. "Think of that."

The rest of the group averted their eyes from the
empty chairs, and Angelo DiLeonardi groaned.

"Of course, you all realize Quirk is right about
one thing," DeGraaf said. "He could not possibly
have done the murders. His garden cart was actually completely wrong. I'm afraid I stampeded him
about the murders because I thought it was important to clear the drug traffic out of the way. If he'd
had time to think, and hadn't been worried that
Nash would set him up, he would have realized he
couldn't have committed the murders on the face
of things.

"In the first place, as Miss Simmons mentioned
and we all must have noticed, his cart always
smelled of manure. He couldn't have carried anybody in it without the victim's clothing smelling of
manure. Besides that, there would have been black
dirt or peat moss or grass seed on the clothes and
the hair. His truck is out, too, because the back is
wide and flat and wouldn't have abraded the
elbows and so on, or bent the body double. That is,
the body was lying on its side during the trip, and
parts such as the front of the knees and backs of
the elbow were rubbed, so he was certainly in a
more confined space than the back of a truck.
Also, there is a spillage of black dirt and manure
and so on in the back of the truck which is another,
not a necessary, pointer. The front seat or floor of
the front of the truck is inappropriate because the

seats would not cause abrasions; they're too smooth. And the rubber mats on the floor wouldn't either. But of course, in addition to that, neither the seat nor the floor would be at all confining for a small child. It simply *had* to be something really quite small.

"So, Quirk's truck and cart are out. And Nash owned no transportation at all. The two of them were clear.

"They were out for another reason, too. Mr. Joyner was certainly moved in the child's red wagon. The tracks were the same, the rust was the same as that on his body, and there was no sign of any other transporting device. There were even tracks at the very edge of the ditch where he was tipped in. Now that was a flat, open, exposed carrier. Therefore he was moved at dusk or dark. Now we know from Quirk himself, well before the Joyner murder took place, that he never worked at dusk or even when the sun was low. He couldn't see well. Indeed, he always arrived very early in the morning and left sometime in the afternoon. Everyone who knew him and had seen him come and go over the past months would have been alerted, would have wondered why, if they had seen him moving around hours past his usual time to leave. I don't mean that they would be suspicious, but they would have remembered. That would have been too much risk to take. If Nash and Quirk had killed Joyner, they would have intercepted him earlier, probably just before he started on the delivery to the Loops, put him in the truck under the tarpaulin, and driven him out of Young Lake. Nobody was checking cars that left the town. Then Quirk could have dumped him anywhere in the desert at his leisure, safely. So there were just too many reasons why Nash and Quirk were not the people we were looking for. I'll bet that the two women he mentioned will confirm Quirk was there the afternoon Tim was killed."

Amy Lane had made a choking sound and then cleared her throat and asked, "That red wagon was Paul's, wasn't it?"

"Yes. We haven't had time to ask, but when did you miss it?"

"We didn't. I noticed this morning that it wasn't in the back yard. But you know how it is with children's toys. If they don't want it, nobody thinks of it. Because you don't exactly *use* it, if you see what I mean."

"Yes. We can always check with Paul about when he last saw it. But I imagine it was borrowed about dusk, when you wouldn't notice anybody in the yard. And the airplane was in it and simply got dumped under Joyner's body."

"Paul's airplane?" she asked in a whisper.

"I'm afraid so."

She turned white, but she went ahead with her question. "Does that mean you're going to think that Paul and Grub killed Mr. Joyner? Out of some idea of *revenge?*"

"Not exactly. Gran, could we have the coffee now? I think we need it after the Quirk and Nash business."

"Certainly, Gerritt," said his grandmother calmly, and she went into the kitchen.

"Amy, certain children were involved in this thing, but in a very complex way. I'm going to have to explain it in some detail—oh, thanks, Gran."

Adelaide put the steaming pot down on the table

near Miss Francot. DeGraaf got up and said, as he reached for a cup, "The whole thing started 'way back before Fib Levinson broke his arm—" De-Graaf, with a cup tilting in his left hand, knocked over the steaming silver coffee pot directly toward Miss Francot and Miss Simmons. Miss Francot, with considerable speed, backed her chair up, and backed right over Abner Milanowski's toes. He shouted, but at the same instant Amy Lane screamed. She was looking at Miss Simmons, who had jumped up at the sight of the boiling liquid hurtling toward her. Miss Simmons was now standing rigid, in full knowledge that everyone understood.

There was total silence. Miss Simmons did not seem to breathe.

"After a time, DeGraaf said, "That's how it was with Joyner, wasn't it? For just a second you forgot to be blind. He came up on your carpeted porch, perhaps, silently. And you turned and he knew you saw him."

Now she sighed, and with the breath, DeGraaf thought he saw the will to fight go out of her.

"I was in the vestibule," she said. "I'd been a little nervous—from the other things. His shadow fell over me and I looked up into the mirror suddenly to see who was there. Our eyes met."

"How did you ever get him inside?"

"He didn't put it all together right away. But I think he had been watching for something like that. I asked him in, to explain, and he came. He came into the kitchen, and I hit him with a tomato soup can."

"A can!" DeGraaf said. "Cylindrical, three or four inches in diameter, and with a ridge at the end.

I had thought of baseball bats with wires around them and poles and pipes. I imagine it's still in the trash can?"

"I suppose."

"I should have thought of it. Well. Then *you* delivered the mail to the next couple of houses?"

"Yes. Just to make it seem Joyner had gone farther along his route. I left him where he was until dusk. And then I borrowed the wagon and took him to the vacant lot. It was right next door. There really wasn't much risk. He would have told. Joyner was very duty conscious. He would have told the insurance company and they would have taken away the money. And probably prosecuted for fraud." And you would have guessed—about the children."

"Yes, I'm sure they would have. Do you want to tell us about the children?"

"All right. I'm not going to fight. It's all over anyway, now. All my life I've had to work. Nobody's ever given me anything. For years and years I got up at six every morning to get to work at the office. A legal secretary is just everybody's slave, anyway. Typing. Research. I did as much research as the lawyers. They'll shout at you to look something up and then run out the door for their glory in court. Well, I tried. The insurance company has plenty of money and it doesn't belong to anybody. It wasn't such a wrong thing to do."

"The children?"

"I was riding my tricycle to the store, going down Saguaro. Timmie must have thought it would be funny to tip over a blind woman. He came out suddenly from behind a bush and shoved a large board in front of the wheel. It would have thrown me right over. I've had years of practice at never reacting as if I could see, but that was too sudden. I swerved before I hit the board, but then, of course, I saw that he knew. I just jumped off and crooked my arm around his neck from behind. Before I thought about it, really. It stunned him. There was no one coming along the street, and no direct view from any house, because of the bushes, so when he fell down I leaned on his throat with my hand. When he was dead I put him in the back of the tricycle. I laid a sweater over him so he couldn't be seen. I always carry a sweater in case it gets cold. Abner was not home, and, anyway, everybody's used to seeing me ride around. I just turned around and went up to the dry wash and dumped him out. It looked as if the ground was hard enough to resist footprints. It had all happened near the Townshends, but I had seen them leave in their car when I first started out of the house, so that was all right. The nurse taking care of that heart patient spends her whole day watching television anyway, so she wouldn't notice anything. There were bushes between me and the street, so that people on the other side wouldn't have seen, I thought. And Tim, of course, had been hiding until he tried to tip me. After I put him in the ravine, I went to the store, as I had planned, and passed Cora Grundler on the way. She didn't look twice at me. I thought I was safe."

"And Libby?"

"Well, I had been to the store the next day in the afternoon, and when I got back a thing happened that really frightened me. I was unloading my groceries. I was in the kitchen, and I noticed that the sugar bowl was in the wrong place. It was right

near the edge of the table, where it could fall off. I
didn't remember leaving it there, but I went over to
put it in the middle. And from behind the breakfast
room drapes, Libby Potts jumped out. She said, 'I
thought so. You can see.' She had shoved the bowl
over and waited to catch me. So I went over and
said that she must find this very odd, but I was
totally blind in one eye and only partially blind in
the other, and so forth. Of course, I was walking
right towards her, so I had to be seeing her. But the
words held her still for just the moment I needed. I
hit her with a can and when she fell I just leaned my
palm on her throat like Tim. Then I got the tricycle
out and took her to the same place.

"They would have told, too. Those children
would have loved to get something like that on one
of us adults."

"And you would have lost your money," De-
Graaf said.

"Life isn't worth living hand to mouth."

"I think it would be best if she were taken away
now, Joe. Maybe Fish can take her in and we can
talk."

It was done. She went without protest.

"When they took Quirk out—were those tears
she was crying just fake?" Ellen Norris Brown
asked.

"I don't think so. Think what she had gone
through. First, she had experienced the great relief
of thinking that I suspected Quirk and Nash. Then
she found that I did, but only as drug dealers. It
was quite obvious that Quirk's alibi was going to
turn out to be true. And she burst into tears. Not
for Quirk; for herself. She had been under a great
deal of strain the last few days. A strain that led her

to make mistakes. She turned it to her advantage
quickly, claiming he was trying to approach her,
too. She was resourceful. She was resourceful
enough to turn the steam pipe explosion to her advantage in the first place. She seized on everything
chance sent her way."

Amy Lane was staring at the rug. "That isn't
coffee!" she burst out. Shakily, she pointed at the
liquid from the overturned coffee pot, which had
been soaking into the rug, but showed no stain.

"It's water. The steam was actually just dry ice in
water. It makes a nice bubbling noise, too. But I
had to tip it over quickly, because in a minute
somebody would have noticed that the 'steam'
went down instead of up, and in another minute
condensation would have started to form on the
outside of the pot. Thank you for your pot, Mrs.
Brown. It isn't damaged, I think."

"Good cause," said Mrs. Brown.

"I take it from the fact that you splashed both of
us, or tried to, that you had decided it was either
Becky or me," said Abby Francot.

"Well, to be honest, yes. It had to be somebody
on the Loops. It had to be somebody with something to hide or a reason to profit. Some of the
people were away and some were sick, and some
had people watching them. Some, like the nurse,
Miss Pettijohn, were on call to another person. She
never knew when her patient would wake up and
call for her. And there was nothing she would have
gained. It was so low a probability that it didn't
pay to spend much time on her.

"DiLeonardi quite clearly lost by what was
going on. Abner Milanowski, who was well situated geographically to have done it, had no dark

secrets, no odd sources of money, nothing. He's the cleanest old curmudgeon I've ever seen. And one doesn't kill out of sheer curmudgeonliness, as a rule."

"And if I did, I wouldn't put the body in my own back yard," Milanowski snorted.

"The same goes for Popeye and Cora Grundler. They were, much to my disappointment, just what they seemed. Their incomes were what they should have been and their backgrounds were clear, as far as it's possible to check. You understand, you never get a hundred per cent certainty on these things. There could be a dark episode in their past we didn't know about. But the likelihood was low. The same is true of Mrs. Brown, the Barkuses, and the Pottses.

"It was possible to eliminate several more people because they lacked the proper transporting vehicle. Aside from what we already have mentioned— small size, moderate roughness inside, somewhat jiggly, partially closed—what do we know or surmise about it? I once told Cornish that I thought it was very important that Tim had milk on his elbow. Where had it come from? He did not have milk at school for lunch. He took only a sandwich and they went on a field trip to an orange grove and drank orange juice. In other words, not only did he not drink milk for lunch, which I already knew from the autopsy, but none of the people around at lunch did either. He didn't have it at home after school with his cookies. And his mother did not have any either. Milk and bread were the main reasons she was planning to go to the store. Now, the milk stain was on his left elbow, and he was lying bunched up on his left side when he was conveyed to the dry wash. This strongly suggested that the container was stained with milk. In other words, it had been used to transport groceries. Where does that leave our suspects now?

"Not only was Miss Carini's car too well carpeted to produce abrasions on Tim, but I could not picture her spilling milk in its beautiful white interior without cleaning it up right away. Also I think milk that had soaked into such a carpet would no longer come off on an elbow. And of course, she would have been very conspicuous pushing a wheelbarrow up to the dry wash. Her car was the only thing she could safely have used. The same was true of Mrs. Brown and Mr. Townshend, whom I already considered unlikely on other grounds. Abner Milanowski's car was not so plush, and he wouldn't carry milk in a wheelbarrow, but since he was so near the wash, he could have simply carried Tim over. He was left out simply by no adequate motive. Quirk's cart, of course, would not have milk in it and did not when I looked at it. Nor would Mr. Joyner's mail bag, Joe. He was exceedingly tidy, very respectful of official equipment, and besides it would have leaked out through the fabric. When I realized that, I was much relieved.

"But a shopping cart was ideal. Miss Francot's on the back of her wheelchair—"

"I carry milk in there all the time," said Miss Francot.

"—or Miss Simmons's on the back of her tricycle. Cora Grundler had a tricycle too, but I had her testimony about what she ate. And I had the testimony of her refrigerator, which was bare of milk."

"And bare of steak and bare of a lot of things," said Mrs. Grundler.

"Yes. I had put aside Amy Lane and the children. I hardly thought Mrs. Lane would kill Tim on the notion that he was a bad influence. And Grub and Paul could not have killed Tim. They hadn't the strength or the weight. Did I forget you, Mr. Chide? You had no motive, either, that I could see. That left Miss Simmons and Miss Francot. Both had disabilities that had brought them large sums of money and both disabilities relied on nerve damage, which can be faked."

"Oh, dear," said Miss Francot.

"And to add to the problem, the night Joyner was killed, Miss Francot broke a pot and the dirt from the pot matched the dirt in Joyner's hair. Where did you get that dirt, Miss Francot?"

"Why, Quirk got it for me from the vacant lot behind the house."

"The lot where Joyner was found. And he got the dirt in his hair from being dropped on the ground."

"Well, I can see how it narrowed down to two, but then why did you say that it started when Fib Levinson broke his arm?"

"You told me that, too," Cornish said. "Were you just being misleading?"

"Me? Never! No, it was an important part of the sequence of events. I just wish we had known the explanation for it earlier."

"I always thought Nash did it," said Popeye.

"Well, you were feeling his hostility to the world," said DeGraaf, "but he didn't do it. The way things happened, that is, the order in which they happened, was this:

"First, there was the background of the feud in town. Both the old people and the children were

upset by it, even those who had nothing to do with
it. Timmie, however, was the kind of child who en-
joyed it. He tipped over Abner's cactus. Abner re-
taliated by putting a more prickly cactus in its
place. That worked. Tim, you see, felt the feud
gave him reason to do the sort of vandalism he en-
joyed doing. He rode his bike repeatedly over Miss
Carini's lawn. Once she put some cholla or some
spiky things there, trying to discourage him. But
that didn't work, so she strung a trip-wire across
the space."

Miss Carini, in the middle of a nice cup of coffee,
choked. Amy Lane looked at her in shock.

"That could hurt a child badly," Amy said.

"It was not at neck level, where it could have
been fatal," DeGraaf said. "It was eighteen inches
at the tree and bush where it was attached, and
therefore, probably a foot from the ground in the
center. It was enough to flip the bike and it was
soon removed. It wasn't there long enough for the
tree to start growing scars. It had cut the soft bark
of the bush but not the hard bark of the tree, so
assume it was not stretched very tightly. Whether
caught Tim or not, I don't know. Maybe Miss
Carini doesn't know. She was at work most of the
time while he was out spoiling."

"I—I took it down that very night. I decided
was an awful idea."

"But we can be pretty sure that Timmie saw it
He hit her lawn most days, just to keep the rut
fresh. Probably he ran into it and fell. It's what he
did then that makes me think he did.

"He set a trap for Miss Carini."

"But wait," said Miss Francot. "Then did she
trip Fib Levinson?"

"I'm coming to that. One day when he got off the school bus, Tim saw Miss Carini walking home. Possibly she had forgotten something. At any rate he ran and got a stick and then lay in wait in the bushes near her house. When he saw her coming along the street, he wriggled through the bushes, and when he heard feet, he pushed the stick through. What he didn't know was that Fib Levinson, running along the sidewalk, had passed Miss Carini in that time. It was Fib who fell over the stick."

"*Timmie* broke Fib's arm?" Amy cried.

"That's right. He probably didn't see Fib coming, while Fib was behind Miss Carini. But we should have guessed when we knew that Fib was running when he was near Miss Carini. He would naturally have had to pass her. The bushes were thick enough so that neither of them saw Tim run away. Similarly, Tim couldn't see who he was tripping."

Cornish said, "Jeez."

"If we had guessed this, we would have had a better idea of what sort of thing Timmie would do. If we had figured that out earlier, we might have saved Libby or Joyner. Because, you see, Tim did exactly the same thing to Miss Simmons. He tried to trip her with a board. We can't know whether he was just exacting revenge on all older people or whether he suspected that she wasn't really blind. I'm inclined to think the second. And that, if he suspected something, he kept it from Grub because he had had a fight with her. But not with Libby. He may have hinted to Libby, and I rather think he must have. That's where it all began. And that's the end of it."

There was silence for a few moments. Then Cora
Grundler got up and poured some more coffee into
Sara Carini's cup. "Come on, Sara," she said.
"Cheer up. We've all done something stupid one
time or another."

Adelaide, who had believed Cora incapable of
an upbeat word, stood amazed. Abby Franco
smiled. But DeGraaf decided then and there that
Cora had thrown the garbage on the lawns.

He turned to DiLeonardi. "You won't hold it
against Sara, will you?"

DiLeonardi shook his head. "No. I haven't the
strength, anyway. Does this mean we're out of the
woods? If we can only end it without too much
publicity!"

Adelaide and Ellen Norris Brown began to pass
the cookies.

"What about the feud?" said DiLeonardi.

"I've got my own opinion about that, for what
it's worth," DeGraaf said. "I've been evading taking a position on it, while everybody gave me their
views. Basically, I believe you have no moral right
to hide out here to escape school taxes. You all
received your own schooling and grew up in communities where the old people of your day were
paying for your schooling. The jobs you found later were in part dependent on the schooling you
were given. But it's not just history. Even here
where you are out of the main stream of things,
part of the reason you can count on stability and
some security is that the children of the country
around you are being educated. This benefits you
because they are not roaming in destructive packs
and because they are moving into careers and jobs
that serve you directly and indirectly. Also you

grandchildren are being provided with an education. In addition, taxpayers someplace are paying, now, for the education of the children from Young Lake, and I don't think it is their responsibility more than yours."

"But what if we can't afford it?" said Cora Grundler.

"Your taxes are adjusted on the basis of what you have. In most jurisdictions, school taxes are based on the value of your house. If you are really penniless, you wouldn't be paying taxes, and neither would you have a house. You, personally, may be too saving, or you may be maintaining too much house. You probably ought to reconsider your whole position on finances."

"Still, I think it's reasonable to have a community without children, even if you were contributing to schools. We don't need the noise and destruction," she said.

"It's been clear the last few days that adults cause noise and destruction, too. And there are more creative ways to deal with children in the community than Young Lake has used. One of Tim's problems, aside from a home difficulty, was that he didn't have anything to do after school. Anyway, it probably won't be long before you get a higher court decision on whether exclusion laws are permissible. I would bet they'll be struck down, but there isn't much point in wondering. I think what you're really after here is not so much a childless community as a safe, orderly community. You want it clean, quiet, peaceful, and you don't want to be intruded upon. You want utopia. That's an excellent idea. Don't we all? But you've been thinking you could buy it or legislate it. You can't.

You can only work toward utopia, and constantly recreate it. Life doesn't grant people a peaceful childhood or a peaceful adulthood, or even, though it seems it should, a peaceful retirement. You don't stop working while you live." He drew a breath and laughed. "How did I get into this? I quit talking, here and now."

Gran Ross decided to pass the sherry.

It was Saturday morning. Cornish, fresh from a very satisfying press conference, joined DeGraaf and his grandmother on the Young Lake beach.

"Abner Milanowski, Peter Pelham, and Angelo DiLeonardi are now representing Young Lake to the national press," Cornish said. "They're trying to come up with a formulation that will explain that our excellent investigation brought not one but three criminals to book, and at the same time not suggest that Young Lake is a hotbed of crime. I'm glad I only had to describe how brilliant we were."

"Sit down and relax," said DeGraaf. "I'm getting a tan before I leave for the north. Which is tomorrow."

"Tell me something. Why is Ellen Norris Brown so touchy? Do you know that, too?"

"She drinks. Her face was flushed at the dance, and she kept spilling things. Dropped the case of ginger ale. Also, she won't let anybody in her garage. Doesn't want them to see the empties. She probably puts out the trash just before the garbage trucks arrive."

"Oh, damn. I found that out this morning from the trash men. I thought I'd catch you."

"Well, I knew something ahead of the rest of

you," said Gran. "I knew that Becky Simmons's blindness was at least partly faked."

"Good God," said her grandson. "She was the one you had in mind? Why?"

"She planted marigolds and zinnias."

"I thought that was because they were upright flowers and she could weed between them by touch. As a blind person, that is."

"She must have thought that was a clever reason. But she never did really understand the psychology of blind people. They want to *get* something out of life, after all. She planted bright, colorful, unscented flowers. Flowers for display. The blind people I have known plant nicotiana or tuberoses, plants with lovely scents. They are upright enough, but rather pallid things to look at. Most heavily scented flowers are pale, you know. It's an evolutionary thing. They depend on the scent to attract pollinators and don't go in for gaudy blossoms. Becky Simmons went in for gaudy blossoms."

"Hmm," said Cornish. "I'll be sorry to see you leave, Gerritt. Come back and visit. At least we'll have your grandmother here."

"I'm afraid, actually, that you won't," said Adelaide.

"You're leaving?"

"Young Lake turned out to be the wrong place for me. Gerritt said it would be when I first thought of it. The people are too old for me. I'm going back to an apartment in Chicago where things happen."